BETWEEN TWO WORLDS

NAT CUDDINGTON

To Taylor

I hope you enjoy!

Between Two Worlds

You can visit Nat's website at **natcuddington.ca**

Find Laura Kulson, the cover artist at **etsy.com/shop/SirenBayStudio**

Title and Chapter font by Vladimir Nikolic
Interior Artwork from Pixabay and iStock:
(Now) Chapter headings by Halyna Lakatosh
(Then) Chapter headings by Mohamed Hassan
Paragraph Breaks by Daniel Roberts

Other Books by Nat Cuddington

For my Tiktok followers.

If it weren't for you, I quite literally would not have written this book.

Author's Note

This book touches on an emotionally abusive relationship, and the death of a parent. If either of these topics are difficult for you, please read with care.

BETWEEN TWO WORLDS

CHAPTER 1
(NOW)

I have never been so flummoxed before in my entire life. And I'm not the smoothest person you'll ever meet. I'm not smooth, period. I get anxious, I stumble over my words when I'm nervous, and I ramble about embarrassing things. Everyone knows this about me. People are not surprised when I talk too much or when I stumble over the same word eleven times. Okay, so maybe eleven is an exaggeration, but the point I'm trying to make is that I quite often come across as baffled. Flabbergasted. Whatever extreme word you want to use for it, that's me. But today, in this moment, it has never been so extreme. I can't find my voice. I can't find my breath for half a second, and I'm worried that I'm going to come across as incompetent. I can't even remember what I was saying. I look down at the tablet that's resting across my arm, at the patient's chart that's backlit on its screen. Right. Now I remember. Flummoxed.

"Oh. Jack," I finally say, my mouth getting dryer by the second. "It's you." Seriously? *It's you?* Of course it's him. He looks exactly the same. I mean, of course he looks a little older, but that's it. His brown skin is still glowing like it always has, and the only thing that's different is his hair. It's shorter, almost shaved to his scalp, but not quite. Which is funny, because my hair is longer. Ugh, that's not funny.

"Hi," he says. But he doesn't say it like a greeting. He says it like he's just as flabbergasted as I am and he doesn't know what else to say.

"It's uh… It's been a long time." Obviously. We both know that it's been a long time.

"Yeah," he agrees with a shaky laugh. He grabs the back of his neck quickly as he looks to the side for a second. He always used to do that when he was unsure of himself.

"I saw your name on the chart, but I didn't make the connection that it would be you." I don't actually the say the sentence cleanly like that; I stumble over words and say 'uh' probably forty times, but I thought I'd spare you the awkwardness.

"Yeah. I knew I was seeing a Dr. Robitaille, and I know you were in medical school when we-" his eyes bulge a little bit as if he's caught himself saying something embarrassing, and he tries to backtrack. "I mean when you… uh, I mean you were in medical school the last time…" he looks away and lets out a breath as if he's admitted defeat. His hand goes to the back of his neck again. When he drops his hand back to his side he finally says quietly, "I didn't make the connection either."

"Well to be fair, there are a lot of Robitailles around here."

"Yeah."

I need to say something else. I can't just start examining him after having not seen him for so long. Maybe I can get a different doctor to do his exam. Yes, that's a good idea.

"So how's it going?" I ask, instead of looking into the different doctor idea I had. "Are you still with Anna?"

"Uh. No. We broke up a few months ago."

"Oh no, I'm sorry," I say. "That's hard."

"Yeah," he sighs. "It had been over for a while before we broke up, but… yeah, still hard."

We stare at each other and I start to fidget with my stylus. He looks away and then back to me, and I smile but actually I want to die.

"So you're a physician for The Mars Group, that's pretty cool," Jack says.

"Oh. Yeah. But I mean, I'm staying here, so it's not as cool as it could be."

"Right."

And then everything gets even more awkward because as I start to say that we should get on with the physical, Jack asks me if I'm seeing anyone. Our sentences overlap and I could probably get away with pretending that I didn't know what he said, but I know what he said.

"What?" I ask, deciding to pretend I don't know what he said.

"Sorry, that was so inappropriate," he says. So he doesn't even want to pretend with me, okay. He totally could have just pretended he said something else, to go along with my pretending that I didn't hear what he said, but I guess he's owning it. "Yes, let's get on with the physical."

So he's not pretending that he said anything else, but it seems he's now taken back the invitation for my response.

"Um. Yeah. The physical," I say.

I start by checking his eyes; shining a little light in them and checking the reaction of his pupils, and then I check his peripherals. We're both staring at each other, and while I'm actually focusing and paying attention to what his eyes are doing, it still just feels like we're staring. Like we're looking longingly into each other's eyes. We're not. I'm not. But somehow it still feels like that. So I say the thing that I sort of wish isn't true in this moment. But it's the thing that's needed to cut this awkwardness from the room, I know it.

"I am." I say quickly. Maybe too quickly. Does he know what I'm talking about? "Uh. Seeing someone," I add. "I am seeing someone."

Jack blinks a couple times and looks a little hurt, but only for a second. He nods and swallows, clears his throat. "Right. Of course you are."

"Why of course I am?"

"Oh, I don't know. Just. I didn't mean it like, 'oh, of course, that's just my luck,' I meant it like, 'of course you are because you're great.'"

I smirk a little and nod, but say nothing. He doesn't know that I'm great. We haven't seen each other in over eight years.

The appointment gets less and less awkward as it goes, and eventually it mostly feels like he's a regular patient and I'm his regular doctor. But by the time we're finished, I feel weird again. I stumble over my words before I can even really get them out of my mouth, and Jack keeps fidgeting with the popsocket on his phone, so he's probably just as uncomfortable as I am. I think he catches me noticing, so he stops and clears his throat.

"I'm uploading your results right now," I finally manage to say to him. "They'll attach to your application automatically." I tap on my tablet and link his information to his profile.

"Oh that's cool. So I don't have to do anything?"

I shake my head. "Nope."

"Cool. Um. Were they good?"

"Were what good?"

"My results?"

"Oh. Yes, of course."

"Okay. That's good."

I nod at him, feeling like I'm supposed to say something else, but usually I just tell the patient good luck and leave. Maybe I'll do that now.

"Good Luck." I cringe as I grab for the door handle because I wish I was able to say something else. Even 'it was nice seeing you again,' would have been okay, but I can't just turn around now and add something else. But then he says my name, making me stop.

"Yes?" I ask.

"Um, just out of curiosity… When you applied to be a Mars Group physician, was it because you thought you were going to be placed on Mars?"

I let out a breath before I answer him. "Yeah. It was."

CHAPTER 2
(THEN)

I was much too drunk. I should have been at home studying, but my roommates dragged me out. It took a lot of convincing and begging, but they finally managed to break me down and make me feel like I needed it. Which I guess I did, I just didn't need it this much. I didn't need to be this drunk. I was very drunk. I think I said that already. I couldn't find my roommates, the ones who said I needed to get out. The ones who brought me here. Where were they? I needed to puke. I stumbled through the crowd and the strobing lights to the washroom. I wasn't even sure I was going to make it in time, but damn I needed to try.

I swung the door open with so much force that I pushed it into someone who was trying to get out.

"I'm sorry!" I shouted. "I need to puke!"

I pushed past them and into the nearest stall before they could even answer me. I kneeled in front of the toilet and pulled my hair out of the way as best I could, but it was short, so chunks of it fell out from under my fingertips. And then it all just started to come out. Puke, not my hair. I was puking, my hair wasn't falling out.

My stomach heaved and I gagged and choked as that night's dinner and drinks made their way back up. It smelled so bad that I had to plug my nose, otherwise I was never going to be able to stop. When I finally got it all out, I took a deep breath and let myself sit fully on the floor, leaning against the stall wall behind me. My hair was stuck to my sweaty and probably paler than normal face, I was shaking, and I could feel even more sweat dripping down my chest. Gross.

"Are you okay?" someone asked, startling me.

I turned my head to see a guy with dark skin standing a few feet away, his hands in his jacket pockets and a worried look on his face. His hair was styled into twists, and his fingers moved through them as he scratched his head.

"I guess so," I slurred. "Why are you in the women's washroom?"

"You're actually in the men's washroom," he said.

"What? No way. The door said ladies on it."

"It actually doesn't say anything on it, it just has a silhouette of a person wearing pants on it."

"That's very outdated," I said, still looking up at him from on the floor.

"Quite."

"I'm very drunk," I added.

"I can see that."

"I didn't mean to puke in your washroom."

"It's not my washroom."

"But you were in here and then I puked."

"I was actually trying to leave, and you slammed the door into me."

"Oh that was you!? I'm sorry."

"It's okay," he said. "It was an emergency."

"It really was."

"Anyway, are you okay? Do you need me to call you a cab?"

"No, my friends are here somewhere."

"Can I help you find them?" he asked.

"Maybe. Maybe I need help walking. I'm much too drunk. I didn't mean to get this drunk."

"It happens to the best of us."

"Are you drunk?"

He laughed a little. "I am, yes, but not as drunk as you."

"I'm much cooler when I'm not a sloppy, barfing mess."

"Noted." He chuckled and started to walk over to me.

"Actually no, that's a lie. I'm super uncool."

"Oh?" He grabbed onto my hand and tried to pull me to my feet but I couldn't do it. He leaned down and grabbed me under both my armpits and got me to stand that way. Once I was on my feet, he put his hands on my shoulders, keeping me steady.

"Yeah," I sighed. "Normally when I see cute guys, I can't function. But I'm talking to you like a normal person. I think."

"You just think I'm cute because you're drunk."

"I swear I didn't mean to get this drunk," I said again.

"Why do you keep saying that? I don't care that you're wasted. I don't even know you."

"Why are you trying to help me, then?"

"Because I don't care that you're drunk means that I also can't care about you as a human and that I don't want to make sure you're okay?"

"I don't know."

He laughed. "Can you walk?"

"I think so."

"Okay. Let's go find your friends."

"Okay."

He linked his arm through mine and together we walked back into the bar with music so loud I swear I could feel it in my brain. The lights were making me feel sick again, but I was pretty sure I wasn't going to puke. As long as we left soon enough.

"Oh my god, Aspen! Where have you been!? Are you okay?" My roommates, Brianna and Carly came running as soon as they saw us.

"I think she needs someone to take her home," the guy said to them.

"What happened?"

"She just ran into the guy's washroom to puke and I wanted to make sure she was okay."

"That's literally the sweetest," Carly said. "Thank you so much."

"Of course."

Brianna linked her arm through my free one, and then the guy smiled at me and stepped away.

"I hope your hangover isn't too bad," he said. And then he waved and got lost in the crowd.

"Who was that?" Carly asked as she linked my arm with hers on my other side.

"Some guy," I said. "I don't know."

"Well, he was amazing."

CHAPTER 3 (NOW)

I walk through the bright hallway towards my office so I can breathe before my next patient. My shoes squeak on the shiny floor and it makes me feel like there's a crowd of people following me and laughing at me. I finally make it to my office and shut the door behind me. I say finally as if my office is a far walk away, but really it took me like 30 seconds to get here. When's my next appointment? I open the Mars Group Med app on my tablet and check my schedule. I have another patient in ten minutes. So I have ten minutes to process what just happened.

But I actually don't, because Shannon barges into my office without even knocking. I had been leaning against the door, and her shoving her way in makes me squeal and stumble into the middle of the room.

"Sorry," she says. Her previously blue pixie cut is now dyed hot pink and it looks awesome against her pale skin.

"Don't you knock?" I ask.

"Sorry. I was just excited."

"About your pink hair?"

"What?" She touches her fingertips to her lightly styled hair and then shakes her head. "No, I got the Infinity Pool tickets!"

"Oh no way! Where are we sitting?"

She bites her bottom lip and I'm afraid that all she could get were seats way in the nosebleeds where you have to watch the entire concert from the big screens in order to see anything, but then she starts to grin.

"Where?" I ask again.

Instead of answering me, she grabs onto my elbows and starts to do a little tap dance thing with her feet. I bounce around with her, hoping she's not messing with me.

"Shannon!" I half shout.

"The floor."

"What! You got us floor tickets!?"

"I did!"

"How!?"

"I'm a genius, that's how!"

"Oh my god. I was freaking out earlier about something else and now I'm freaking out about finally seeing my favourite band and you got us floor seats? Really? So we could like, stand right in front of the stage if we wanted to?"

"Their sweat will probably fly off their hair and hit us in the face!"

"No!"

"Yes!"

"I have to go!" I shout in the same excited tone we've been using.

"Where?"

"I have a patient!"

"Oh! Then yes! Go!"

My tablet beeps just as I open the door, letting me know that my patient is waiting in exam room 4.

It smells like pizza and garlic bread as soon as I step into my apartment after work. I'm excited at first that David made us a treat, or ordered in for us since it's Friday, but when I step into the living room I see that he's already started without me. The pizza box is open on the coffee table with three or four slices already gone from it. David's slouched back on the couch with a plate in his lap, just half a piece of garlic bread left on it.

"Oh," I say.

"Oh?" He straightens up a bit and looks at me.

"You ordered pizza without me?"

"It isn't without you, there's still more than half of it left."

"But like, you didn't want to wait until I got home until you ordered it?"

He shrugs and takes a big bite of his garlic bread. "You were late."

"My last patient went a little longer than normal, sorry. I texted you."

He shrugs again. "I had already ordered it by then."

I sigh and pass him to get a plate in the kitchen.

"Really?" he says. "You're mad at me? I ordered pizza for us and you're mad at me because you were late and I didn't want to eat mine cold?"

"I didn't even know you were ordering pizza!" I throw my arms up in frustration. He always does this.

"It's not a big deal, Aspen. God." He finishes his garlic bread and turns off whatever he was watching to go back to the Netflix home screen. "Grab your plate and come pick a movie with me."

I let out a breath and get a plate from the drying rack beside the sink. The pizza isn't quite cold yet, which annoys me even more. He could have kept the box closed and waited another ten minutes for me. I lean back on the couch and tell him to pick a movie.

"Nah, I'm not falling for that," he says with a hint of playfulness in his voice. "You can pick what we watch. I'll enjoy anything you choose."

I roll my eyes and we end up going with a new romcom that was in theatres not too long ago. We both laugh throughout the movie, and I even cry at one part. David notices and gently brushes the tear away from the corner of my eye with his thumb. I turn to look at him and he smiles at me.

"It's just a movie," he says.

"I know." I smile and hit him in the shoulder, but his thumb is still at the edge of my eye, the rest of his hand wrapping around the side of my head. He kisses me then, and the way he does it so gently makes me feel like he really loves me. Like maybe he didn't mean to hurt me earlier with the pizza and I was overacting. He pulls my ponytail out of its hair tie so he can run his hands through my hair. My hands find the hem of his shirt, lifting it over his head. He starts to kiss me a little harder, and the way his hands move across my body makes me feel wanted. I pull myself into his lap and straddle him on the couch, and then lift my arms over my head as he takes my shirt off.

I pour myself a bowl of Shreddies in the morning, and David sits at the kitchen table with a cup of black coffee.

"Oh!" I say. "I forgot to tell you!"

He looks up from his mug and gives me a half smile. "What?"

"Shannon got us tickets to see Infinity Pool!"

"All three of us?"

"No, you said you didn't want to go." I take a bite of my cereal and some milk drips down my chin. I wipe it away with my pyjama sleeve.

"I never said that."

"Um. When I told you about it, you snorted and said it sounds expensive."

"Yeah, but I never said I didn't want to go."

I stare at him for a second, completely gobsmacked. "You… I-I'm so confused."

"Just because I said something sounds expensive means I don't want to do it?" he asks.

"You…" I can't think of what I want to say. Surely the concert's sold out at this point, and even if it wasn't, there's no way we'd be able to get him a ticket on the floor with us. I feel bad for leaving him out, but I honestly thought he didn't want to go. "You sounded very aggressively uninterested," I finally say.

"Aggressively uninterested?"

"What was I supposed to think? I was excited to tell you about the concert for my favourite band, and you made me feel bad for wanting to go because I would spend a lot of money on it. I asked you if you wanted to go, David."

"Sounds like you didn't listen to my answer."

"Don't do this to me. When you said it sounded expensive, I said 'so you don't want to go with me, then?' and you shrugged."

"That doesn't mean no."

"Why didn't you tell me you wanted to, then?"

"I had to think about it."

"This isn't my fault, David. I'm going to the concert with Shannon because you made it sound like you didn't want to go."

"Whatever."

I'm not even hungry anymore. I get up and dump my cereal milk into the sink and put the soggy Shreddies in the compost.

I start to walk away, but before I make it past the kitchen table, David says, "The bag's going to leak."

I sigh and go back to the counter and grab the compost bag from under the sink. I stomp to the door and don't even put my shoes on to head down to the waste room. It's where we put all our garbage, recycling, and compost. It's almost as cold as a freezer in this room so the piling compost from the entire building doesn't stink or attract flies, which is genius. I toss my small bag of compost into a bin and then head back to the elevators.

CHAPTER 4
(THEN)

I was still hungover. It was Monday morning and I still felt like barfing as I walked across campus. At least it was nice and crisp out, so the cool air felt good on my head. I took in a deep breath and let it out slowly, trying my best to bury any feelings of nausea. *I will not be sick today*, I told myself. *I will not be sick today*.

"Hey," someone said from beside me.

I jumped a little and looked over to see the same guy from Saturday night, the guy from the washroom. At least I thought it was him. I was very drunk when we met.

"Ah, you don't remember me, do you?" he asked.

"Um, bathroom guy?"

"So you do remember." He smiled and straightened up a little.

"Yeah. Uh, I'm sorry you had to meet me at such a low point."

He waved me off. "It's fine. You were just drunk."

"Yeah, and puking. And I looked awful and my hair was all stuck to my face and stuff."

"Who says you don't still look awful?"

I almost choked, completely at a loss on how to respond.

"Kidding," he said, putting his hands up in front of him. "I'm kidding. You didn't look that bad. And your hair looks great today."

"Oh." I immediately felt myself blushing. My auburn hair was short, and the choppy layers curled around my ears. "Thanks."

"Of course. How was the hangover?"

"Still going," I said. I laughed a little because I was suddenly nervous even though I knew I didn't have a reason to be.

"Oh man, that sucks." He hooked his thumbs around his backpack straps and slowed his pace to match mine when he saw that I was lagging behind him a little. "What are you studying?"

"Biology. Uh, for pre-med."

"Wow, that's amazing. So you must be super smart, then."

"No."

He smirked and sort of laughed. I felt like he didn't know what to say and I made him uncomfortable with my awkwardness.

"I'm Jack, by the way," he finally said.

"Aspen."

"Are you going to make it through the day, Aspen? You're not dissecting things today or anything, are you?"

"No."

"I'm sorry, I'm bothering you," he said, grabbing at the back of his neck.

"No you're not," I said.

"Are you sure? Because I can leave. Actually…" he stopped and looked around for a second, at the vine covered building in front of us, and at the path that continued to our left, toward another, smaller building. "I don't even have classes in this building. Or that one."

"Why did you walk over this way, then?"

"Because I recognized you and I wanted to say hi."

"Oh."

We both stopped walking and I looked up at him. He was quite a bit taller than me, but nothing about him seemed threatening or intimidating. His smile was warm and soft, and he had a dimple in his left cheek, which was quite adorable. His cheeks were a little chubby, making him seem innocent. Also, I really liked his hair. Even though I didn't know him, I thought it suited him.

"Hi," I finally said.

He smiled. "Hi."

We stood and stared at each other for a good fifteen seconds, his mouth curled in a cute grin, and mine probably gaping open like a loser. I shook my head and then held out my hand. Because I'm a loser.

"Nice to meet you when I'm not drunk off my ass," I said.

He laughed pretty loudly at that and actually threw his head back. "Nice to meet you too." And then we shook hands.

"I'm going to keep going to class," I said.

"Okay," he said, nodding his head once. "I'm going to turn around."

I couldn't help but smile. "Okay."

"I hope you feel better."

"Thanks."

I watched him turn back the way we came, and once he made it to the curve in the path that started to take him around the Jackson building, I went on my own way. I shook my head and laughed at myself, hoping I didn't sound too nervous or weird. I thought I seemed pretty normal. I was normal, right? Fuck, I probably wasn't normal.

I found myself always on the lookout for Jack after that. We obviously seemed to have classes on different parts of campus, but if we ran into each other one time, it would probably happen again. Plus not all of my classes were in the sciences, so maybe we'd have a class together in the future. I didn't even ask him what he was studying. I didn't even know if he was in the same year as me.

It was a week until I saw him again. We ran into each other at the bus stop after dark. It was raining so I was huddled inside the bus shelter with my arms crossed over my chest for a little warmth.

"No umbrella?" he asked me.

"Even if I had an umbrella, being in here is the better choice."

"Touché." He smiled and came inside to wait with me. The rain pelted the roof, and some stray drops came in through the opening, spraying our feet.

"Did you just get done with class?" I asked.

"I was working."

"Oh."

He smiled and slid his hands in the pockets of his jacket, the handle of his umbrella hooked over his left arm.

"I just work at the little store by Westin," he said after about a minute of silence. Westin was one of the dorms. It was the dorm everyone wanted to be in because it was so close to the variety store. It was one of the oldest dorms on campus, so it wasn't that nice, but people loved the convenience of it.

"Oh. Sorry, I should have asked," I said.

"No, don't worry about it."

"My brain doesn't work sometimes."

He raised an eyebrow at me, but didn't say anything in return.

"Sorry. I mean my head. My thoughts. My thoughts and my mouth don't communicate properly sometimes." I covered my face with my hands for a second, completely embarrassed. "Words are hard."

That made him laugh, and I wasn't sure if it was because he thought I was funny, or if it was second hand embarrassment. Or because he was making fun of me.

My bus came around the corner and I stepped closer to the opening of the shelter at the same time that Jack moved.

"Are you getting on the 95 too?" he asked.

"Yeah."

The corner of his mouth curled up into a soft grin. "Well. Would you look at that."

CHAPTER 5
(NOW)

It's been a week since I saw Jack for his application physical. We didn't exchange numbers or anything, and I haven't looked him up on any socials. It seemed weird having not been mutuals on anything like that in years, and then just adding him again out of the blue. And I know it's not really out of the blue; we just saw each other, but I still push it to the back of my mind. Seeing him again was… I don't know what it was. Weird. Weird? Nice? I mean I absolutely made a fool of myself, so that's not good. But I can't stop thinking about him, and that is most definitely not good. I mean I'm not thinking about him in a sexual way or anything, I just keep thinking about what he might be doing. What he thought of seeing me. I shake my head and try harder to push him to the back of my mind. If we were meant to be friends then we would have stayed friends. And we didn't. So it doesn't matter. Plus he's applying to live on Mars, so it really doesn't matter.

"Hey, do you want to get dinner before the Mars Send Off tonight?" I ask David as I put my shoes on for work.

"Oh, that's tonight?"

"Yes, David, it's tonight. We were talking about it yesterday. And they happen every six months."

"You say that as if I've had so many opportunities to forget about it."

"Well they've happened twice a year since I got this job, so yeah, you've had, what? Six opportunities to forget about it?"

"Oh come on, Aspen. I went to your first one with you. It was all exciting then because it was for your new job, but like, who cares? Really?"

I stare at him for longer than a few seconds, and he doesn't even seem to register that what he said was hurtful. "I do," I say. "I care."

"It's just a party, Aspen."

"It's not just a party. It's my job, and it's important to me. And it'll be more fun with you there."

He sighs and sort of rolls his eyes. "We'll see."

"That means no," I say under my breath. I leave the apartment without saying goodbye or even glancing back at him. I clear my throat a couple times on my way to the elevator to stop myself from crying, and when I get to my car, my phone beeps. I take it out of my back pocket to see that David has texted me.

I love you ♡

I don't reply.

David does not come to the Mars Send Off Party. I go alone, again, and mingle with the few people I know from work and then stand there awkwardly with a drink in my hand. The music isn't too loud, and the lights aren't too dim. It's more of a professional party, if that makes any sense. They hold them the night before each new group goes off to Mars, which is every April and October. Because I work for The Mars Group, I'm obligated to attend. I'm not technically required to go, but it's frowned upon if I don't. I'm always hopeful that each party is going to be more fun than the last, and I'm not really looking for anything exciting to happen at them anyway. But this time I'm in an awful mood. I can't bring myself to smile at anyone. Even the Mars Party Members who are having such a good time don't rub off on me. Even though I'm kind of secretly jealous of them, they've always made me happy. Not today, though.

"Hey! Aspen!" I hear from behind me. I turn around, and of course, it's Jack Duncan. "Er, um, I mean, Dr. Robitaille," he quickly corrects himself when I smile at him.

"Hey Jack," I say. "And Aspen's fine."

"Right. Sorry. We haven't seen each other in so long, and I wasn't sure."

"You're ridiculous."

"Sometimes."

I smile and take a sip of my beer. I don't know what else to say to him. What do you say to someone you used to be in love with but haven't seen in eight years?

"So do you come to all the Send Off Parties?" Jack asks.

"Yeah, ever since I've been working for them. I kind of have to."

He nods.

"Do you?" I ask. "Uh, come to them all?"

"No. Actually, Anna and I used to come to them sometimes, but I haven't been to one in a few years."

"Well hopefully you'll be at the next one too, but as a Mars Party Member!"

"Yeah!" He smiles, but only briefly. "Hopefully," he adds, in a less excited tone. As if he feels bad or something. As if he's remembering the end of his exam when he asked if I had applied for The Mars Group because I thought I'd be placed on Mars. As if he's remembering all our talk about going to Mars when were younger, and he feels bad for me. "But I don't get to find out for a couple of months yet," he continues.

"That time'll go by in a flash," I say.

"Yeah, probably. So where's your boyfriend? Doesn't he normally come with you to stuff like this?"

"He wanted to come, but he had to work," I lie. I'm not even sure why I do it. "He usually comes to them." Another lie. He never comes to them.

"Aw that sucks," Jack says. "I'm sorry he had to miss this one."

"Yeah. It's not a big deal. I mean it's not like I'm the one going to Mars, right?"

"Right. And hey, at least now we get a chance to catch up! You know, as friends."

"Yeah. I could always use another friend."

"Until I go to Mars, that is." Jack laughs, and I know that he's joking, but I can't do more than smile. "Sorry, that wasn't funny."

"It's okay, I'm just not having the best day. But tell me, what did you apply for on Mars?"

"Everything," he says. "I wanted to up my chances of being accepted. But I really hope I get accepted for photography. It's my dream to do all their marketing pictures."

"That would be so incredible. Just being out there taking pictures of the Mars landscapes."

I imagine him out there in the red sandy hills, smiling through his space helmet and holding his camera in front of him, waiting for the lighting to shift to get the perfect shot. He was always so passionate about photography when we were in university. It was like looking through a camera lens was his way of escaping.

"You know," I say, "even if you don't get a photography job, you could still go out and take your own pictures. Maybe you'll become this famous Mars photographer."

"Yeah, that would be super cool."

"Is that what you're doing now? Photography? Instead of-"

"Yeah, sort of," he says, cutting me off before I finish my question.

"Sort of?"

He shrugs. "I work for a marketing company. I take pictures of cereal and cheeseburgers."

"I'll bet you make those things look really good, though."

"Oh, I do." He grins. "And I guess it's not a bad job. Like, I don't hate what I do or anything, it's just not that creative. There isn't much freedom in taking pictures of food, or sunscreen, or watches."

"Right."

"But it's still challenging, which is nice. And I still take my own pictures outside of work."

"Are you on any photo sharing apps?" I ask.

"Yeah, I've been trying out Photodump. I was skeptical at first, but all the other photo apps switched their focus to videos and this one hasn't."

"Right? So annoying. Like I just want to share pictures with my friends, I don't want to watch people I don't even know dancing or lip syncing."

Jack nods and smiles, and I think for a second he's not going to give me his username. "Uh, it's just Jack Duncan Photography," he ends up saying.

"Excellent." I pull out my phone and bring up the app.

"You're not following me right now, are you?"

"Yes, I definitely am."

"Oh god, that's embarrassing. My pictures aren't actually that great."

"Stop lying," I say as I hit the follow button under his name on his profile. And as I put my phone away and smile up at him, I realize how comfortable I already am with him again. It's like we never stopped being friends.

We're interrupted by the countdown for all the Mars Party Members to leave. There's a big clock on the wall with digital numbers moving from 10 to 9 to 8, and everyone is counting down with it like it's New Year's Eve. When they get to 1, everyone turns on their red sparklers, and the group leaving for Mars comes through the doors at the top of the grand staircase in their space uniforms with the Mars Group logos on their chests. Everyone cheers and waves their sparklers in the air, the chemicals in them creating an illusion of sparking hot fire when really it's just some kind of smoke and flashing lights. They look real, though. I forgot mine somewhere near the bar so I just clap and cheer for them, but Jack's got his and he waves it around in excitement for all the people leaving.

"Hey, how was your thing?" David asks when I come home close to midnight.

"What thing?"

"What do you mean 'what thing?', your work thing."

"Oh, you mean the Mars Send off that you didn't want to go to, even though I said it was important to me."

David sighs and closes his eyes for a second. "Yeah," he says slowly.

"It was good," I say with a smile. "I caught up with an old friend."

"Oh yeah? Do I know her?"

"Uh no, I don't think you've met him. His name is Jack. He's a photographer."

"Oh really?" He sounds unimpressed. I wonder if it's because he doesn't want me to know that he's jealous, or if he actually doesn't care.

"Yeah. It's too bad you didn't want to come."

"Yeah…"

"Anyway, I'm beat, so I'm going to head to bed." I force a smile at him and walk past him to our room.

I can hear him shuffling around in the living room as I get into my pyjamas and I wonder what he's doing. If he's mad. I'm the one who should be mad. But I'm not mad. At this point I expect this of him, which isn't good for either of us, but I guess it's worse for me. I am hurt, though. I'm hurt that I don't seem to take priority in his life anymore. It's not even like he did something else while I went to the party that he didn't want to attend with me. He just stayed home and watched TV and had a few beers. I wish I was mad. I think being mad would be easier.

I crawl into bed and bunch the blankets up under my chin, trying not to cry. A few tears escape onto my pillow, but nothing else. I take a few deep breaths to calm myself and I fall asleep before David comes to bed.

Did David come to bed at all? I wake up and reach across for him but his side is empty and cold. I look at the alarm clock to see that it's four in the morning.

"David?" I ask. I look into the dark room around me trying to find any shapes of him, but all I can see is the bedspread and his pillow. "David?" I call a little louder.

I get out of bed and open the door which opens into the living room. David is sleeping on the couch. Why is he sleeping on the couch?

"David, what are you doing out here?" I ask.

He snorts a little and then wakes up, not looking surprised at all that he is where he is. So he didn't fall asleep out here by accident, then.

"Is this not where you want me?" he asks.

"What?"

"You're mad at me for not going to your Mars party."

"Did I say I was mad at you?"

He sits up a little and props himself up on his elbow. "No, but you didn't have to."

"So you know that you did something to upset me, but you're not going to do anything about it?"

"I did do something about it. I slept on the couch."

"Why can't you just apologize to me?" I can hear my voice cracking and I hate it.

"I shouldn't have to apologize for not wanting to go to a stupid party."

"Wow."

David deadpans. "What?"

I let out a breath and shake my head, but he still doesn't seem to think he did anything wrong.

"What?" he asks again.

"You're unbelievable, you know that?"

"Why?"

I turn around and head back into our room, and that's when he calls after me.

"Aspen," he says, but I shut the door on him. "Aspen!"

He can just open the door; it's not like I locked it. But he doesn't. I'm not sure if he stays on the other side of the door wondering what he should do, or if he immediately goes back to the couch, but he doesn't come into the room. He doesn't even try the doorknob. I watch it for about a minute, hoping to see it jiggle or start to turn, anything that tells me he still cares about me. But nothing.

I try to get back to sleep but I can't.

CHAPTER 6
(THEN)

Turned out Jack and I lived in the apartment buildings across the street from each other. He laughed and suggested that it would be fun if our bedrooms or living rooms lined up so we could send each other messages with flashlights through our windows.

"We can just send each other messages with our phones," I said.

"Yeah, but if we could look at each other at the same time that would have been funny."

"I guess so."

"We can't exchange messages though, if neither of us has the other person's number."

"Right," I said, blinking at him.

"Here, give me your phone and I'll put my number in it."

I pulled my phone out of my pocket and handed it to him, watching him with a pounding heart as he swiped and tapped on my phone. He smiled as he gave it back to me and I almost put it back in my pocket right away but then decided to look at how he put his name in. He inputted it as Jack with a smiley face. I smiled up at him and then looked back down at my phone. I tapped on his name and sent him a message.

Hello there

He took his phone out of his front jeans pocket, because guys have pants with front pockets big enough to comfortably hold a phone I guess, and looked at my message. He smiled and tapped out a response.

I read that in Ewan McGregor's voice.

I laughed out loud and covered my mouth with my hand that wasn't holding my phone.

"Oh come on, it wasn't that funny," he said.

"It was to me."

"Well I'm glad I make you laugh. But I should head home."

We had been standing at the bus stop in between our two buildings ever since getting off the bus and realizing where we lived, on my building's side of the road.

"Yeah, me too," I said. "I have class in the morning."

"Well, have a good night."

"You too."

I watched him cross the street, and watched as he turned around to wave before going into his building. I waved back, let out a deep breath, and went home.

"Heeey," Brianna said to me when I got inside. "How was class?"

"It was fine. I ran into bathroom guy at the bus stop."

"The guy who helped you when you were drunk?" Carly half shouted, coming out of her room.

I laughed and turned to her a little. "Yeah. He lives across the street. And his name is Jack."

"Nice. You don't meet many Jacks these days."

"Well I meet this one all the time."

Brianna narrowed her eyes at me in sort of a question.

"I also ran into him last week at school," I said.

"Maybe he's stalking you," Carly suggested.

"No way." I shook my head. "We go to the same school and live across the street from each other, it makes sense that we'd run into each other a few times."

Brianna and Carly giggled with each other. I just rolled my eyes and went to my room so I could start getting ready for bed.

Jack and I ran into each other more frequently after that, but they were planned run-ins. He texted me that he would be catching the bus at 8:10 for his first set of classes, and would I be on the same one. I would reply and tell him I might possibly be on the same one, and maybe I'd see him. Of course we'd see each other at the bus stop. He would text me that he was getting coffee at the Tims on campus, and I would text him back telling him that maybe I was heading over there too, and was he a mind reader? He would reply with a winking emoji and I wouldn't know what to say so I wouldn't text back. I would just go meet him at Tims.

"Can I get you a drink?" he asked.

"Sure. I'll just get an iced coffee."

He nodded and walked up to the counter, where he ordered an iced coffee for me, and a coffee with two milks for himself.

"I can't believe we keep running into each other," he joked as we sat down.

"Yeah it's so weird," I said, playing along.

"Maybe we should run into each other again tomorrow."

"Yeah." I smiled at him, happy that he was confident enough to do this. All our meetups had been his doing. I'd thought about texting him in the same manner but could never work up the courage. Which I knew was silly because he was doing it with me, so obviously he wanted to hang out, and obviously he would have played along in the same way, but I just couldn't do it. What if I suggested something stupid, or what if the one time I did it was the time he decided he didn't want to play this game anymore?

"I do have to study for midterms, though," I said after about a minute of silence.

"Oh right. Yeah, I should study too."

"What are you studying? Sorry, I never asked before."

"Oh, I'm majoring in English and I'm going to teacher's college when I'm done."

"Oh, that's great. What year are you in?"

"Second."

I smiled. "I'm in second year, too."

"Cool."

"Are you going to apply for teacher's college here?" I asked.

"Yeah. I mean I'll still apply other places too just in case, but I like it here."

"Me too."

"Are you going here for med school? I know they have a good medical program here."

"They have so many strong courses here," I said. "But I'm the same. I'll apply everywhere, but I hope I get in here. I want to do my residency at the hospital over here too."

"That would be perfect."

I noticed in that moment how comfortable I was getting with him. I didn't feel as nervous with him as I had previously. My words were coming out a lot easier, like they did with Brianna and Carly. I wanted to keep seeing him.

"We could study together," Jack said.

"When you say study…"

He raised an eyebrow at me.

"Um, I mean, uh, when you say study, you actually mean study, right?" I asked slowly.

"Of course, what else would it mean?"

"Oh, I don't know, just a lot of people use that as a euphemism."

"Ah. No, I meant study. I don't want to stop you from doing as well as you could."

"Right. Okay. Do you want to study in the library, then? Tomorrow?"

"Yeah, that sounds great."

I was nervous again to meet him in the library, but I knew I was being silly. He was the one who suggested studying, and he said it wouldn't be anything else. I didn't have anything to be worried about. I was going to study with a new friend. That's all. I took in a deep breath and let it out slowly. I shook my head and grabbed onto the big metal door handles of the campus library and walked into the old, warm building. I looked around at the towering mahogany bookcases and the sturdy tables in the middle, but didn't see him anywhere. I must have just gotten there before him. I found an empty table closest to the front so he would see me, and sat down.

I waited for about ten minutes before I started taking my stuff out of my bag, and another ten minutes before I thought about texting him. Did I get the time wrong? I opened our conversation and double checked that we had agreed on 4:30. We had. And it was almost 5:00 now. I didn't know if I should send him a message or not. But just as I was about to start typing, a message came through from him.

Hey where are you? his text said.

I'm at the library where are you?

The library

Did you book a study room?

No he replied. **I'm at a table right inside.**

What? I looked around but I didn't see him at all. There weren't a lot of people in here and there were only people at four of the tables, including the one I was at. He was lying. Why was he lying?

So am I. I said.

That's weird. I don't see you. And then he sent a picture of a very open library that I wasn't in. But it wasn't the campus library. Was he at the city library?

What library are you at? I asked.

Peterson. he replied.

Peterson?

Yeah on the west side of campus by the newer buildings.

Our university has more than one library!?

Are you at a different campus library? I didn't know we had more than one either

We're such losers I joked.

Where is yours? I'll come to you.

Jack came through the library doors about half an hour later so I took my earbuds out of my ears and smiled up at him as he made his way to my table. He put his bag down by his chair and took a seat next to me.

"What're you listening to?" he asked, gesturing towards my earbuds on the table.

"Infinity Pool," I answered.

"Oh nice, I like them."

"Me too."

He blinked at me a couple times and then grinned. "I would hope so. Otherwise listening to them is a strange hobby."

"Oh. Ha. Right."

"Anyway, this library is way nicer than the one I always go to." Thank you, Jack, for being so good at changing the subject away from my awkwardness. "It's all old and magical."

"You think it's magical?" I asked, smiling, because obviously I also thought it was magical.

"Well, yeah. Because it's all old. The arches over the windows, and the dark wood everywhere and the old tables and stuff makes me feel like I'm in a novel."

"A magical one?"

"Of course."

"I'm glad you think so," I said. "I love this library. Sometimes I come here if I need to destress. It's so calming."

He smiled at me and took a binder out of his bag.

We studied for three hours, first quietly on our own, with occasional glances and smiles at each other, and then together, by using each other's notes to ask quiz questions. Well, I used his notes, he used my flash cards that I made earlier in the week.

"You have flash cards?" he asked when I pulled them out of my bag.

"Yeah."

"Did you make them?"

I felt my face going red. "Yeah."

"That's so cool." He took them from me and started to go through them, looking at both sides. "Okay, are you ready?"

And suddenly I was no longer nervous about what our study session might or might not turn into. I didn't feel like a loser for making my own flash cards, and I didn't feel silly for not knowing that we had more than one library on campus. I felt like I was in the exact place that I needed to be, with exactly the right person. Someone who made me feel perfectly okay about who I was.

He quizzed me for a while and I already knew most of the answers, but any time that I didn't, he tried to give me hints instead of telling me the answer, which was cute. I couldn't really ask that many questions to Jack in return because a lot of his exams revolved around opinion answers and just having the information to back them up. He said that giving him the opportunity to explain himself to someone else still helped a lot, though.

The library was empty and quiet by the time we decided to start packing up, and I looked at my watch, startled at the fact that I hadn't even eaten.

"It's late," I said.

"Are you hungry?" Jack asked. "Do you want to get something to eat on the way home?"

We stopped at Wendy's because there was one two stops away from our buildings, and we walked the rest of the way with our burgers in one hand and drinks in the other.

"Thanks for helping me study," I said.

He was still swallowing a bite of his Baconator, but he smiled around the food in his mouth and nodded.

"We should do it again for finals," I added.

"Definitely."

We walked in silence for a few minutes, just eating our food and sipping our pop from paper straws. When I finished my burger, I crumpled up the wrapper and put it in the open bag that I had pinched between my fingers and my cup.

"This was a silly idea," I said after almost spilling my drink everywhere as I reached in the bag for my fries.

"It was. I don't know what I was thinking." Jack laughed and took my cup from me, balancing it between his own cup and take out bag.

"We can just sit somewhere to finish eating."

"Where?" He looked around at the almost empty road, void of any benches.

"On the sidewalk?"

"You want to sit on the sidewalk to eat your fries?" he asked.

"What's wrong with sitting on the sidewalk?"

"Nothing. Let's sit on the sidewalk."

"Well okay then."

I smiled at him and he smiled back, and then together we planted our butts on the hard concrete below us. The nights were a little chilly with it being the middle of October, but the days were still really warm, so the sidewalk wasn't cold. There was no chill seeping through my pants. Just hardness on my tailbone. We sat for a little while longer after we finished our fries, and long after our straws started making noises because there was nothing left in our cups. We laughed and talked about life, and I never once stumbled over my words.

CHAPTER 7
(NOW)

I'm trying to decide what to make for dinner tonight as I stroll through the aisles of the grocery store. David and I usually go grocery shopping together after having made a list of what we each want to eat that week. He picks half the meals and I pick half, and we try to make them together. We haven't said much to each other since last night though, after our stupid 4am fight. So here I am at the grocery store on my own, trying to think of something we'll both like, and something I don't mind making on my own because I don't think I want to make dinner with him right now. We usually end up fighting about something stupid while we make food together anyway. Maybe I'll just get Thai takeout for myself and he can figure out his own supper.

I turn the corner into the next aisle and see Jack up ahead reading a box of frozen meatballs.

"Jack?" I say.

He turns around and smiles when he sees me. "Aspen, hey!"

"We're just running into each other everywhere, aren't we? So random."

"Yes, because the medical office that you work at, and the party put on by your work are such random places to meet."

"Well, okay, you got me there. But the grocery store is random."

"Is it?"

"Well I don't know. Maybe it is. I haven't seen you in like, eight years and now I've seen you three times in less than two weeks."

"Well maybe I'm stalking you." Jack smiles and it reminds me of when we used to joke around when we were younger.

"You're not doing a very good job," I say.

"I would say I'm doing an excellent job. We've run into each other three times in less than two weeks."

"Yeah, but if you're stalking me, I'm not supposed to catch you doing it."

"Oh yeah, that makes sense. To be honest, I don't know how stalking's supposed to work."

"Because you're not actually a stalker," I clarify.

He nods. "Correct."

I can't help but smile. "Okay, that's good."

"You're not, are you?"

"I'm not what?" I ask.

"A stalker."

"Oh. No."

"Okay good," he says.

"Yes, it is a good sign that neither of us are stalkers."

Jack laughs and I step a little closer to him.

"So what are you getting?" I ask, eyeing the meatballs still in his hand. "Are those any good?"

"Oh, I don't know, I've never had them before. I was just getting a few things for the rest of the weekend. I usually do a grocery shop after work on Monday but I don't have much food left in the house."

"I usually do a grocery shop with my boyfriend but I'm, uh," I pause, suddenly embarrassed to tell him about having a fight with David. We don't really know each other anymore; I don't want him to think that David is always awful to me. "I thought I'd get us something fun for supper tonight, but turns out I don't even know what qualifies as a fun meal."

"Pizza rolls and homemade poutine."

"Oh, that does sound fun."

"It is. I had it a lot in university. Minus the cheese and gravy."

"So you just had a lot of pizza rolls and fries, then?"

"Yes, but I was poor when I was in university. And lazy."

I laugh and start to turn my shopping cart around.

"Where are you going?" he asks, following me.

"To get pizza rolls, of course!"

Jack walks beside me as I hunt for the best frozen fries and gravy mix to use, and he walks with me to the deli section where I was sure they would have cheese curds, but don't. We walk all the way back across the store to the dairy fridges and still find no cheese curds. I get a brick of mozzarella instead and promise Jack that instead of shredding it, I'll break it into pieces. I follow him around while he gets his food, which just ends up being the meatballs, a bunch of bananas, some bread, and Kraft natural peanut butter. We use the same lineup to check out, and then separate in the parking lot.

"Enjoy your pizza rolls and poutine!" Jack calls as we head in different directions.

"I will! Enjoy your meatballs and bananas!"

"I will!"

I'm a little nervous to go inside. I'm just afraid that I'm going to try to talk to David and he's going to get defensive or blame stuff on me. He smiles at me when I walk through the door, and then he gets up and grabs my grocery bag from me.

"What'd you get?" he asks.

"Pizza rolls and poutine stuff." I try to sound excited when I say it, but it comes out like I'm trying not to cry.

David doesn't seem to notice and just says, "Nice!" as he heads to the kitchen.

I watch him unpack the reusable bag and wonder what our life would be like if I had been given a position on Mars. I would have been living alone in an apartment for the first six months, but we would have been preparing for David to join me almost the entire time we were apart. Deciding whether or not we wanted to put the rest of our stuff in storage or if we should get rid of it. Getting David a new job, and getting ready for him to arrive. There was a lot of paperwork for spouses to join too, so we would have been dealing with that. But that would have been almost four years ago at this point, we'd be so deep into Mars life by now, we wouldn't even question it anymore. I wonder if we would fight about the same things if we were on Mars. Or if there would be different things for us to fight about. I wonder if we would fight at all.

David puts the pizza rolls and fries in the oven and starts on making the gravy right away. I watch him from the other side of the kitchen, thinking about saying something to him about last night.

"David," I say slowly.

"Yeah, babe."

"So about last night…"

He huffs and turns around to face me. "Are you still upset about that?"

"Well we didn't really resolve it."

"There's nothing to resolve, Aspen. I thought you wanted me to sleep on the couch, so I slept on the couch."

"That's not what I was talking about."

"What, then?"

"The Send Off was important to me. I told you it was, and you still didn't go, even though you had nothing else going on."

"Okay, I'll go to the next one with you."

I let out a breath and nod.

"Why don't you seem happy? That's what you want, isn't it?"

"I want you to want to go with me, David."

"You want me to just change my opinions about something?"

"No," I say slowly. "I want you to take an interest in me."

"I do take an interest in you. I'm very interested in you."

"Then why don't you want to go to the Send Off parties with me?"

"Look, I said I would go to the stupid party, I don't know what else you want from me."

"Fine. Yeah. Whatever."

It's a little unfair that I applied to work on Mars and instead I was hired to work on Earth, performing physicals for people who are applying for the same thing, and for people who are accepted and about to leave. I was rejected from Mars and I have to say "Congratulations" to half of my patients before I leave the room. Congratulations for getting the life I wanted. I'm so happy for you.

"Hey, when's your first patient?" Shannon asks, barging into my office without knocking.

"In fifteen minutes, why?"

"I brought you an iced coffee."

"Oh. Thanks!" I take it from her and take a sip. It's way too sweet, but I smile and continue to drink it anyway.

"Did they make it right?" she asks.

"Um, it depends, what did you ask for?"

"Dammit, they didn't make it right. I asked for no sugar."

"It's fine. It's still delicious."

"Are you sure?"

"Yes. And it's also free, which makes it extra delicious. Plus I used to drink iced coffees with sugar when I was in university. Brings me back."

"Oh, well if I can make you feel young again, then I'll take it. I'm like a fairy godmother."

"Is that what fairy godmothers do?" I ask, raising my eyebrows at her.

She shrugs. "If that's what'll make you happy, then sure. Yes."

I laugh and open the Mars Group Med app on my tablet.

"My patient's already in her exam room," I say. "I'm going to go now. Maybe if all my patients are early, I'll be able to get out of here early too."

"Okay see you later."

"Yeah, see ya. And thanks for the coffee."

"And making you feel young again."

"Yes, that too."

And off I go to spend the day clearing people to continue applying for their dream jobs in a dream location. Should be fun.

That was sarcasm, by the way, in case you didn't catch it.

CHAPTER 8
(THEN)

I walked into my apartment after my last midterm and almost screamed. Ryan Reynolds was in my apartment. Well, a cardboard cut-out of Ryan Reynolds was in my apartment. But it took me a full three seconds to realize that it was cardboard and not a human who had probably broken in while my roommates and I were all at school.

"What is this!?" I called, hoping that someone was home.

"What's what?" Brianna came out of her room and scrunched her face at me. "What's what?" she said again.

"This!" I pointed to the six-foot-tall flat celebrity occupying our entryway.

"Oh, that's Ryan Reynolds."

"I know that it's Ryan Reynolds, Brianna, I want to know why he's here."

"That's not what you asked. You asked what it was."

"Why is it here?"

Brianna shrugged. "Carly got it. You can't make her get rid of it, it cost her like 250 bucks."

"250 dollars for cardboard!?"

"That looks like Ryan Reynolds!"

"Well it scared the shit out of me."

"Me too, actually. I thought someone broke into the apartment when I got home."

"So I'm not being unreasonable then."

A knock at the door made us both jump and I squealed a little. I shook my head at Brianna, who narrowed her eyes at me.

"Don't answer it," I whispered.

"Why not?"

"What if it's an intruder?"

"Yes, because intruders love to knock before breaking in."

"It's an easy way to get us to open the door, is it not?"

"Maybe it's Channing Tatum." She smiled and opened the door.

"Hi!" Jack stood in the hall with a big smile on his face. "Is that Ryan Reynolds?" He leaned to the side a little to see past Brianna.

"It is!" Brianna said. "But he's made of cardboard."

"Ah."

"Yeah."

"Anyway, is Aspen home?"

"I'm right here." I raised my hand and watched his face fall completely as he realized I was basically right in front of him.

"Oh. Doy. Hi, Aspen."

"Hi."

"How was your last midterm?"

"It was good! Pretty sure I told it who's boss. How were yours?"

"Same."

"We rock."

"You two make me sick," Brianna said, heading back to her room.

"Do you want to come in?" I asked Jack.

We hung out in the living room and watched sci-fi movies on streaming services, and when Carly came home and asked to use the living room to do her yoga, we moved to my bedroom. I had a TV in there, so we could continue our movie marathon no problem.

"Maybe we should get something to eat first," Jack said. "Before we pick the movie back up."

"I have Mr. Noodles in the cupboard."

"Excellent."

So we stood in the kitchen and waited for the water to boil, not saying much to each other, but stealing awkward glances every now and then. *I* felt awkward, at least. I either couldn't think of anything to say, or had too much to say. I was starting to like Jack, but we'd been hanging out as friends for a few weeks now, with no indication of him wanting anything more. I didn't want to tell him that I was getting a crush on him and scare him away. I liked having him as a friend.

We carefully carried our bowls of hot noodles back to my room and sat beside each other on my bed. We didn't say anything during the rest of the movie, and when it was over, Jack smiled, thanked me for sharing my food, and headed out.

"So what's going on with you and that Jack guy?" Carly asked after he'd been gone for about twenty minutes.

"What do you mean? Nothing, we're friends."

"So you wouldn't mind if I asked him out, then?"

"Well no, I mean, yes, I would, but-"

"So something is going on?"

"No, nothing's going on. But we haven't been friends for that long, and I'm enjoying getting to know him. Can I not take it one step at a time with him?"

"Only if he also wants to take it one step at a time."

"What do you mean?"

"If he doesn't want to take something slow, he probably won't wait around for you."

"That sounds kind of harsh," I said. "But I'm not asking him to wait around for me, I just don't want you to ask him out."

"Because you're going to?"

"I don't know. Maybe."

Carly rolled her eyes and went back to her own room. It was at that moment that I questioned how good of a friend she actually was.

"And can you move that Ryan Reynolds thing, please?" I called out to her.

"He's for all of us to enjoy!" And then I heard her door shut.

I flopped down on my bed and looked at the ceiling, wishing I had a hobby besides studying. I didn't have any studying to do, and I was all movied out, so I opened my phone and scrolled through social media. A celebrity I didn't even follow was in one of my feeds, sharing an article put out by a company called The Mars Group. It had a picture of two women in red space suits sans helmets, smiling at the camera. The headline read 'Secret Mars Program not a Secret Anymore.'

I opened the article link and read that a secret project had been in the works for over ten years, getting ready to build a community on Mars. Now that it had been somewhat established, they were encouraging people of all backgrounds to apply to be a part of it. They were in the midst of putting together a town of sorts, and would need people of all education areas, not just scientists and astronauts. There were pictures of what had already been set up, which looked like big, clear and white bubbles, connected by long stretches of clear bubble hallways. They sat on red dirt with cliffs in the distance, covered by a hazy, greyish-purple sky. I swiped to see more pictures of people in space suits, smiling and giving thumbs up and peace signs, standing atop rock faces and peering into craters. Photos of happy faces inside their bubbles, cuddled in blankets on couches with Mars behind them outside. Everyone looked so happy to be there, and they all looked so comfortable with each other. Like they all created a new family up there, and they were happy to finally share it with everyone. I kept swiping to see concept photos of future apartments and businesses, run with solar power and energy-banking technology.

I sent the link to Jack and waited to see if he thought it was as cool as I did.

For the next few months, all Jack and I talked about was going to Mars. I mean, we studied a lot too, but if we weren't studying, we were talking about Mars. Study breaks consisted of Mars sci-fi movies, Mars documentaries, stalking all The Mars Group social media accounts, or talking about going ourselves.

We wanted to go. We wanted to go so bad. We said we would wait until more of a community was established, until there was more for us to do there on our days off, and easy ways for us to explore. But we also didn't want to wait until we were too old, so that it wasn't all humanized completely before we got there. We wanted to be able to experience the Marsness of it all before us Earthlings wrecked it too much. Before we made it too much like Earth, really.

"How long did it take the first group to get there again?" Jack asked one night as we lay on my bed with music playing softly on my Bluetooth speaker. Our class notes were strewn across my blanket, and this was his first non-school related question in about an hour. We hadn't said anything about Mars since he came over after class, and somehow I knew exactly what he was talking about.

"Forty days," I said. I was lying on my back with my head hanging off the edge of the mattress, making me dizzy. Even though I could feel all the blood rushing to my brain, I couldn't bring myself to get up. "But they're saying when the next group goes out, their new ship will be ready and it'll only take them twenty-seven."

"Twenty-seven days to get to Mars? That's wild."

"I know, right?"

"Get up, Aspen, I swear your head's going to explode."

"It feels good," I said.

"How does that feel good? I feel like it's not good for it." He grabbed onto my wrists and pulled me up so that I was sitting in front of him.

"Okay yeah, that's better," I said with a laugh. "But now my head kind of hurts."

"I'll get you some water."

"No, let's go get some coffee."

"Coffee? But it's 11pm."

I shrugged. "I'm going to be up until three studying anyway."

"No, you should get some sleep. You'll do better on your finals if you sleep."

"I've been doing fine so far without any proper sleep."

"Please?" he asked. "For me?"

"For you? What do you get out of it?"

"I won't be worrying about you as much."

"You worry about me?"

"Yeah, of course I do."

I wanted to kiss him so badly. It would have been easy, too. We were sitting so close to each other. We'd been hanging out for the better part of three months, and now here he was, telling me he cared about me. All I had to do was lean forward a little, and he would know what I was doing. He'd finish closing the gap for me and we'd kiss and it would be great.

Except that I couldn't do it. If I thought about it for more than two seconds, my heart started to pound, my mouth went dry and gross, and I felt like I couldn't breathe. Thinking about us kissing was lovely to me. I imagined us kissing quite often, but if I ever told myself that I had to do something in order for that loveliness to happen, I clammed up with anxiety. I wanted to kiss him. I just didn't want to be the one to do it.

"Anyway, I should probably go," Jack finally said after I hadn't said anything in response to him caring about me.

"Oh. Um. No."

"No?"

"I mean, I didn't mean to not say anything."

"Not say anything about what?"

"For when- I mean when- Uh," and then I started laughing because I couldn't seem to do anything else.

"Are you okay?" Jack asked.

"I'm fine. Of course I'm fine, I'm totally 100 percent fine. Excellent."

"Okay." He smiled and got off my bed. "Get some rest. We can go to the library tomorrow morning to study if you need to."

"Yeah, okay."

"I'll text you."

I nodded and watched him leave my room. When I heard the apartment door shut, I got up and locked it behind him.

Of course we studied in the library the next morning. And of course it was a Saturday so I had to sneak out of my apartment so as not to wake my extremely hungover roommates. Although I should have done something to wake them, since they woke me up with their crashing around and puking when they got home at 2am. I ultimately decided not to return the favour, and closed the door quietly before locking it with my key.

Jack met me at the bus stop with an iced coffee for me.

"I figured you'd need it," he said.

"You went to Tims to get this before coming to the bus stop?"

He shrugged. "It's just around the corner."

"Still."

He smiled and took a sip of his own drink.

"Thanks," I said.

The bus came by then, so we both got on, showing the driver our passes before walking down the cramped aisle to the back. There were no seats so we held onto the overhead bar with one hand and clutched our drinks in the other. I looked out the window so I wouldn't get motion sick, but sometimes I glanced at Jack, who was looking at me so intently.

"What?" I asked.

"How are you going to fly to Mars if you can't even ride the bus without feeling nauseous?

"I don't feel nauseous," I said, looking past him and out the window again.

"Right, because you're looking out the window. Look at me and tell me you don't feel sick."

"I always feel sick looking at you," I said with a smile.

"Oh is that how it is?"

"Yeah, that's how it is."

"Look at me," he said.

So I did. I turned my gaze on him, and stared into his eyes. He stared back, and I could tell that he was smiling. I tried my hardest to keep a straight face but it was hard. I felt a smirk make its way to my mouth, so I pulled my lips in, trying to stop it.

"That's cheating," he said.

"How is that cheating? You said I had to look at you, you didn't say anything about the kind of faces I needed to be avoiding."

He sighed very dramatically. "I guess you're right."

"I am right."

"Motion sick yet?"

"Yes. But I can handle it."

"Right. Just like you can handle the takeoff for Mars."

"Damn right."

CHAPTER 9 (NOW)

The smell of garlic fills my apartment. I walk through the door into the warm living room and then across to the kitchen to find the table set, with a vase of wildflowers in the middle.

"David, what's going?" I ask.

"What do you mean what's going on?"

"What's this, why did you set this up?"

"I just thought I'd do something nice for the woman I love." He kisses me on the forehead and then grabs an oven mitt to pull a tray of garlic bread out of the oven.

"Oh. That's nice. Thanks. Do you need help with anything?"

"No, you just sit down and relax and let me bring everything to you."

I pull my chair out and sit down, watching him plate the garlic bread and then use a pair of tongs to put a pile of spaghetti next to them. He ladles the sauce on top and brings both plates at once.

"Is there parm?" I ask, starting to mix the sauce into all the noodles.

He huffs and goes to the fridge, pulls out a container of Kraft parmesan cheese, and practically slams it on the table.

"Um," I say.

"What?"

"I don't understand why you're mad at me."

"I'm not mad at you."

"You just huffed when I asked if there was parm."

"You didn't even let me finish. I was going to bring it out after I put our plates down!"

"Okay. Sorry. Thank you for doing this, it's nice."

He doesn't say anything, instead he shovels some spaghetti into his mouth and nods.

"So you don't have any other reason for this?" I ask quietly.

"What's that supposed to mean?"

"Nothing, I'm just, it's just… is there something you're trying to avoid?"

He stares at me. "What?"

"You have this pattern of only doing nice things for me after we've had a fight or after you've been an asshole," I say.

"What, I'm not allowed to make you dinner now?"

"No, I didn't say that."

"Sure sounds like it."

"I'm just trying to understand. It seems like when you do stuff like this, it's so you don't have to apologize."

"Apologize for what? What is it with you and apologizing?"

"There isn't something with-"

"I can't win with you," he interrupts. He gets up from his chair and throws his arms up. "You get mad at me when I don't pay attention to you, and you get mad at me when I do!"

"I'm not mad at you," I say quietly, trying not to escalate this. Which is pointless. It's already escalated.

"Then what are you?"

"I'm nothing. Confused, I guess."

"You're confused because I made you dinner?"

"No, I'm just- I just-"

"You know what?" he says. "Enjoy your romantic meal by yourself."

He kicks his chair as he walks past, making me jump a little, and then he storms out the door. He slams it behind him and I take in a deep breath, trying not to cry. It doesn't matter though; I should just let myself cry. He's not here to see it, so who am I trying to hide it from? Maybe I'm trying to hide it from myself. I know that doesn't really make sense, but I've been with David for almost five years and it hurts to think that I've been with him for that long just because he did nice things sometimes and told me he loved me. It hurts to admit to yourself that your boyfriend makes you cry more than he makes you laugh.

I'm about to get up from the table when my phone goes off, so I pull it out of my back pocket and open my notifications. Jack has sent me a picture on Photodump.

The picture is of a night sky, taken away from the city lights, with a silhouette of trees lining the bottom of the frame. The sky is a deep blue with so many stars it would be impossible to count them. There are lighter spots in the sky, like lighter blues with grey tones, and soft purples, which I think is the Milky Way.

Jack's message says, **I thought you might like this picture I took of the sky last night. You can see Mars.**

I have no idea which one Mars is, but I'm not about to tell him that. So I reply with, **That's gorgeous. I wish I could live there.**

His response comes almost immediately. **On Mars?**

Yeah. But mostly just anywhere but here.

My phone starts to ring and I blink at it, confused. Is Jack calling me on Photodump? Can you call people on Photodump? Maybe we should have just exchanged numbers the last time we saw each other.

"Hello?" I say, answering his call.

"Hey, are you okay?"

"I'm…" I pause, wondering if I want to dump my problems on him. I'm sure he doesn't want to hear about how my boyfriend's a royal dick. "I'm okay," I end up saying.

"Are you sure?"

"Uh, yeah. I'm uh, I'm just not having a great night. But I'm fine. I promise."

"Alright." He sounds hesitant.

"Thanks for checking, though."

"No problem."

"Have a good night, Jack," I say quietly.

"You too."

"Oh, uh," I add before he hangs up, "thanks for the picture."

"No problem."

And then he hangs up. I sit at the kitchen table with my phone to my ear for longer than is necessary but I just don't know what to do at this point.

I finally let myself cry, but I don't do it loudly or anything. No sobs, just tears and some sniffles. I'm not hungry anymore so I get up from the table and start to put the spaghetti into glass containers so we can at least have something for lunch tomorrow. I wrap the garlic bread in tin foil and then I start to clean the kitchen. I scrub the pots and pans David used to make supper and then I wash our plates and cutlery, and then I wipe down the countertops and the stove. I feel like I'm on a roll and cleaning is really distracting me, even making me feel a little better, so I get out the vacuum and start in the kitchen, working my way to the living room. I move the couches to the middle of the room so I can get the floor where they normally sit, and there's so much crap it's ridiculous. There's used tissues, dust bunnies, popcorn, even a few peanut M&Ms.

Just as I'm about to move the couches back, David comes in. I stop and look at him, my thigh pressed against the armrest of the love seat so I can shove it back to its spot.

"You doing all this to make me feel bad, too?" he asks.

"What?"

"Are you going to get mad at me, saying I wasn't here to help you clean?"

"What the fuck is wrong with you?" I cry. "I was upset so I just started cleaning! I needed something to do!"

"Just thought it would easily be another thing on your list, since you get mad at me all the time."

"David, I get mad at you because you're not supportive of me!"

"How am I not supportive of you? Is it because I didn't go to that stupid party? Are we still on that?"

"It's not just the party, and you know it!"

"What, so you wanna break up, is that it?" he asks, a smug tone to his voice.

My voice cracks when I answer him. "Yes."

"Wait, really?"

"Yes, David. You make me feel like a bag of shit all the time."

"I make you feel like a bag of shit?"

"Yes! You only do things to please yourself, and it's like being an ass to me is one of the things that pleases you! I don't get it! We used to get along. You used to love me."

"I do love you!"

"No," I say, shaking my head. "I don't think it's possible to treat someone you love that way. You don't love me. You just love being loved."

He stares at me with his mouth open for a few good seconds, but seems unable to come up with a response.

"It's okay," I say, "I love being loved too. I think that's why I stayed with you for so long. Because any time I questioned our relationship, you would come in with your romantic dinners, or tell me I'm beautiful, and I didn't want that part to go away."

He scrubs his hand over his face and shakes his head. Looks away for a second. "Please," is all he says.

"No, you don't get to do this to me." I make my way to the bedroom and start pulling clothes out of my dresser.

"What are you doing?" he asks, following me.

"Getting some of my stuff packed up."

"You're leaving?"

"Yes, that's how breaking up works, David. One of us has to leave."

"Then I'll leave."

I shake my head. "I don't want to be here alone when you come back to get your things. I don't want to stress about whether or not you're coming."

"It's not like I'm going to hurt you! Fuck!"

"I don't care," I say through tears. "I think it's best if I leave and you just keep the apartment. I'll be back with Shannon to get my things when I've found somewhere permanent to stay."

"This is so out of the blue!" he yells, throwing his arms in the air.

"It's really not, David. This has been coming for a long time." I throw some clothes and underwear in a backpack and stop when David doesn't move from out of the doorway. "Please move," I say, not looking him in the eye.

"Please stay."

"Why?"

"I'll miss you."

"You'll get over it. Move, please."

He huffs and moves to the side, so I slip between him and the doorframe and half-run to the bathroom to grab my toothbrush.

"Where are you going?" he asks.

"I can afford a hotel for tonight."

"And then where? Shannon's?"

"I'm not telling you, David."

"I'm not going to follow you!"

"Then why does it matter?" I slip my shoes on and grab onto the doorknob that leads into the hallway of the building.

"Fine. Whatever. Leave. I hope it makes you happy."

I give him a forced smile. "So do I."

I should have brought my bathing suit. The hotel I checked into has a pool, and it's open until 11. Maybe I can run to Walmart and get a cheapy one. Instead of going down to my car, I scroll through the Walmart website on my phone, checking to see if they have any in stock that I might like. I end up falling asleep before I even get to the second page.

Luckily I wake up in the middle of the night so I have a chance to set my alarm for work. I get out of bed and make my way to the bathroom, deciding if I want to have a shower now since I'm up, or just have one in the morning. I think having a shower will feel nice so I turn on the water and wait for the bathroom to steam up before I get in.

"I'm really happy for you, to be honest," Shannon tells me the next morning.

"You hardly even knew him," I say.

"Yeah, and you were together for how long after you and I became friends? I should have known him."

"Yeah, you're right. I know you're right, that's why I left."

"It was the right decision. I know it's hard to leave someone, even if they're raging assholes, so I'm proud of you. Put yourself first, girl."

I smile at her and check my med app. My first patient just cancelled. Twelve minutes before their appointment, isn't that nice. I roll my eyes and set my tablet down on my desk.

"I suddenly have a free forty minutes if you're not doing anything," I say.

"I could always use a cup of coffee."

"Sounds great."

We take off our coats and leave them both in my office so we can head down to the Tim Hortons that's in the building. We get breakfast and sit at one of the wooden tables set up in the lobby. Shannon asks me more about David and what was said when I left, and I tell her about it seeming like he wanted to follow me.

Shannon shakes her head. "Don't worry about it. If you need to stay with me for a while, it's totally fine. I mean do you really think he would hurt you?"

"No," I say. "But the thought of him knowing where I am still bothers me for some reason. And if something happens, I don't want you caught in the middle of it."

"That's nice of you. But I'm fine. If it's for you, I'll happily be caught in the middle of it."

CHAPTER 10 (THEN)

"They released new pictures of the community on Mars!" Jack leapt off my bed like it had turned to lava and jumped up and down a few times, holding his phone out.

"Why are you moving away from me!?" I shouted. "Show me!"

I sat up on my knees and Jack bent down in front of me, holding his phone for me to see. I took it from him and swiped through the pictures myself, and Jack ended up sitting next to me on the bed, leaning into my side a little. His face came in really close to mine and I could smell his breath. Which was nice. It didn't smell like much, just sort of like the pasta we had earlier, and also sort of like him. It had been about six months since we became friends, and I'd gotten familiar with his scent. The way he moved. The way he smiled when he thought something was funny but felt insecure about laughing. Even the way his footsteps sounded. I leaned my shoulder into his so that we were pressed up against each other, but he just breathed next to my face and pointed at the pictures as I scrolled through them.

It was pretty futuristic looking. There was a row of white apartments in three stories, with walkways across the fronts and stairs at each end. They had trees set up inside this little compound, with benches and paths that wound around the apartments and into the little town. There was a grocery store, which sold things exclusively made and grown on Mars, according to the caption, an import store, which had things imported from Earth, a research lab, and a gym. In the photos, people were running along the footpaths wearing generic workout clothes, and giant smiles on their faces. People were in the grocery store, smiling in the well-lit aisles that held produce and fresh baked goods. And then there were pictures of the greenhouse, of the factory that made—

"Hold on," I said. "They've created meat?"

"What do you mean?" Jack asked.

"They have a facility that grows meat with some kind of cloning technology!"

"I'm still confused."

"They clone animal parts! But just the parts, so no live animals are hurt. They literally grow meat. It's real meat but it's not real animals."

"That's absurd! Why can't they do that on Earth?"

"I don't know! Why can't they do any of this on Earth? Their little town looks so sustainable and healthy. And happy."

"Well it's all just propaganda," Jack said.

"What do you mean?"

"They're just showing us what they want us to see. And those people's smiles? Those aren't real. No one smiles like that at the grocery store, even if it's on Mars to buy healthy, natural foods. And those runners? No one's ever happy to be running!"

"Maybe if you were on Mars, you would be."

He laughed. "Maybe. But I don't think so. It's still running."

"Yeah," I said. "You're right. But I still want to go."

"There's nothing wrong with that. I want to go too. I think it would be so cool to live on Mars. It would be like living in a sci-fi movie. And because of the compound walls being clear, you always get two views."

"I still don't understand why they can't grow meat on Earth."

Jack shrugged and that's when I realized that our sides were still pressed together. I didn't want to move away. Surely if he wanted more than friendship, he would have done something about it by now. Right? If he hadn't tried to kiss me by this point, it was because he didn't want to, right? If I leaned in to kiss him, it would be unwanted. He would pull away and ask what I was doing. He would say that he never said we were more than friends, and why would I think that we were more than friends? We've studied and watched movies together for the last six months, why would that make me think that he wanted to kiss me?

I leaned away a little and handed him his phone back.

"We should get back to studying," I said quietly. "I know this final's going to kick my ass if I don't get into gear."

"Oh stop, you're a genius."

"I'm really not."

"You know more of this stuff than I ever could."

"That's because I go to the classes. If you went to the classes, you would know it too."

"Nope. Guarantee I wouldn't."

"Just flash me, already," I said.

"W-what?"

"My flash cards."

"Oh." He picked them up off my comforter and held them in the palm of his hand. "Right."

"So can I ask him out, or what?" Carly asked after Jack left.

"What?"

"You obviously got shot down, so can I ask him out?"

"Who?"

"Jack. Who else?"

"You still want to date Jack?"

"Well I don't really want to date him, if you know what I mean."

"Ew. Gross."

"How is that gross?" she asked, sounding hurt.

"It's Jack. He's my friend. I don't want to know that you guys have done it the next time we hang out."

"Why not? What's wrong with him having sex with me?"

"I don't know. I guess gross is the wrong word, sorry. But that's if he even wants to have to sex with you."

"Why wouldn't he want to have sex with me? Is there something wrong with me?"

"No, Carly, nothing's wrong with you. He just doesn't seem like the type of guy who would just sleep with some random girl."

"I'm not random! We've met like twenty times!"

"Right. Sorry, I didn't mean it like that. I just mean that he doesn't strike me as the type who would have a one night stand, or sleep with someone just because."

"Is that why he hasn't slept with you?"

"What? No. I don't know. What's that supposed to mean?"

She shrugged and went into her room.

What did that mean? Did that mean she didn't think I was good enough to be his girlfriend? Did she mean that she didn't think he would want to be in a relationship with me? Was I stupid for assuming that he didn't want to be more than friends? Maybe I should have told him. Maybe that's what I should do tonight. March over to his apartment, knock on his door, and then tell him I have a big fat crush on him. One of two things would happen: He would tell me he also had a big fat crush on me, and then we would kiss, or he would tell me that he just thought of me as a friend, and I would be a little embarrassed, but it would be okay. Right? This wouldn't ruin our friendship or anything, would it? Did I wait too long? I definitely waited too long.

"Alright, well I'm going to invite him out drinking," Carly said, coming out of her room.

"No, don't."

"Why not?"

"Because I'm going over to his apartment right now."

"Why? He was just over here."

"Because he just texted me and asked me to," I lied.

Carly raised her eyebrows at me, and the corner of her mouth started to curl.

"So I'm going," I continued.

"Okay. Well good luck, girl. Give me all the details!"

I smiled and straightened out my shirt, which I realized was an oversized crew neck with our university logo on it. It was essentially my pyjama shirt.

"After I change," I said, darting into my room.

Okay, what does one wear to tell one of their best friends that they have feelings for them? I didn't want it to look like I was trying or anything, but I also didn't want to look like a slob. Not that I looked like a slob, but I didn't want Jack to think I was a slob. Jack wouldn't think I was a slob; he'd seen me in these clothes all the time. I never dressed up for him, so it wasn't a big deal.

Maybe that's why he never thought of me as more than a friend. Because I was always dressed like a teenage boy who never left his bedroom. I took my sweater off and looked at myself in the mirror. My hair was all staticky so I smoothed it down, and then ran my brush through it. Then it looked stupid. The top was flat and the rest was waving in weird directions. I messed it up with my fingertips and tried to separate the layers. Okay, the waves and slight curls looked a little better so I stopped playing with it. But I still didn't know what to wear. I guessed I could go over in the t-shirt I had on underneath the sweater; it was just a fitted blue shirt with capped sleeves. Did it smell, though? I lifted my arms and pressed my nose as close to them as I could, and as far as I could tell, they didn't smell. I put on some new deodorant just in case, and then did a spritz of perfume. Was my breath okay? If I told him I liked him and he tried to kiss me, would he then be repulsed by my bad breath? I ran to the bathroom and quickly brushed my teeth, and then I grabbed my purse off my bed and left.

My heart was pounding. I couldn't believe I was actually going to tell Jack that I liked him. That I wanted his mouth on my mouth. That I wanted to be more than friends. That I wanted to keep studying with him and going for coffee, but during our breaks I wanted to do other things. Um, to him.

I shook my head and buzzed his apartment, and someone buzzed me in without asking who it was. I wondered if it was Jack or one of his roommates. I held my breath in the elevator because I was so nervous, and for some reason I felt like that would help. Of course it didn't help. I was panting and wheezing when the door opened and an older lady came in. She looked at me as if I'd lost my mind. I smiled at her and tried my best to breathe calmly for the next two floors until it was my turn to get off.

When I knocked on the door, I could see my hand shaking. I tried to make it stop, but then Jack opened the door. Oh god. I couldn't do this.

"Hey, what's up?" he asked.

"Um. I just wanted to hang out."

He narrowed his eyes at me and laughed a little. "Okay." And then he stepped aside so that I could come in. "Are you sure nothing else is going on?" he said once we both made it to his living room.

"No. Nothing at all. I just thought you left too early."

"It's past midnight, Aspen."

"Right. Yes. You're right. But it's Saturday night. The bars don't have last call until two."

"You want to go drinking?"

I shrugged. Maybe it would be easier to tell him about my feelings if I was drunk.

"Okay. Um. Give me a sec," he said.

I stood in front of his couch and watched as he disappeared into his room.

"What's going on?" someone said from behind me, making me jump.

"Oh my god," I said, turning around to see his roommate, Brad, sitting on the couch in the corner. "I had no idea someone was in here."

"I am in fact here. So what's going on?"

"What do you mean? Nothing. Nothing's going on."

"Doesn't seem like it."

But then Jack came out of his room wearing a fitted, black button down and dark jeans. "Alright, let's go," he said. He turned his attention to Brad and asked if he wanted to join us.

"I'm good, man. You two have fun." Brad smiled and got off the couch. He winked at me as he passed by, and I hoped that Jack didn't notice.

"So what made you want to go out so badly?" Jack asked as we waited for the bus.

"I don't know. I haven't been drunk since the night I met you, and I thought it would be fun."

"We could have gotten drunk at home. It's way cheaper."

"I don't have booze at home, are you kidding me?"

"Why don't you have booze at home?"

"Because I would never drink it. Do you have booze at home?"

"I do."

We were silent for a minute or two, and then I said, "Do you want to just drink your booze?"

"We could do that." He smiled down at me and I smiled back. And together we walked across the street and back to his apartment.

"That was fast," Brad said when we got in.

"We decided to stay here and drink instead. It's cheaper."

"Right on."

"Okay, let's go." Jack tilted his head in the direction of his room and I followed him, butterflies working their way up my throat. "I like that shirt on you, by the way."

"Oh." My stomach practically shot up to my throat. "Thanks."

Jack got out a bottle of rye and some Coke cans from his mini fridge, and poured us each a drink. He sat next to me on the bed and turned on his TV, which was still paused on some video game. He switched the input and turned on Netflix, where a Mars Community Documentary was being advertised on the top panel.

"Oh no way," I said, sitting up straighter. "A documentary on building the Mars Community!? Can we watch this, please?"

"Fuck yes we can." Jack pressed play and I leaned back against his headboard, the rye and coke still in my hand.

We sipped our drinks slowly, and didn't have another one once we were finished. We did binge four episodes of the documentary though, before I fell asleep. Jack shook me awake, and I opened my eyes to see his face real close to mine. It was so close I couldn't even make out his features.

"Hey," he whispered. "It's like, 5am."

"Is it?" I could hear how groggy my voice was.

"Do you want me to walk you home?"

"I'm so tired."

"Do you want to just keep sleeping?"

"Mhmm." I wanted Jack to keep whispering to me. I wanted him to whisper in my ear that he wanted me to stay over. That he would sleep next to me under the covers and we would sleep together there until the end of time.

"Okay," he finally said. "I'll go sleep on the couch."

"No, stay," I managed to say.

"What?"

"I want you to stay." If I wasn't half asleep, I don't think I would have been able to say that to him.

"Alright."

And then he got under the covers. The covers that I was already under. I felt his body heat immediately and smiled at the thought of being kept warm by him. I wanted him to move closer, but I was so tired I couldn't keep my eyes open anymore let alone say more. I could feel him next to me though, and somehow that was enough.

CHAPTER 11
(NOW)

Shannon is driving me to David's in a moving truck. The only apartment I could find that's available is a studio, which is obviously not ideal. But it's available now, and the price is right. So whatever. I can live in a studio apartment for a while, right? It'll be cozy. I can lie in bed while I wait for the water to boil when I make Kraft Dinner. Excellent. The best of both worlds.

David is pretty quiet while Shannon and I take my books, my clothes, my computer, and pack them into boxes. He watches from the couch until Shannon kicks the side under the armrest.

"We'll be taking this," she says.

"What?" he asks, looking up at her.

"You have two. Aspen can have one and you can have one."

"She can buy a new couch. She's got money."

"That's not the point. And she's not rich, you idiot."

"Don't call me that."

"What? An idiot?"

"Shannon, it's fine," I say. "I'll just use my bed. I mean, the bed… I mean… Fuck, I don't have a bed."

"Fine, you can have the couch," David says. He stands up and clears his throat.

"Great," I say, ignoring the fact that it looks like he's trying not to cry. He's probably doing it for show, so that I'll feel bad. "I'm just going to grab some towels and toilet paper from the bathroom."

David huffs and follows me. I continue to ignore him, and instead pay attention to the sounds of Shannon out in the living room taping up boxes. I fill a cardboard box with eight rolls of Costco toilet paper, three bath towels, a hand towel, and the soap dispenser from the sink. He can get new soap.

David doesn't even help us move anything; he continues to watch us as we struggle to fit the couch out the door, and then I assume he sits on his loveseat in the living room while we take it down to the truck.

I assumed right, because he's sitting on it when we get back.

"Are you going to help us?" Shannon asks.

He just snorts.

"We'll be gone faster if you help us, you know. Two people can only carry so much."

"Whatever. Fine." He gets up and immediately picks up a box. He grunts as he walks past me to put his shoes on, and he stomps down the hall in front of us.

"Okay great, now let's get the TV," Shannon says with a smile.

We cover the tv in a blanket and carry it to the elevator.

"We should have taken this last," I say once we get outside. "I still have a bookcase up there."

"If he notices, I'll buy you a new one."

"I can't let you buy me a bookcase."

"Sure you can."

I roll my eyes at her and slide the TV into the truck in between boxes. We run back to the elevators and hope that David hasn't noticed the TV missing. My heart is hammering in my chest imagining him blowing up at us and us having to run back to the truck and drive away with the rest of my stuff still in his living room. But he's not in there when we get back. Shannon and I look at each other and shrug, but continue to get the last of the boxes. Shannon puts them in the stairwell so that if we don't get a chance to come back into the apartment for them after bringing the bookcase down, we'll still be able to get them. We carry my bookcase into the hall together and shove it into the elevator, with no sign of David the whole time.

"Maybe he's taking a shit," Shannon says as the elevator moves from floor 5 to floor 4.

Shannon helps me get everything into my new apartment and we even unpack most things and get it all set up, minus a bed that I still need to get. But Shannon is so supportive and helpful, and we tape a spot for it on the floor so we can figure out where everything will fit. It's definitely going to be a little tight. But it'll work. We'll make it work.

"We should go to IKEA. We can get you a mattress and a bed frame, and a tiny little two seater kitchen table."

"Yeah, we should. Next weekend?"

"You want to go all week without a bed?" she asks.

I shrug. "I have the bigger couch, I'll be fine."

After Shannon leaves, I grab my purse and head out. I know it's getting late, and I haven't been this exhausted in a long time, but I really need to escape. Being in my tiny apartment that doesn't even have a bed is not what I want right now. So I go to the only place I've ever been able to really escape since graduating university. The bookstore.

I'm four books deep, already having trouble keeping them in my arms as I pull new ones off the shelf to read the synopsis, when I spot Jack farther down the same row as me. I take a step forward just to make sure that it's actually him before I say anything, but it's definitely him.

"Jack?" I ask.

He's literally mid-pull when he hears me, and he stops, his arm in the air, his hand grasped onto a small hardcover. "Oh. Hey, Aspen."

"What are you doing here?"

"At the bookstore?" he drops his arm, the book now at his side. "Oh, you know, just thought I'd come see a movie."

"A movie?" But just as I say the words, I realize that I asked him a stupid question, and he was being funny. "Oh," I say, shaking my head. "I see what you did there."

"Yeah," he says slowly.

"I just meant why are you here?"

He narrows his eyes at me and tilts his head to the side, probably trying really hard not to say something that could come across as mean. Why am I so stupid?

"Okay, never mind," I try. "It's just weird, us somehow always being in the same place all of a sudden."

"Maybe we've been in the same places a lot before, and we just never noticed. Maybe it took us actually interacting for us to see each other."

"Hmm. Maybe."

"I also just moved back to this area a few months ago."

"Oh, and look at you trying to be all philosophical!" I shove him in the arm a little and almost drop my books.

"You alright there?" he asks.

"Yes. Fine. Sorry. I just tried to be cool and obviously failed."

"Aw come on, don't say that. You're obviously very cool."

"Ha, ha," I say slowly.

"But anyway, I have been here for a few months, and I swear I wasn't hiding this whole time. I've still been out and doing stuff since before we… uh, I mean before you- uh, before my appointment."

I smile at him and his awkwardness. It makes me feel better about myself that sometimes he seems too nervous to form a proper sentence as well. It doesn't seem to happen to him nearly as often as it does to me, but when it does happen to him, it makes me feel more human.

"Alright, alright," I say with a bit of a laugh. "I guess your philosophical moment is still justified."

"Thank you." He beams at me. "So what are you doing here?"

"At the bookstore?"

"Yeah."

"Actually, the bookstore is sort of my escape."

"Your escape?"

Jack knew that the library was one of my escapes in university, especially the one on my end of campus. The one that felt like you were in an old castle. I wonder if he forgot about that, or if he just assumes that I've moved on to other things at this point.

"Yeah," I reply, not really wanting to elaborate.

"Escape from what?"

"Oh, you know. Life."

He looks at me for a few seconds and nods slowly. He doesn't believe me. I can tell he doesn't believe me. He takes in a breath like he's about to say something serious, but I start talking first.

"So what books are you getting?" I ask.

He looks down at the one in his hand, the thin hardcover, and then back to me, holding the book up.

"I've read that one," I say. "It's really good. There's a whole bunch in the series, and they're really fast reads since they're so small. You should get the next one in the series too."

He smiles at me and then turns back to the shelf. "Okay." He starts to take one off, but I can see that it isn't the right one.

"That's the third one," I say. "They don't have them in the right order on here." I scan the books and find one with a grey spine. "Here." I pull it off the shelf for him and hand it to him.

"Thanks."

"No problem."

"I know it's late, but do you want to get a coffee?"

We buy our books and head over to the café that's in the bookstore, and wait in line quietly. There are still a surprising amount of people here considering it's almost 9pm. Who gets coffee at 9pm? Well, I guess we do.

"Hi, I'll get a medium coffee with two milks, and," he turns to me, "an iced coffee? You still like iced coffees?"

"Yes," I say, "but with no sugar."

He turns back to the barista. "And a medium iced coffee with none of that sweet syrupy stuff you guys put in it."

"You got it," the barista says with a smile. "It'll be ready over at the counter on your left."

Jack pays and then we both shuffle to the left and wait quietly for our drinks to come. I wonder what he's thinking about. I wonder if he's wondering what I'm thinking about. I'm about to open my mouth to ask him a question, but our coffees are ready and the barista calls out Jack's name. He smiles at me and goes to grab our drinks, so I follow him.

"Should we sit?" he asks. "They're open till ten."

"Yes. Let's sit."

I walk beside him and let my arm brush against his. I wish I could do more than just let our arms brush against each other. He smiles down at me and sits at the nearest table, so I sit across from him. I take a sip of my iced coffee and contemplate asking him about his Mars application. I decide against it though, because I'm jealous of him and I don't really want to talk about him going to Mars when I thought I was going to be there more than three years ago.

"So what brings you to this part of town?" I ask him instead.

"An apartment I could afford."

"Ah. Sorry."

"Don't be sorry," he says. "I'm okay."

I nod at him and take a sip of my drink.

"Do you come to this bookstore often?" Jack asks.

"Too often, probably."

"No such thing; I shop here a lot too. I'm actually surprised that we haven't run into each other before now."

"I'm not. I've never run into an old friend so many times before."

"We're not old friends anymore though, are we?"

"What do you mean?"

"I'd like to think we're friends. We've talked and seen each other enough in the last little while, I think we count as friends again."

"Okay, fair," I say. "We're friends. I mean that's all we ever were, right?" My tone is a little snarky and I'm not even sure if it's on purpose or not.

He scrunches his eyebrows at me for a second. "What?" he asks.

"Nothing, never mind." I say quickly, suddenly deciding that my comment wasn't fair, snarky or not. "I don't know where that came from. Let me rephrase. I've never run into a friend so many times before." I put emphasis on the word friend, I guess to point out that I didn't use the word 'old' in front of it. "Unless you are stalking me," I add with a bit of a laugh.

He puts his hands up in mock surrender. "I swear I'm not."

"Okay. But anyway, I should go." I grab my bag of books and stand up from my chair.

"Boyfriend expecting you home?" Jack asks, looking up at me.

"Um. Yeah." I don't know why I lie. It wasn't my plan; it's not like I came here with the idea in my head that I was going to make Jack think I'm still in a loving relationship. I just don't want to talk about it, and saying something like 'he's actually not my boyfriend anymore' or 'no, he isn't expecting me home' will bring questions. Questions that I don't have the energy to answer right now. And even though I feel like I know Jack pretty well, the fact is that I haven't seen him in over eight years. So I don't know him. I know Jack from a decade ago. I have no idea what Today-Jack is like at all.

"Alright," Jack says. "Have a good night."

"You too." I start to turn away when I realize that even though I don't want to talk about my break up just yet, doesn't mean that I don't want to talk to Jack at all. I can't get to know Today-Jack if I don't allow myself to talk to him. "But hey, um," I start up again, "if we were to run into each other again, I uh, I wouldn't mind."

"Neither would I," he says with a warm smile, showing off his dimple.

"I need to go to the mall tomorrow. Pick out a new comforter."

"Oh yeah?"

"Yeah. I'll probably go after lunch."

"Well maybe I'll run into you."

"Yeah. Maybe."

I get home and let out a deep breath so I don't cry. I look around my tiny apartment and try to imagine a bed taking up even more space in this little room. As if I live in a cramped studio apartment. I put my new books on the kitchen counter and head to the washroom to have a shower.

At least the bathroom is a decent size. The shower has a deep tub and a clear curtain, but I'll probably buy a new one to go over it, one with a fun design on it. I pull my hair out of its ponytail and then turn on the water. I let it run for a bit so it can get hot, and then I step in, almost slipping on the bottom. I grab onto the shower curtain rod over my head and slip again, my feet coming out from under me completely. I keep a grip on the curtain rod and manage to right myself, but now my shoulder feels like it just came out of the socket. It didn't, but it hurts a lot. I rotate my shoulder around and let out a whine as I do it, trying even harder not to cry at this point.

It doesn't work. I realize that I don't have any shampoo, so I cry as I let the hot water run over me.

CHAPTER 12
(THEN)

"I can't believe you still haven't done anything!" Carly cried. "The only reason I didn't ask him out was because you said that he wanted you to go over to his place! You made it seem like he wanted to fool around with you!"

"I thought he wanted to!" I lied.

"Well now that you know he doesn't want to, can I ask him out?"

"No!"

"Why not!? He's never going to sleep with you!"

My jaw dropped. I was so offended and I hated that I didn't even know what to say to her. Tears ran down my face, hot and fast, so I wiped them away with my sleeve. It was pointless though, because more just followed.

"You're so pathetic, Aspen," Carly said. "You're a full grown adult and you just study and hang out with the guy you're secretly in love with. And you won't even let me do anything about my feelings for him! Feeling that *I* don't want to keep a secret!"

"You don't have feelings!" I shouted at her. "You told me that you just wanted to have sex with him!"

"Those are feelings!"

"Why do you think it's okay to sleep with your friend's crush?"

"Why do you think it's okay to stop your friend from doing something about *their* crush?"

"You don't have a crush on him, Carly! It's not the same!"

"Maybe it isn't the same for you, but it is to me! You can't keep him all to yourself and not even do anything with him! Like, what? He doesn't want to sleep with you so he's not allowed to sleep with *anyone*? No, you know what? You don't get to tell me what to do. You don't control him. If I want to sleep with him, then I'll sleep with him."

"Fine!" I yelled.

She threw her arms up in the air. "Fine!"

"Good luck," I added sarcastically, and more loudly than I meant to.

"Thanks. But I don't need it." She smiled and left the apartment.

I wanted to scream. As if she was doing this to me right now. It was okay though, because Jack wouldn't say yes to her. Would he? No, of course he wouldn't. Jack and I were friends, and he knew that Carly and I were friends – at least *were* friends – and he wouldn't do anything with her. He would either feel weird about it, or would know that I would feel weird about it, and he would say no to her. But why would he think I feel weird about it if he didn't have any suspicion that I liked him? And if he had a suspicion that I liked him, he would have done something about it, wouldn't he? I guess he only would have if he liked me back.

Fuck. Jack was going to sleep with Carly.

I needed to text him. I needed to do something; I couldn't just let this happen. I pulled out my phone and opened my conversation with him, but my thumbs hovered over the keyboard. What was I supposed to say? Carly's going to come over and try to sleep with you? That sounded ridiculous.

I typed **hey** and pressed send.

Hey he replied.

Okay. Good. This was good. We could work with this.

What's up? I asked.

The little typing bubble came up and stayed on the screen for a while, and then it went away. I watched my phone like a cat watching a squirrel, and waited for the typing bubbles to reappear. They didn't. I watched my phone until the screen turned black, and then I turned it back on, and he still wasn't typing again. Where did he go? Did Carly make it to his apartment? Did she even know which one was his? How would she know which apartment to buzz? Oh my god, had she been over there before? Did she have his number? Did they text?

"Hey, what are you doing?" Brianna asked, making me practically jump out of my socks.

"Oh my god you scared the shit out of me," I said.

"Sorry. Is your phone broken or something?" She put her bag down by the door and walked over to me.

"I wish," I said.

"What do you mean you wish?"

"Carly's trying to sleep with Jack."

"What? Why?"

I shrugged. "She says she likes him."

"But you like him," Brianna said.

"But she thinks because I won't do anything about it, she should get to."

"Excuse me? What a bitch. Well you know he's not going to, right? He's totally in love with you."

"Really? You think so?"

"Oh my god, Aspen, how are you so dense? Both of you have the hots for each other and you're both too chicken to do anything about it. I see the way he looks at you when he's over here studying with you."

"I don't believe you."

"Okay. Whatever. When he doesn't sleep with Carly, then will you believe me?"

"Maybe."

"And then will you do something about it?"

"Maybe."

"I still can't believe Carly would do that."

"I can."

"Really?"

"I thought she was great last year… before…" I stopped for a second and bit my lip. "Before we lived together."

"You're right," Brianna said. "I definitely didn't know her as well as I thought I did."

I nod.

"Maybe we should talk to her about it," she suggested.

"About her being a bitch?" I asked. "No way."

"Why not?"

"I can't tell the guy I like that I like him, how do you think I can tell the girl I live with that I think she's a bitch?"

"Well you don't have to say it like that, Aspen. And we can do it together."

"Great, two people telling her she's a bitch."

"Oh my god, we're not going to tell her she's a bitch," Brianna said, rolling her eyes. "Just that we think she needs to be more mindful of us if we're going to keep living together next year."

"Right. Okay. That works. We can do that."

"Of course we can."

"Now we just have to wait for her to finish having sex with Jack."

"She's not having sex with him."

She definitely had sex with him. She'd been gone for two hours and still wasn't back. What were they doing over there? They had to be having sex. Or doing sex related things. What else would they be doing?

Unless she wasn't over there and just wanted me to believe that she was. Maybe he told her to leave and so she wandered around the city on her own, hoping I would be super jealous by the time she got back.

Or they had sex.

"Stop thinking about them," Brianna said. "There's nothing you can do at this point."

"Except to think about it." I sighed and leaned my head back against the couch behind me. I stared up at the ceiling, imagining a life where Carly was at my study sessions because she couldn't leave Jack's side. I imagined a life with Carly everywhere and I cringed. And then I imagined Carly and Jack having sex on the table at the library on top of all my flash cards and I just about screamed.

"You should have laminated them if you were worried about them getting wrecked," anxiety-dream Carly said to me.

"No." I stood up from the couch. "No no no."

"No?" Brianna was on the other end of the couch, cuddling a stuffed animal.

"I have to go over to his apartment! It's been too long!"

"If she's there, do you really want to see her with him?"

"You're right," I said.

"I know I'm right."

I heard Carly creak the door open well after I'd gone to bed. I checked the time on my alarm clock: 2am. She was not at Jack's until 2am. I refused to believe it. There's no way that Jack even allowed Carly to be in his presence for that long. Right? Ugghhhh.

I groaned and tried to get back to sleep. Which I obviously failed at.

My phone was going off. Notification after notification. What time even was it? I grabbed my phone off my nightstand and swiped the screen to see that I had actually slept in and I was late for class. Oh my god, I was late for class! What the hell! Why didn't my alarm go off!? I checked my alarm clock, and it wasn't even set. Did I seriously forget to set it last night? I must have been too wrapped up in Jack and Carly possibly doing it to remember. I didn't even have time to shower! Was I even going to make it by the time I got there? There was no way. I swiped on my notifications to see what they were.

Texts from Jack.

Hey, I missed you on the way to class this morning. I usually see you on Wednesdays.

And then: **Are you okay?**

Then: **Sorry I didn't answer you last night. It's a bit of a long story.**

What was I supposed to say to him? What should I do? I could at least make it to my next class, so I should get in the shower. I did that first and thought about how to reply to Jack. Of course all the answers I came up with in the shower were unacceptable, and when I got dressed, I had to settle with: **I slept in.**

Oh no came his reply. **Did you miss class completely?**

My first class, yes. I'll make it for my next one though I said back to him.

Glad to hear it. Study after school? Or we could watch more of that Mars Community Documentary since we haven't watched any more of it yet.

Yeah. Mars Doc sounds good.

He replied with a smiley face and I finger brushed my wet hair before heading out to catch the bus.

Carly was in the hall. I didn't know how to approach her, and I kind of just wanted to pretend that I didn't see her, but that was clearly impossible and also rude. It was a small hallway and it would be obvious that I was ignoring her on purpose.

"Your friend is really good with his hands," Carly said as we got closer.

"What?"

"Jack? His fingers are magic."

"What?" I said again.

She rolled her eyes as she passed me. "Never mind."

"Wait," I said, turning around to keep facing her. "You didn't… How much did you… I mean…" She smirked as I stammered.

"What didn't we do, is the question you should be asking," she said.

"Carly!"

"What! There's nothing wrong with two consulting adults having sex!"

"It is when you're supposed to be friends with me!"

"Honey, I don't need your permission to sleep with a boy I find attractive."

"I can't believe you." I felt my eyes well with tears, and Carly's face dropped a little. She looked at the ground for a second, then back at me, and she looked really… unsure. Her eyes seemed a little sad, or maybe ashamed, like she actually felt bad for what she did. But then she smiled at me and turned back to our apartment.

There was no way I was going to be able to hang with Jack that night. Him and Carly were all I would be able to think about. I wouldn't be able to enjoy the documentary, or even enjoy just being in his presence. Carly really ruined everything.

I decided something in that minute that I never thought I would do. I decided that instead of continuing to make my way to school so I could go to class, I was going to march back down the hallway and tell Carly to fuck off. Or ruin her cardboard Ryan Reynolds.

"Carly, what the fuck!" I yelled, storming into the apartment.

But she didn't say anything because she was… crying? Was she crying?

"Carly!" I yelled again, making my way to her bedroom. I knocked on her door, but she didn't answer, she just kept crying. "Carly?" I asked, this time in a softer tone.

I didn't want to just open her door without her telling me to come in, but now I was worried. Why would she be crying? She just had amazing sex apparently, so what was going on?

"Are you okay?" I asked, pushing her door open slowly.

"No! Do I look okay!?"

"N-no. But you seemed excellent in the hall."

"Well I wasn't! Okay!?"

"Okay…" I hesitated for a few seconds and then said, "What's happening? I'm so confused."

"Nothing is happening! Just go away!"

"O-okay." I backed out of her room and quietly went to mine. I took my backpack off and pulled all my notes out of it so I could at least study if I wasn't going to go to class. I went through all my flashcards and made some new ones. I tested myself with them and did a few practice questions from my anatomy textbook.

I jumped a little when my door creaked open a few hours later. Carly was standing in the doorway, her eyes red and puffy from crying. I sat up on my bed and crossed my legs, waiting for her to say something to me.

"Nothing happened with Jack," she finally said.

"Oh?"

"Yeah. I lied to you in the hall. Because I was embarrassed."

"Why would that be embarrassing?"

She shrugged and looked away for a second. "I don't know. Because I was so confident that he would want to. And it hurt my feelings that you didn't want me to, and I wanted to make you mad."

"It hurt your feelings that I didn't want you to get involved with one of my best friends?"

"Yeah."

"Carly, that's silly."

"I just," she paused for a second before continuing, like it was hard for her to open up about this. "I've had a thing for Jack for probably as long as you have."

"What?"

"I know it's not the same, because I'm not close with him like you are, but I see him every time he comes over, and I've run into him on campus a few times and I never wanted to do anything about it because I thought you guys would end up getting together. But then you never did anything about it, and when you said I couldn't, I just thought you were being selfish, and that my feelings didn't matter."

"You didn't think that maybe what you did made me feel like *my* feelings didn't matter?"

"I don't know. You weren't going to do anything about liking him, and I… I don't know. I'm sorry."

I let out a deep breath. "Thanks."

"Thanks?"

"Yeah. For apologizing."

"I don't think that's what you're supposed to say when someone apologizes. You're supposed to say that it's okay."

"Only if it is."

"What?"

"It's not okay, Carly. What you did was absolutely not okay. Especially in the hall, lying about it and trying to rub it in my face. Why would someone do that to a friend?"

"I don't know!"

"Well, I appreciate you apologizing."

There was a minute of silence and I looked back down to my notes. But then Carly spoke and it made me look back up at her, taken aback. "He said he liked someone else."

"What?" I asked.

"Jack. When he told me no, he said he liked somebody else."

CHAPTER 13
(NOW)

So Jack and I didn't actually plan a time and place to meet. We really didn't think this through. I decided to stop at the Tims in the mall entrance and get something for each of us, just in case he showed up. I did say that I'd probably come after lunch, but what is after lunch? I guess it's the most common to think that people eat lunch at noon, but some people might eat later or earlier depending on when they wake up, or what they're doing that day. And telling Jack that I'd be here after lunch implies that he's supposed to know how long it takes me to eat lunch. What if I'm a slow eater and I'm not done my lunch until after 1:00? Is that an acceptable after-lunch time? I look at my watch. It's 12:37. That's an acceptable after lunch time, right? Oh I don't know.

I start walking towards Homesense and then realize that I could just message him on Photodump. Unless he doesn't have push notifications set up for Photodump DMs. He wouldn't see it until he opened the app for leisure purposes.

"Hey, funny seeing you here," I hear from behind. Oh good, it's Jack. I turn around and smile at him.

"Hey!" I say with a little too much enthusiasm, handing him his drink. "I got you a coffee. Two milks, right?"

"Oh yeah, thanks. But what if I didn't end up coming?"

"Then I'd be a little sad and have an extra coffee."

He smiles but doesn't say anything. Am I coming off too strongly? Should we not be acting like we did when we hung out in University? I know that I still need to get to know him again before I open up to him more or tell him more personal things, but a big part of me feels like I already know him so well. Like our friendship is muscle memory. But if I'm the only one who feels that way then I need to be careful.

"Sorry," I say, "Is it weird that I got you one? I just got myself one and I thought that-"

"Of course it isn't weird," he interrupts. "It's nice. Thanks for thinking of me."

"No problem."

"So what are you picking out a new comforter for?"

"Oh you know," I say, sort of stammering. "It's… time."

He pauses for a second, probably thinking about how weird I am, and then says, "Why isn't your boyfriend helping you pick it out?"

"Because he's not going to be using it," I say without thinking. I try to backtrack but I've already said the words. "Uh, I mean," I stammer, "It's just for me."

"Okay," he says slowly.

"Yeah. So help me pick out a fun one!" I immediately start walking into the store and I feel Jack following me. I want to talk to him. I want to get to know him again. Seeing him again has made me feel sort of at home. Even thinking about going back to my tiny shithole apartment isn't so bad right now, because Jack is walking through Homesense with me, and I can smell his cologne. It's different from the one he wore when we were younger, but it's got some similar notes to it. It's a little spicy and warm, and makes me want to breathe him in.

"So have you heard anything from The Mars Group yet?" I ask, trying to shake away my feelings. I literally just broke up with David, I can't be thinking about breathing in Jack.

"I have, actually," Jack says.

"Oh yeah?" I immediately regret asking him about it, but try to pretend that I'm excited.

"Yeah. No job yet. Just a bunch of questionnaires to fill out."

"That seems like a good sign."

"Yeah, I thought so too."

"I never got to fill out any questionnaires after I applied, so I would say that it's definitely a good sign. You'll be a Martian before you know it."

He takes in a little breath and smiles in a way that sort of resembles the cringe face emoji, and crosses his fingers in front of his face. "Fingers crossed."

I cross my fingers too. "Fingers crossed."

We stare at each other for a couple of seconds and all I can think about is the fact that everyone is getting to live my dream. Jack's going to get accepted to The Mars Group and get a job on Mars just like everyone else, and I'm going to be stuck here in my tiny studio apartment, doing the same routine checkups on people every day.

"Hey, are you alright?" Jack bumps my arm with his elbow.

"Yeah, of course I am."

"You sure?"

"Yeah." I turn my attention to the shelving in front of us and point at a bed-in-a-bag set that has soft green and yellow polka dots. "Hey, this one's cute!"

"It's a nice one. What size do you need?"

"Queen."

He grabs the bag and moves it around, looking for a size, which we both find in the corner. "Queen. You want this one, or do you want to keep looking?"

"I'll grab it for now, but let's keep looking."

"Good idea."

We shop around the store for about an hour, looking at comforters and also at knickknacks and kitchen stuff.

"Oh, this dish set is super cute," I say, pointing to a box with a picture of a blue plate, bowl, and mug on the front.

"You need a new dish set too?"

My heart hammers a little. "No. Of course not. I was just saying." We walk past and into another aisle. I can get dishes at the dollar store.

Jack takes my cup from me when he sees that it's empty and puts them both in a trash can as I line up to pay for my bed-in-a-bag. We wander the mall for a while afterward, laughing and joking as we go into different stores, and I wish that when we decide to leave, he would invite me over instead of us separating in the parking lot. I want to see where he's living now. I want to know more about what he's doing. What he's been doing. I linger under the covered entrance, hoping he'll notice and not continue walking to his car. He realizes that he's alone after he's stepped off the curb, and he turns back to me.

"What are you doing?" he asks.

"You wanna get dinner?"

"It's 3:30," he says.

I shrug. "The restaurants won't be busy. Might be nice."

He sticks his hands in his jeans pockets and looks around. At what, I couldn't tell you. It's just a big open parking lot with subdivisions behind it.

"Yeah sure," he finally says. "You're right. It might be nice."

"So did you end up getting a job as a teacher at all?" I ask once we sit down at East Side Mario's. "I know you said at the Send Off that you were working for a marketing company, but you went to teacher's college."

"Yeah, I was teaching grade 9 and 10 English for a few years, but I was so into my photography that Anna convinced me to take a two-year photography course. I went to half days for teaching, and managed to snag all afternoon and evening classes. It was tiring, but worth it, I guess."

"Do you like your photography job better than your teaching job?"

"I like that I have more free time," he says. "I really liked interacting with the students when I taught. They were all such great kids. But there was always the marking, and the lesson planning, and after school events, plus I coached the Junior Boys soccer team, which took up a lot of time."

"I can imagine."

"Yeah. Of course I had to stop coaching when I went back to school, but all the extra curriculars were so much work. And now I get to go into work, leave at 5:00 and not have to worry for the rest of the evening."

"That's nice. I like that I basically get to do the same thing, too. I did my residency in emergency medicine, so my schedule was all over the place, and work was almost always hectic. When I applied to work on Mars, it was a mix of like, GP and emergency medicine, doing arrival physicals and also working in their little hospital, which I was really looking forward to. But then I got hired to work here, doing intake physical exams."

"That's gotta be really boring compared to working in emerge."

"Yeah. I couldn't pass up the pay, to be honest. And it's nice and calm, at least. And there aren't any surprises."

"Until I'm in your exam room."

I laugh once out loud, like a cartoon "ha," and I'm a little embarrassed, but then Jack laughs and I start to giggle. We're laughing at each other when our server comes with our food, and she looks at us like we've lost our marbles.

"You wanna do a photoshoot sometime?" Jack asks when we're waiting for the bill.

"Like what kind of photoshoot?"

He shrugs. "Any kind of photoshoot. Like we did back in the day."

"I wouldn't consider those photoshoots." I scoff a little and look away.

"Are you undermining me as a photographer, Aspen?"

"No, I guess I'm undermining myself as a model."

"You were always the best model."

I can feel myself blushing and I look down at the table. "Okay there," I say quietly.

"We don't have to. If you're uncomfortable with it-"

"Why would I be uncomfortable with it?" I ask, cutting him off.

"Well, just, I don't know, you have a boyfriend and I can see how he might get the wrong idea. You know what, forget I asked. I'm sorry."

"Oh. Um. That's okay. No worries."

He smiles at me but it seems forced. "Why is the bill taking so long?"

I shrug at him and watch as he turns in his seat, looking for our server. She comes out of the kitchen almost right away and drops our bill off.

"I can pay right now," Jack says to her.

"Sure." She hands him the portable machine and he presses a few buttons and then taps his card. She smiles at him, thanks him as she rips his part of the receipt, and walks away.

"I could have paid," I say.

"Don't be silly."

"I was the one who invited you out."

"Oh. Right. Well that's okay. You can get it next time."

"Right. Okay."

Jack and I walk across the street back to the mall where our cars are parked, and I wish I could lean my shoulder into his bicep. I wish I could reach out and grab his hand. Everything that I felt in university is coming back in a giant wave and sometimes I feel like I have to stop and take a deep breath before it crashes over me. I had never felt as strongly for someone as I did for Jack, and hanging out with him is making me feel like we never spent any time apart. I'm not even thinking about David at this point. If Jack wasn't in my life, it's not that I would be sad about David, or wishing we were back together, but our breakup would be playing constantly though my head. But it's not. I'm just thinking about what it would be like to stand on my toes and press my lips against Jack's mouth.

CHAPTER 14 (THEN)

Jack texted me at 4:30, asking if we should watch the Mars Doc at my place or his. I didn't really want him to come over if Carly was still there, and I was sure Carly didn't want him to either. I told him I would come to his place.

But the whole time that I got ready, all I could think about was that he told Carly he liked someone else. He didn't tell her who, and when she asked if it was me, he didn't answer. She told me that he pointed to the door and asked her to leave. But then his roommate, Brad, came in and told her she didn't have to go if she didn't want to, and she went into his room with him. She said they didn't have sex, but that they hung out and fooled around a bit, and she fell asleep in his bed. I asked her if she was going to see him again and she said it would probably be awkward with Jack there, so most likely not.

So Jack's place it was, then. With the question of whether or not I was the one he liked, just burning in the back of my mind.

"So what happened last night?" I asked him as I stepped into his apartment.

Brad was on the couch, and seemed immediately interested in our conversation.

"Let's just go to my room," he said quietly.

"Um. Okay." Was he going to tell me that he liked me? That he has wanted me this whole time we've been friends? That for the last six months I'm all he's been able to think about?

We went into his room and he shut the door gently. I sat on his bed and tried my best to breathe calmly. This was not a big deal. It was not a big deal. I could handle it. Better yet, I would be good at it. We would both be good at it, and we would wonder to ourselves how we even waited this long.

"So yeah," Jack started, sitting in his computer chair across from his bed. "Carly kissed me last night."

"What? She kissed you?"

"Yeah." He grabbed at the back of his neck and looked away a little, a nervous looking smile across his face. "I didn't kiss her back," he added quickly.

"Oh."

"She basically attacked me. She came in and said she needed to talk so I said sure, but then she just… kissed me. She tried to push me against the wall too." He laughed, but I could tell he felt uncomfortable.

"Jack, that's horrible. I had no idea she did that. I'm so sorry."

"It's not your fault. Anyway, I pushed her shoulders away from me a little and pulled back. I told her I was sorry."

"She should be the one apologizing."

"It's fine. She was just trying to put herself out there, I guess."

"It's not fine."

"But it doesn't matter, I'm pretty sure she slept with Brad."

"She said they just fooled around a little."

He raised an eyebrow at me. "Oh she told you about all this, did she?"

"Yeah," I said slowly. "She was pretty upset."

"Geez. Now I feel bad."

"Don't feel bad. She threw herself at you. That's not acceptable."

"Yeah. Anyway, that's why I didn't text you back. I was so flustered after that. I left and went for a walk, and when I came back, I heard them in Brad's room, and I just put my headphones on and went to bed."

"Oh."

"Yeah. I completely forgot. I'm sorry."

"Oh. No, it's okay. I get it. That was a lot that happened to you."

He laughed. "Yeah, I guess it was. So, Mars Doc?"

"Yes. Mars Doc. Please."

He turned his TV on and I fluffed up a pillow against his headboard and leaned into it, fully expecting him to sit next to me on the bed. But instead he crossed his arms and watched from his computer chair. What was he doing? We always sat on his bed together. Why was he suddenly keeping his distance from me? I watched him throughout the show, and it didn't seem like he looked at me once during it. I mean I guess he could have looked at me when I wasn't looking at him, but I feel like I would have seen him out of the corner of my eye. I would have noticed him looking at me, and he didn't. Maybe I wasn't the person he liked.

I lingered when we were done binging the documentary, trying to come up with a way to ask him who he liked, or even get more out of him from when Carly was over. I didn't know how to do it without sounding like I knew more than he thought I did, or like I was too invested. I didn't want him to think I was a creep about it.

"I should probably get to bed," Jack finally said, still in his computer chair.

"Yeah. It'll be more comfortable than where you watched that documentary from."

"What?"

"Your chair. How was it comfortable sitting in that thing the whole time?"

He shrugged. "Oh, it was fine. It's a pretty comfortable chair."

I nodded and got up, grabbing my bag as quickly as I could. He barely said goodbye to me as I slipped out his door.

I didn't see Jack much throughout finals. I was so stressed, and I was too nervous to ask him to come study with me. I know, it was stupid, but I couldn't help it. He texted me a few times asking me if I needed a coffee break, or if I needed someone to read my flashcards to me, so the night before my last final, we met at the library.

There were still quite a lot of people in there, probably also getting some last-minute cramming done. It was quiet though, and the fans spread out in front of most of the tables lent a nice white noise to reduce distraction. I knew that wasn't their purpose; it was an unbearably warm May and this old building didn't have any air conditioning.

Jack and I set our stuff down at the closest empty table and without even saying anything, Jack smiled at me and held out his hand.

I stared at it for a second, confused. Did he want me to shake it? Hold it? What was happening?

"What's this?" I asked.

"Flash cards?"

"Oh. Right." I rolled my eyes at my own stupidity and grabbed them from my backpack. I shuffled them like they were a deck of cards and then gave them to him, my heart thumping in my chest for reasons I couldn't even explain. I always studied with Jack. This was nothing new. I liked Jack. I was comfortable with Jack. I wasn't even planning on telling him about my feelings, so why was I nervous? Was it just anxiety of the thought of him never feeling the same way about me? Of us never being more than friends?

"Hey, are you okay?" he asked me after about twenty minutes.

"Yeah, why?"

"You seem off."

"Off?"

He raised his shoulders. "Yeah. I don't know, you seem distracted. Are you nervous about your exam?"

"A little, I guess." And about other things.

"You're a rock star. You'll do amazing."

"Thanks."

"Hey." He grabbed my shoulder and shook me a little. "It's true. You've got this."

I smiled at him and then without warning, I started to cry. My eyes just welled up and tears fell almost immediately.

"Aspen," he whispered. "What's going on?"

I shook my head, wishing I could say what I wanted to say. Wishing I could just open my damn mouth and tell him that I was falling in love with him. What was wrong with me?

"Come here." He pulled me into him and wrapped his arms around me, and it felt so good I almost couldn't breathe. I had never felt so comforted in the arms of someone else before, not even my mom's when I was sick. There was something else there, something else I had never experienced, that came to life and cocooned me so safely when he hugged me. I hugged him back, and when I squeezed him tighter, he did the same for me. I rested my cheek on his shoulder, trying not to make any noise while I cried. I sniffled a little and closed my eyes, wishing that we could stay like this forever.

"You can tell me anything, you know that, right?" he whispered to me, still keeping me wrapped in tight.

"Yeah," I said through a deep breath.

"And you don't have to. You don't have to tell me anything if you don't want to, but I'm here, okay? If you do want to."

I nodded against his shoulder but didn't say anything. I just let him hold me in the library while a big metal fan blew cool air on us.

"It's because you're going to miss me so much over the summer, isn't it?" Jack said after a few minutes.

I laughed and pulled back, straightened up in my own chair. "You caught me." But I was going to miss him. I didn't know how I was going to last almost four months without him. I don't think I'd even been such close friends with someone before, even Brianna and Carly. Well no, maybe not Brianna and Carly. But it was close. I'd never been such close friends with a guy before, that was for sure.

And now we were going to have to spend the summer apart. Maybe that's all my anxiety was about. It wasn't about him not having feelings for me, it was just about having to go home until September.

"We can plan a day to meet up for the day or something. Halfway between you and me. Is there a beach in the middle or something? Or you could come to my town for a visit. We have a really cool Laser Tag place."

"You would really want me to come visit you?"

"Yeah, why wouldn't I?"

"I don't know."

"You're ridiculous, you know that?"

Jack was right. I aced my exam. My parents came to pick me up the next day, where I had most of my stuff packed up. Brianna and I talked about maybe getting a place of our own for next year, but all the two bedrooms were almost the same price as the three bedrooms, and it would be a lot harder to afford without Carly. So we asked Carly if she wanted to sign another lease for the same apartment and she said yes. I hoped any awkwardness between us and Jack was gone by the time we all came back.

Jack and I talked on the phone and texted a lot, and we tried to plan a visit, but we never seemed to have the same days off. Like, ever. So instead, we talked on the phone while we watched the same movies, trying our best to press play at the same time.

I sent Jack pictures of the beach by my parents' house, and he sent me pictures of the pizza restaurant he worked in. The pizza always looked so amazing; I wished I could have had some. I didn't send him pictures of my work, because I just worked at the grocery store, and that wasn't at all interesting.

He got a camera halfway through the summer because of his photography class that he was going to have in the fall. The school provided cameras for it but he said he wanted one of his own. He sent me pictures of sunsets, black and white photos of the inside of his restaurant, of people eating and laughing without knowing their picture was being taken.

You haven't taken this class yet? I texted to him.

No why?

They're incredible. They look like they're out of a magazine or something.

Thanks. I'm just messing around.

Well you have a very good eye.

"Are you staying in the same apartment this year?" I asked him on the phone one August evening.

"Yeah. I'm pretty excited about not having to move again. It was a pain moving into res in first year and into the apartment second year."

"Tell me about it."

"Now it's just mostly my clothes and computer that I have to move."

"I brought a lot of stuff back with me," I said.

"Like what?"

"My bed, for one."

"Your bed?"

"Yeah, I wasn't going to buy a new bed for school. So I brought my bed from home."

"What did you do when you went home for Christmas?"

"Slept in my room on an air mattress."

"Cozy."

"It was, actually."

"Alright," he laughed. "Well I'm sorry you have to move your bed again. That sucks."

"Yeah. But anyway, I'm moving back the last week of August so I can get settled in before school starts. Are you going back early?"

"No, I'm just going down the weekend before."

"Oh. Okay."

I think he could hear the disappointment in my voice. "We're hanging out immediately though, when I get in."

"Okay," I said.

"I'm serious. You better be waiting outside for me when I get there so we can enjoy a night on the town right away."

"A night on the town?"

"Or a night in my room. Whatever."

"A night in your room sounds nice," I said quietly.

"Okay then. A night in my room it is."

I couldn't stop smiling after we hung up. I'm pretty sure I fell asleep smiling.

Jack texted me when he was about to arrive so I slipped on my shoes and ran down to the front of the building. I came out just as he was getting out of his parents' car, so I hung back a little and stayed in the building lobby. I had never met Jack's parents before, and it's not like we were dating or anything, but it still felt weird to me. I hoped he didn't see me through the window in the door. I pressed myself against the wall like an idiot and held my breath. When I couldn't hold it anymore, I let it out slowly, and then checked my phone. He hadn't texted me again, so was he just waiting for me to come over? Was he even being serious about me going over to see him immediately? He was probably joking, and if I showed up now, he'd think I was too intense or clingy. I let out another breath and headed back upstairs.

"I thought you were going to Jack's," Brianna said, looking up from her book in the living room.

"Yeah. But he was unloading the car with his parents."

"So? You didn't want to help?"

"No, I felt weird about it."

"You're silly." She smiled and went back to her book. I was really anxious, so I went pee and then splashed water on my face. And then I peed again. I was about to go flop onto my bed when my phone beeped.

It was a text from Jack. **Are you coming over or what?**

Yeah, sorry. On my way.

😊

Jack practically tackled me when we met in his doorway. He wrapped his arms around me and pressed his cheek into the top of my head, so I stood on my toes and hugged him back. We stood in his doorway hugging for at least a minute, and I didn't want either of us to let go. I would have held on to him forever if I could. He finally loosened his grip on me, so I started to let go, but then stopped when I realized he wasn't actually letting go. He rubbed my back a few times, but he didn't let go. What was happening?

I decided in that instant that I was going to kiss him. I was just going to do it. So I pulled back a little so that I could look up at him, and then he immediately pulled away.

"Come on, I want to show you my camera," he said, running to his room.

"Oh." I followed him, a little confused, but happy that he was excited to show me something.

"I missed you a lot this summer." He was kneeled on the other side of his bed, and he looked up at me from across his mattress.

"I missed you too."

"I know I sent you a lot of pictures that I took, but I wanted to show this to you so badly. Do you want to do a photoshoot?"

"A photoshoot?" I asked.

"Yeah."

"Like what kind of photoshoot?"

He shrugged. "Whatever. I can take pictures of you, if you want. We could go for a walk. Or I could take pictures of you here."

I didn't really know what to say. What would happen if we took pictures in his apartment? In his room? What kind of pictures did he want to take of me? I liked the guy and wanted to kiss him and everything but I didn't want to take my clothes off or like, pose or anything.

I guess I was taking too long to answer, because he swallowed and looked away, then put his camera back in its bag and stood up.

"Sorry, I didn't mean to freak you out" he said. "I just realized how that probably sounded. I was just excited. And you're my best friend and I wanted to share it with you."

"I'm… I'm your best friend?" I asked.

"Yeah, of course you are."

There was no way I could kiss him now. I couldn't kiss a guy who just called me his best friend. So instead I smiled and nodded.

"We can take pictures if you want. But I don't know how to be a model," I said.

"You don't have to do anything. Just be you."

"Just be me?"

"Yeah. Just sit on the bed like you would if we were going to watch a movie." He picked his camera up again and brought it to his eye, one hand on the side of the camera, ready to hit the shutter button, the other hand wrapped gently around the lens.

I sat on his bed and scooted back towards the headboard, looking up at him with an awkward smile.

"Well you don't have to look like you're in pain," he said from behind the camera.

I laughed at him and I heard the shutter in his camera almost immediately.

"That's perfect," he said.

"It is?"

And the shutter went again.

"Yes," he said.

I brought my knees up to my chest and wrapped my arms around them, and Jack stepped back a little.

"Can you rest your chin on your knees?" he asked.

"Um. Sure." So I did, and he took a picture.

"And now, turn your head, like, put your cheek on your knee, and look that—"

I did what he asked before he finished his sentence, and I heard the shutter click a couple times.

"Perfect. You're perfect."

"Okay," I laughed.

"Do you want to see them?"

I shrugged, feeling a little insecure. "Don't you want to edit them or something?"

He looked down at the screen on his camera. "Yeah, probably. I think these would be really good in black and white."

"Show me when they're done."

Jack smiled. "Okay."

"So do you want to watch a movie?"

The pictures that Jack took of me in his room were amazing. He showed them to me the next week after learning some basics on editing. The black and white made them feel moody and dramatic, and I actually felt pretty in them. I couldn't stop staring at his computer screen. I looked amazing. And all I did was sit on his bed.

"These are amazing," I said quietly.

"Thanks. I had an amazing subject, though."

I felt myself blushing so I looked away a little and took a step back. I hit his bed frame with the back of my legs and sat down. If he liked me instead of thinking of me as his best friend, this would have been a perfect opportunity to kiss me. Imagine the guy you had a crush on telling you you're an amazing photography subject, and then just grabbing the sides of your face, slipping his fingers into your hair, and kissing you.

"Aspen?" Jack asked.

I realized in that moment that I had been imagining Jack's fingers slipping into my hair, and Jack's mouth pressed against mine, and I shook my head, trying to get rid of the image.

"Sorry, what?" I said.

He laughed a little. "I just asked if you wanted to do more."

"More what?"

"Photoshoots? Do you want to go take pictures in the library or something?"

"That sounds wonderful."

He grinned. "Let's go, then."

We took the bus across town to the University and walked along the pathway together, moving aside every now and then for the few people going by on bicycles. Jack hung back a few times too, to take pictures of me walking, and he told me to turn around, or to face away and just turn my head and shoulders to look back at him, sometimes he said to smile, sometimes he didn't. Sometimes I would laugh at him and hear the shutter go before I calmed myself. He took pictures of me as he walked towards me, catching up, and then he held the camera out in front of us, taking a selfie with the two of us huddled closely so we could both get in the frame. He took pictures of me outside the library, of me standing with my hands in my pockets and the wind blowing my hair across my face. He took photos of me inside, sitting in front of a bookcase. Of me studying. He took pictures from far away so that you could probably see most of the library, and just me somewhere in the middle, he took pictures close up, ones where I pretended that he wasn't there, and ones where I looked right at the lens, ones where I looked past the lens, at him smiling at me.

I watched him every time he looked at the preview on the back of his camera, and his smile was so soft and easy, like he was in his own little happy place. Like he didn't even have to think about what he was doing, he just did it. He held the camera so effortlessly, like it was a part of him, like it was something missing before now. What was he doing majoring in English?

After we spent about an hour taking different pictures, we actually studied, and Jack went through my new set of flash cards to quiz me.

I was glad that Jack was my friend, and even though I distracted myself more than a few times by imagining us kissing, I was glad that it was at least out in the open that we were nothing more than friends. I still wished I could kiss him, but him telling me that I was his best friend took off any anxiety I had about wondering if I should tell him about how I felt. Now I knew that it was best for us to remain friends, like we had been for the last year. Friends usually last longer than boyfriends anyway. I would get over the fact that I wanted to kiss him. That would go away.

It did not go away. When Jack showed me the library batch of photos that we took, I wanted to jump him. He smiled when he showed them to me, and I was of course blown away. The pictures were incredible. Most of them were in black and white again, but some of them had colour with high contrast, and some with washed out colour. All his colouring choices seemed to fit each individual photo so perfectly, and I don't want to sound full of myself, but I was stunning in every single one. My favourites were the ones that had me laughing, but one serious one that I really liked was just me sitting at a table with my chin in my hand. I was looking to the side, and the photo was taken from far away in portrait format. There was so much of the wooden beams and arched windows behind me and above my head, that it just looked magical. Like I was in fan art for some fantasy-esque dark academia novel.

Jack was so talented. Knowing that he was the one who took these photos, these perfect photos that felt so magical and cozy, made him even more attractive than I already thought he was. He grinned up at me from his computer chair as I stood behind it, and I almost leaned down and kissed him. Almost.

"These are amazing," I said instead. "You don't need a photography class; you already know what you're doing."

"Thanks," he said. "But I think the class is still really helpful. I'm glad I took it."

"So am I."

CHAPTER 15
(NOW)

Jack and I have been texting a lot. I'll comment on his pictures on Photodump and he'll reply to them, and then one of us will just text the other and we'll talk until past midnight. I should really tell him that David and I broke up. It's not fair to him, is it? What if he thinks I'm cheating on David by secretly texting Jack about photography, and my favourite band, and the current books I'm reading until the wee hours of the morning? Jack hasn't asked about him at all, and I wonder if it's because he's trying to pretend that he doesn't exist. I wonder if Jack would do anything with me if he thought we were still together. I hope he wouldn't. I hope he doesn't think that I would, either. Jack from university wouldn't dare do anything if he knew I was with someone. But we are different people now, aren't we? Sort of.

"Who are you texting?" Shannon asks at lunch.

"Oh. No one."

She raises an eyebrow at me. "No one? You're texting no one?"

"Okay, it's someone, but it's not a big deal. Just an old friend."

"I think the fact that you said no one, and then called it 'not a big deal' makes it a big deal. Who is it?"

"No one," I say again. "Just someone I went to university with."

"Ooh, another doctor?"

"No," I say with a smile. "A photographer."

"Oh! That's fun!"

"Yeah, I guess."

"So do you still want to go to IKEA this weekend?" Shannon asks.

"Yeah, we probably should. I can't keep sleeping on my couch."

"You should ask your photographer friend if he wants to come."

"Who said he's a he?" I ask quickly, feeling a little defensive.

"Is he not a he?" Shannon gives me a head tilt and a smirk, and then adds, "I mean, you just said yourself he's a he."

"I did not."

Shannon doesn't reply. Instead she continues to smile at me like she's won something.

"We're still reconnecting," I say with a sigh. "I think it would be weird."

"I knew it."

I roll my eyes and hit her in the arm, and we both laugh.

When Jack asks me what I'm doing this weekend over text, and I tell him I'm going to IKEA, I choke and say that it's for my friend. I don't know why I can't just tell him that David and I broke up. He didn't even know David, it's not like I would have to deal with him picking sides or anything.

I guess if I tell him that I'm not with David anymore, this whole thing will have just gotten more real. The fact that I'm single, the fact that I'm already imagining myself with Jack again. The fact that if Jack knows I'm single, something could happen between us. I know I could still say no if I didn't want something to happen, but I don't think I would. A huge part of me wants something to happen between us, but if it did, it would just hurt even more. He's going to Mars and I'm not. I don't want to sleep with him or fall in love with him and then literally never see him again.

Not telling him until after he's gone is the better decision. Yes.

I was going to go down to the water and take pictures he says.

Oh that's cool

If you're back from IKEA do you want to join me?

Yeah maybe. I'll let you know.

Shannon picks me up on Saturday morning and we drive to IKEA after stopping for coffee. We walk through the entire showroom, lying on every bed, sitting on every couch, and pretending that we're making dinner in every kitchen. We have drawer closing races on all the soft-close drawers, and I admire nice bookcases that I can't get because they won't fit in my apartment. We pick up a few knickknacks downstairs, like scrub brushes for my dishes, a cheese grater, a candle holder, and a lamp. Then we venture into the warehouse to find my bed frame, mattress, and tiny, two-seater kitchen set.

Shannon helps me carry everything in and build my bedframe and table right away. We unroll my mattress and push my couch back against the foot of the bed. My apartment actually feels cozy now that I have all my furniture set up. I could watch TV from my bed or from my couch, but I can see myself never getting out of bed on weekends this way. The couch will probably just end up being where movies are watched from if I have guests over. Although if Shannon came over to watch movies, we would probably use my bed.

I wonder if Jack ever came over to watch movies if we would sit on the couch, or get comfortable on my bed like we did at school.

"You want to go for dinner?" Shannon asks.

"Oh. I'm actually pretty tired. Is it okay if I just hang out alone?"

"Yeah of course. See you on Monday?"

"Yeah. See you on Monday."

She smiles and starts to open the door.

"Thanks for today," I say before she leaves.

"Of course. It was fun."

I watch her leave and then get up to lock the door behind her. I turn around and lean back into the door, looking at my apartment in front of me. It needs twinkly lights. I wait a few minutes so I don't run into Shannon and make it seem like I was lying to her about wanting to stay home, and then I head down to my car.

I drive over to the Canadian Tire to look for lights to put up, and have a hard time finding them since it's the middle of May, and I end up wandering the store for about an hour, just looking at everything they have. I find an area with bedroom décor, and pick up a box of LED fairy lights on a flat string. It doesn't give off the vibes I was looking for, but I take them up the register anyway to try them out.

My phone beeps while I'm walking across the parking lot so I check it when I get into my car. It's a text from Jack.

How was IKEA?

Fun I reply.

What are you up to now?

Just heading home.

Okay. Have a good night.

I want to hang out with him. I want to tell him that I live alone now and I just finished furnishing my new apartment. I want to tell him to come over and see it. My thumbs hover over the keyboard on my phone for longer than a minute, and he texts me again before I get a chance to even think about what I want to say.

Sorry for bugging you.

You're not bugging me I type back.

The three dots show up in the corner of the screen and stay there for a little while and then they disappear. I sigh and turn my car on, check my phone one more time to see if he starts typing again, which he doesn't, and then drive home. My phone goes off when I'm halfway to my apartment and it takes everything in me not to pull over and see what he said.

As soon as I park at my apartment, I check my phone; I don't even turn my car off first.

Okay.

That's it!? That's all he said? Okay? Okay? He was typing for all that time and all he said was okay? I shove my phone in my purse, grab my stuff from Canadian Tire and head into the building. I shake my head to myself as I pull the string lights out of their box, and I mumble to myself about how stupid I am as I hang them from the corner of my ceiling over the tv, and down the wall on each side. The lights are a bit more yellow than I was expecting and now I'm disappointed. I wanted them to be really white but it looks like my walls are peeing. Ugh. I don't have the energy to take them down so I flop onto my bed, which is more comfortable than I remember, and open Photodump on my phone.

Jack posted a new picture. It's a black and white photo of a very happy golden retriever running towards the camera. I comment the heart eyes emoji and Jack likes my comment almost immediately. He's probably not going to be the first one to text me, since I've shot him down every time he's asked to do something the last couple times. If I want to continue to reconnect with him, I need to reach out.

Sorry for being so distant I type to him. **I didn't mean to.**

Oh don't worry about it. I get it.

You do?

Yeah he says. **I'm sure your boyfriend doesn't appreciate me just inserting myself into your life again.**

You say that like you're doing it against my will, or like you're pushing your way in.

Sometimes I feel like that's what I'm doing.

Is that what you're doing?

No he says. **I'm just interested in being your friend again. I'm not trying to come across as pushy or annoying.**

You're not coming off that way, I promise. If I made you feel like that, it wasn't my intention.

You didn't make me feel like anything. I made myself feel that way when I realized your boyfriend is probably uncomfortable with me being in your life.

At this point I feel weird telling him that David isn't my boyfriend anymore. He's mentioned my boyfriend so many times, if I tell him we've broken up now, he'll just feel stupid. Maybe we can go for lunch and I can tell him then. And I can tell him that we've been broken up for a few weeks now and I just wasn't comfortable telling him yet because we were still becoming friends again. I don't want to just hang my dirty laundry in front of people I hardly know. I'm sure if I tell him this week and explain it to him, he'll understand. But I certainly can't tell him right now.

Nothing like that is going on I say. **No one is uncomfortable**

If you say so

I do say so. What are you doing on Monday? Do you want to go for lunch?

I've been nervous all morning at work knowing that I'm going to tell Jack that I'm single. I'm afraid that he's going to be hurt about the fact that I've been lying to him, and I'm afraid it's going to make everything harder when he inevitably moves to Mars. Maybe he won't be accepted. Maybe he'll have to stay here like me and we can just fall in love on Earth and have a life here together.

But we always talked about going to Mars, and now that I think of it, we didn't even talk about going together. Like we did, we talked about both going, and both living there, and hanging out together when we weren't working, but we never talked about when we would apply, or if we would apply together or even at the same time. I guess it was just something so far in the future that it wasn't something we needed to consider yet. It was a possibility, sure, but it was far enough away for us that it still didn't fully feel real. And now it was real and he was doing it without me.

"Uh, Aspen, there is a very cute man waiting for you at reception," Shannon says to me as I'm getting ready to leave. "He says his name is Jack."

I smile at her from my chair, where I'm closing out some appointments on my tablet. "Yeah, we're going to lunch."

She smiles at me and raises her eyebrows like she's expecting me to tell her something juicy.

"Why are you looking at me like that?" I ask.

"Is this the guy you didn't want to tell me about before? The guy you went to school with?"

"Yes," I say slowly.

"So you're going on dates now?"

"It's not a date, we're friends. We're still reconnecting. And he doesn't even know that David and I broke up." I look back to my tablet and log out of my Mars Group Med app.

"Excuse me? Why doesn't he know?"

I just shrug.

"Oh come on, Aspen, there has to be a reason for you to be close enough with a handsome man who is interested in women-" she sort of cuts herself off and then says, "Yes?"

"Yes," I say to her.

And she continues. "Okay, so there has to be a reason for you to be close enough to a handsome man, who is interested in women, to go out for lunch with him and want to 'reconnect' with him, but not tell him you're single."

I don't know what to say. I raise my shoulders and take in a breath as if I'm about to answer, but really I don't have anything. She pulls up the second chair in my office and sits down in it.

"Spill," she says.

I sigh. "It's a long story. And there's nothing to tell."

"Which is it, Aspen? A long story or a nothing story?"

"A nothing story."

"Come on, I know it's not a nothing story. It's a long story and I want to hear it."

"I don't have time, Shannon."

"Do you have a patient right now?"

"No. Because I'm going to lunch." I pack up my tablet and start to stand.

"With the cute man who thinks you have a boyfriend," Shannon says.

"Correct."

"Aspen, you're killing me."

"Ugghh okay fine. We met when I was in pre-med, and I had a huge crush on him. But I was really busy with school and also way more shy and awkward then than I am now, even, and I didn't do anything about it. We were friends. We watched Mars documentaries and he helped me study."

"Aw, that's cute."

"Sure. Okay, I'm going to lunch now."

"Ah nice try, that's not the whole story."

"I'm not telling you the rest right now, Shannon. Plus it doesn't even matter, because he's going to Mars."

"Oooh," she says, realization in her voice. "That's why you want him to think you're still with David. Aspen, that's hard."

"It's really not," I tell her. "We haven't seen each other in over eight years. It's not like we've been friends this whole time. I barely know him."

"I think you're lying to yourself a little bit."

"Lying to myself?"

"Yeah. You told me on the weekend that he was basically nobody, and now you're saying that you barely know him. I think the eight years you two spent not being friends has done nothing to your feelings of closeness with each other."

I narrow my eyes at her. "How do you know?"

"I don't know, I just said I think. I *think* your time apart hasn't done anything to your closeness."

"Okay well you're wrong. We're practically strangers."

"Strangers who are going to lunch?"

"Yes, Shannon. Strangers who are going to lunch."

"So you're telling me you're upset about this guy moving away to Mars, but you're just strangers."

"I'm not upset about it," I say quickly.

"You sound upset about it. Are you sure you two haven't, you know, done anything? Since reconnecting? Like you haven't…" She moves her arms around in circles in front of her to imply sexual things, I'm sure.

"No! He thinks I have a boyfriend!"

"Right," she says, nodding. "You should tell him you don't."

"Why? So we can fall in love and then live on different planets?"

"You don't have to live on different planets." Shannon shrugs. "And also maybe the only reason he's leaving is because no one on Earth has told him that she wants him!"

"Okay, I don't want him," I say.

"Are you sure about that?"

"Yes! I said we're practically strangers, Shannon!"

And then she just stares at me. She stares at me with this sad, pity smile, like she feels bad that I can't admit feelings. She looks like she's going to call me sweetheart if she says anything else to me.

"Okay, maybe I want him a little bit," I say. "But he's not going to give up living on Mars for me."

"How do you know?"

"It's… It's Mars! It's Mars, Shannon!!"

"You gave up living on Mars for David."

I look at her for a second and scrunch my face a little in confusion. "No I didn't."

"But you changed your application at the last minute."

"No I didn't. I was just placed here."

"Aspen, I was on the hiring committee that year. We wanted you on Mars, I remember."

"And I'm the one who applied! I remember! The only reason I applied for The Mars Group was because I wanted to go to Mars!"

"Then who logged into your Mars Group account and changed your application?"

"Not me! I didn't-" But then it hits me. I feel my eyes bulge, and I gasp, not wanting it to be real.

Shannon's face matches mine, and we stare at each other in mild horror for a few seconds before either of us says anything.

"You don't think it was David, do you?" I finally ask.

"Who else would it have been?"

"What the hell, Shannon!? You're telling me I could have been on Mars for the last three years and instead I've been in a toxic relationship? I could have been on Mars this whole time, and instead

I've been watching everybody else go to Mars while the guy who secretly made me not be able to go was making me cry every night? Are you fucking kidding me, Shannon?"

"Okay, hang on. I know I just said I agreed with you that it was him, but maybe there was some kind of glitch in the system. I didn't know you then. I didn't know your plans, and so I didn't think it was weird that you changed your mind. You weren't the first person to change your mind. I mean, going to Mars is a big deal."

"Right, so David was the one who changed his mind, and instead of talking to me about it he just hacked my account and made it a non-issue."

"Or there was a glitch."

"Have you had glitches like this happen with other people? Before or since?"

Shannon stares at me with her mouth open a little and then slowly shakes her head.

"Right, that's what I thought. David changed my application. I can't believe he changed my application! This is fucking ridiculous!" My voice is getting louder with every word that comes out of my mouth and I'm very aware of it but very unable to control it. People in neighbouring offices are probably concerned for my wellbeing. "I can't believe I could have been on Mars this whole time! This whole time!" I try to bite back the tears but I'm so frustrated.

"But you wouldn't have met Jack again if you were on Mars."

"Yes I would have! On fucking Mars!"

Shannon bites her lip a little and lets out a deep breath. "Right. But things might have been different. Maybe it wouldn't have worked out if you were on Mars."

"Oh, because it's going to work out now?" I ask. "Also it doesn't matter! David still did that to me!"

"Yeah," Shannon says quietly. "That was really shitty of him."

"Probably the shittiest thing anyone has ever done to me." I take a deep breath and shake my shoulders out a little. I watch Shannon's eyes follow me as I pace back and forth a few times. I look at the clock on the wall and feel my stomach tighten. "Is my mascara all messed up?" I ask. "I have to go."

"Go? Go where?"

"I have to go to lunch! Jack is waiting for me!" I can't believe I'm still yelling almost all of my sentences.

"Here." She motions for me to move closer and she takes a Q-Tip and moisturizer from her purse. I close my eyes as she lightly rubs away the smudged makeup from under my eyelashes.

"You could reschedule your lunch, you know," she says when I open my eyes and look at her.

"Do I look that bad?"

She shakes her head. "No, you look great. But you're obviously upset."

"It's fine. I'm fine."

"Are you sure?"

I let out another deep breath and nod my head. "Yes. Maybe going for lunch will distract me a little."

"Okay. Ooh, tell him about your troubles and maybe he'll comfort you."

"You did not. You are not going there right now."

Shannon's lips pull closed tightly and she shakes her head. "You're right, I'm absolutely not going there."

I close my eyes for a second, trying to calm myself down a little more before opening the door to the hallway. "I'm okay," I say.

"You're okay." She smiles and nods, and I head down to the lobby to meet Jack, whose face falls as soon as he sees me.

"Is everything okay?" he asks.

"Yeah," I say, but I can tell it doesn't sound convincing at all. "Sort of," I correct. "Okay, not really."

He opens his mouth to say something but I don't let him.

"Let's just go," I say. "I don't want to talk about it here."

"Okay." He nods and follows me out of the building.

We walk across the street to a deli restaurant that I like, and Jack had said he wanted to try. We wait in line without saying much outside of what on the menu looks good to us, and after we order, we take our trays to a table in the back of the restaurant.

"So what's going on?" Jack asks after we've both taken a few bites of our sandwiches. "Are you okay?"

"I'm actually not okay. I'm pretty shaken up by something, but I uh, I'm- I don't…" I let myself pause and take a breath before I continue. "I actually don't want to talk about it right now. Is that okay?"

"Yeah of course. We don't have to talk about anything you don't want to."

"Okay. Thanks."

"I actually have exciting news," Jack says, and it almost comes out like a question.

"Oh? Please tell."

"Before I start though, I do want to make something clear. I'm so happy that we've reconnected and become friends again. And I'm so happy to be your friend. But like I said before, I'm sure your boyfriend isn't thrilled about it, and I don't want to give either of you the wrong impression, so just in case I wasn't clear when we were texting, I wanted to make it clear now that my feelings for you don't go past that. Past friendship, I mean."

It's like University all over again. I've finally gotten the nerve to say or do something about how I feel and he goes and tells me how much he loves being my friend. I'm always just someone's friend, aren't I?

"Oh," I say.

"I just didn't want you to think that I had ulterior motives. Or for… uh…" He looks at me like he's waiting for me to tell him said boyfriend's name.

"David," I fill in for him.

"Right, I didn't want David to think I had ulterior motives either."

"Right," I say. "Um. About that. David and I actually broke up."

"Oh my goodness, I'm so sorry. Is that what you're upset about?"

"No," I say slowly. "We broke up a few weeks ago."

"A few weeks ago? Why didn't you tell me?"

"I don't know," I lie. "A lot of reasons, I guess. But mostly I think the main reason is just that I needed a friend. And I was just afraid that if you knew I was single, I wouldn't know if your friendship was genuine or not?" What a stupid thing to say.

"Don't you know me at all?" he asks, his voice quiet.

"I used to know you," I say. "I'm not sure how well I still know you."

"I'm the same Jack I always was."

"I'm not sure I'm the same Aspen."

"Of course you are. You've grown up since we last saw each other, and you've had a lot of different experiences, which shapes the way you think about things, but you're the same Aspen I knew in university. You're still the same person. And I know you said you don't want to talk about it, but you're kind of worrying me."

"No, you don't have to worry about me. I'm sure I'll be fine with time. I'm just not right now. But what's your exciting news?"

He hesitates and looks away for a second, grabs at the back of his neck quickly before dropping his hand to the table.

"Come on," I say. "I need to hear something good. What is it?"

He takes another few seconds before answering. "I got accepted into The Mars Group. For a position on Mars."

CHAPTER 16
(THEN)

"There's a party for the first group of people going to Mars!" It was the beginning of April in third year, and Jack ran over to my apartment to tell me this news. We had spent the school year doing what we always did: studying, watching sci-fi movies or Mars docs, and our new photography thing was sprinkled in there too. And I guess this new information he had for me was too exciting to express over text and he had to tell me in person, and it had to be immediately.

"Where is this party?" I asked, letting him into my apartment.

"Just outside of town at their headquarters! It's all public information now, Aspen! It's incredible! We have to go!"

"Of course we have to go! When is it?"

"Tonight!"

"Tonight?" I asked, looking at my watch. Which was a ridiculous thing to do, because it was Friday. It's not like I had to be up for class the next day.

"Yeah, let's go! We can grab dinner on the way! It'll be so cool! There's a big send off for them when they leave at the end of the night, too, with confetti bombs and lights and everything! It's going to be amazing!"

"Okay, okay, let me get changed. Oh my god, what should I wear!?"

"I don't know, I don't even know if it's formal or not! I don't think it is."

"Where did you find out about this party? Do we need an invite? Is the dress code on the invite?"

"No, everyone's invited! I saw it posted online!"

I ran into my room and opened my closet, trying to find something presentable but not too fancy. I didn't want to look like an idiot showing up in a gown if everyone else was going to be dressed casually.

I settled on a pair of dark jeans and a knitted off-one-shoulder sweater that I hardly ever wore. Jack looked at me the way he looked at some of the Mars pictures we looked up together. I wasn't trying to be full of myself, but I swear he was looking at me like he was mesmerized. I'd seen that look on his face before. Maybe he was just excited about the party, and it had nothing to do with me.

We were both giddy the entire bus ride there, and we got off a stop too early and had to walk. We laughed when we realized what we did, and I fell into him a little, out of breath and unable to hold myself up.

"Okay, it's not that funny," he said, wrapping his arm around my waist and holding me steady.

"Yes it is," I wheezed. I didn't want him to let go of me. I tried to laugh more so that I could 'accidentally' lose my balance and get to feel his grip tighten on me, but I couldn't bring myself to force it. So I straightened up, took a deep breath, and sighed when his hand dropped from my waist and went back to his side.

"This party's going to be great," I said, trying to hide the disappointment in my voice.

"Hell yeah it is."

"Aw, we should have invited Brianna or Brad."

"Nah," he said with a shake of his head. "I think it's better just us two. Plus they're not into this Mars stuff as much as we are."

I smiled up at him. "Yeah."

He nudged me with his elbow and then nodded ahead of us. "There it is."

I stopped walking so I could look at it and take it all in. The building was pretty cool looking; a modern architectural structure of three floors, with big glass doors and angled windows and overhangs. It had a lot of grey and white concrete, and a big tree in the front.

"Do we just walk in?" I asked.

"I think so."

We continued along the path to the main doors and could already hear music as we approached. I could see my hand shaking as I reached out to pull on the door handle, and I was surprised when Jack put his hand over mine.

"Let's open it together," he said.

I nodded, and together we pulled the door open, his warm hand on mine.

The party was in the main lobby and branching hallways of the building. It was crisp and clean inside, with white walls and shiny floors, and a big curved staircase off to one side, which had a red velvet partition rope across the bottom, as if they wanted to be fancy about not letting us upstairs. There was a woman with a neat ponytail standing behind a large glass desk near the entrance, stopping us from going right in immediately. She smiled at us and welcomed us to the first Semi-Annual Mars Send Off. She gave us each a bracelet and a drink ticket after seeing our ID, and we walked past her into the party. There was music playing but it wasn't too loud, so it was still easy to have conversations. The bar was set up at the back by the elevators, which had a lineup, so we decided to walk around for a bit first.

We wandered into the halls that had groups of people standing and chatting with drinks in their hands, and people with white shirts and black bow ties walked around with trays of appetizers. One of the servers walked by me while I had started trailing behind a little, and then asked if I would be interested in prosciutto wrapped bocconcini and I almost gasped.

"Yes please," I said, reaching for one. "That sounds fantastic." I grabbed one of the toothpicks that was coming out of a cheese ball and then I grabbed another one. "For my friend," I said.

He nodded at me and went on his way to the next group of people.

"What'd you get?" Jack asked, turning back to find me.

"Heaven on a toothpick," I said, shoving the second one in my mouth.

"Oh. I want heaven on a toothpick."

"That guy's giving them out."

We laughed and ran towards the server, asking him for more. He smiled and lowered the tray for us and we each took two. I guess he didn't care if the same people hogged any appetizers.

"This is the best thing I've ever had in my mouth," I said.

Jack snorted a little and then laughed, and then he snorted again. I couldn't contain my laughter, and we were both snorting and wheezing in the middle of this party, surrounded by pretty professional seeming people. I finally realized that a few people were looking at us, so I shushed him and we quieted down, trying our best not to get kicked out. We hadn't even used our drink tickets yet.

"You'd think people here would be having more fun," Jack said. "I mean it's a party for people going away to Mars; that's pretty exciting."

"Right," I agreed.

We walked through more halls, getting away from the party and the people who probably thought we were drunk. We admired framed photos of astronauts and awards on the walls and peeked into offices with shut off lights and locked doors.

"This is so cool," I said, opening the door to a stairwell.

"We're just going to go upstairs?" he asked, following me.

"Why not? We've already left the party. And if they didn't want people to look around, they should have locked these doors. Or had the party somewhere else."

"True enough."

The second floor had a lot of doors without windows, and a few boring offices, so we headed up to the third floor, which had more offices but also another reception area with exam rooms.

"Hey maybe you could be a doctor here," Jack said, sliding through an open door and sitting on the exam table inside.

I shook my head and walked towards him. "Nah, I'm going to be a doctor on Mars."

"Do you want to be a surgeon?"

"No way. Medicine, definitely. Maybe emergency. Sometimes I like the idea of pedes, but I'm not totally sure yet."

"Why pedes?"

I stepped closer to him. "I don't know. Kids are always scared of the doctor. It would be nice if I could be a fun doctor that kids aren't afraid of. If I could show them that going to the doctor isn't that scary at all."

"That's nice."

"Yeah."

"I hate the doctor."

"Why?" I asked.

"I'm not sure. It always gives me anxiety. Even if I'm going for something routine that's not a big deal. I feel like my heart's going to fly out of my chest or I'm gonna throw up. My hands shake and everything."

"That's no fun."

"No, not really."

I looked down at his hands that were resting in his lap. I swallowed and slowly reached down and touched his index finger. I didn't look at his face so I wasn't sure of his reaction, except that he lifted his finger a little, and then I slipped my hand under his, holding onto it.

"Your hands aren't shaking right now," I said.

"Well you're not a doctor yet," he said quietly. I swear I could hear his voice shaking, though.

"No, I guess not." I carefully put his hand back on his lap and looked in his eyes. "But you're in a doctor's office. Gives the same vibes. It smells like a doctor's office. The smell alone gives a lot of people anxiety."

"Maybe I'm not nervous because you're here."

I looked back down at his hands, then back at him again. "Maybe."

I wanted to kiss him so badly. It seemed sort of like he wanted to kiss me, too, but I was so bad at reading people. What if I really was just his best friend?

"Let's go back to the party," Jack said. "We can't have the opportunity for a free drink and not use it."

"Okay."

We turned the light off before we left and put the door in the same spot as it was before we opened it all the way. He shoved his shoulder into mine a little, so I shoved him back, and together we walked back to the Mars Send Off.

We got beer as our free drinks, and then we decided to buy another drink each, and by the time the Mars Party Members were making their entrance, or I guess exit would be a more accurate word, we were sufficiently drunk. The lobby went dark, so coloured lights could flash across the floor and walls, and we counted down with everyone like it was New Year's Eve, watching a clock on the back wall. We cheered with everyone and clapped as the Mars Party Members came down the main staircase, which now had the velvet rope partition opened and clipped to one of its posts. They all smiled, walking down into the lobby in their red uniforms. They waved and took pictures with party guests, and people shot confetti into the air with little confetti poppers that they were supposedly handing out while we were upstairs. Everyone seemed to stick around after the Mars Party Members left, and I wanted to stay longer too, but Jack squeezed my arm a little and leaned into me.

"We should go," he whispered. "I'm really drunk."

I smirked at him. "So am I."

"I don't want to make a fool of myself by accident."

"We already might have," I giggled.

"Right. So let's go home."

I nodded, and followed him out into the night.

"What would you do if Infinity Pool moved to Mars?" Jack asked me as we walked to the bus stop.

"What? No. They wouldn't. They could never. They would never."

"Does that mean you don't want to live on Mars anymore?"

"No, how does that translate to me not wanting to live on Mars?"

He shrugged. "If you lived on Mars, and they lived on Mars, you would probably run into them. Often, even. They would have concerts. Multiple concerts."

"But most of their fans live on Earth. That would be mean. Literally no one would be able to see them perform anymore."

"Not literally no one."

"Most people," I corrected.

"So you'll have to see them live before you move, then."

"Before *we* move." I realized what I said as soon as I said it, but it was too late. I couldn't take it back. My heart was all of a sudden in my throat, because I didn't mean to make it sound like we were going to move together, like as a couple, just that we would both move. We both wanted to go to Mars so we were both going to move there. Yes?

"Right," Jack said with a nod.

And everything inside of me settled almost instantly. Either he knew what I meant, or he felt the same way that I secretly felt. What if he felt the same way that I secretly felt? He smiled at me, and I smiled back.

I wanted to close my eyes and lean my head on his shoulder during the bus ride home. It would be so easy. He probably wouldn't mind either. Since I was his best friend, he wouldn't even see it as romantic. Just two tired friends riding the bus home together. With about ten minutes left until we were home, I finally worked up the courage to just do it. I leaned to the side and pressed my cheek against the edge of his shoulder, and felt him lean his head in towards mine almost immediately.

"Are you okay?" he asked quietly.

"Just tired," I said.

"Okay." And then he fully rested his head on top of mine. I felt like I couldn't breathe for half a second. And then all of a sudden it was like breathing was the easiest thing in the world. Being this close to Jack was so comforting, so quiet, so safe. It was like no one could touch us while we were together. All those nervous feelings I had thinking about doing it, had completely melted away. It was like I could literally feel my worries slipping out of me, and could feel myself start to relax. All this time I'd been so worried to bring myself closer to him, but I should have just let myself do it sooner. I should have known that it would have felt like this.

My hand was resting on my thigh, and his fingers slid between mine, holding it gently.

Ohmygod.

I squeezed his hand back and nuzzled my head into him a little more, but then the bus jerked and I fell to the side a little, and Jack pulled me back.

"Shit, I think we missed our stop," he said, standing up in his seat. He pulled his hand from mine and looked out the window, and then pulled the yellow cord. "We did miss it. We'll have to do a little walking."

"I'm okay with walking," I whispered. For some reason I couldn't find my regular voice in that moment.

I stood up and grabbed onto the handrail, anticipating our stop. Once the bus started to slow down and pull over to the side, Jack and I stepped over to the door.

"Thank you!" we both called as the doors opened and we stepped off.

The bus driver waved a little and smiled at us in the rear-view mirror. We turned back the other way to make it back to where we were supposed to get off, and without even thinking, I grabbed onto Jack's hand. He linked his fingers through mine and we walked hand in hand towards our apartment.

All I had to do was turn to the side, stand on my toes, and press my face into his. I could get real close and then ask if I could kiss him. I could do it. He would say yes, and it would be just as cozy as sleeping on his shoulder on the bus. Cozier, even. It would bring so much life into me, I knew it would, it would be like we had our own little confetti canons, and it would be amazing. I knew it would. But I still couldn't do it.

It's a good thing I didn't though, because he walked me to my building, opened the door for me, and said, "Goodnight, Aspen," as soon as I walked through the doors.

I stopped in the lobby, a little taken aback, and turned to him. "Oh. Um, goodnight."

He smiled at me. "I had fun."

"So did I."

Then he nodded, let go of the door, and turned away. I watched him through the closing door as he made his way to the road, and I watched him through the door window as he crossed the street and went into his own building. I was still his best friend. We leaned on each other on the bus and held hands because we were best friends and we were drunk. He didn't want me to be his girlfriend.

He even told Carly last year that he liked someone else. I had thought for a second that maybe it was me.

Of course it wasn't me.

CHAPTER 17 (NOW)

So Jack is for sure going to Mars. There's no way I can tell him about my feelings now. That would ruin both of our lives. Okay, maybe that's a bit dramatic. It probably wouldn't ruin Jack's life. He wouldn't care; he's going to Mars for crying out loud! My life, it would ruin. Definitely.

I force a smile and try to sound as genuine as I can. "Jack! That's amazing! Congratulations."

"Thanks," he says with a growing grin.

"Are you going to be a photographer?"

"No, I got hired on as an English teacher at the high school."

"Oh. Well that works. You said before that there was a lot about teaching that you liked, right?"

"Yeah, definitely. And the workload might be different on Mars. There are way less kids."

"Right." I nod and take a sip of my water.

"But like you said, I can still do photography on the side. Maybe I can even start a photography club at the school."

"That would be amazing. Plus this way you can take pictures of whatever you want, instead of what you have to. It'll be more freeing that way."

"Yeah, probably."

"So when are you leaving?" I ask.

"With the next group. So in just over four months."

"Oh wow. I don't know why I'm surprised; that's usually how it happens."

"Because we just found each other again. Seems a little unfair."

"Yeah," I say. "Just a little."

We're quiet for a little bit as we eat our sandwiches, and I look around the restaurant. There are a few other occupied tables, and the lineup has really grown since we came in.

"Wow, we came in at a good time, eh?" I say, pointing to the line that's almost out the door.

"Oh yeah. Man, this place is popular."

"Well they do have excellent sandwiches, so it makes sense."

"Aspen, are you okay?"

"Yeah. Why? What do you mean?"

"You were on the verge of tears when we met in the lobby, and you told me that you and David broke up, and now here I am telling you that I'm going to Mars."

"Jack, it's fine. I'm happy for you."

"But are you happy for you?"

I take in a breath and think about my answer for a few seconds. "I don't think I've been happy for me for a while."

He reaches across the table and grabs onto my hand. I look down at our intertwined hands, and then back up at Jack. His face is full of hurt, like he's genuinely worried for me. He starts to rub the back of my hand with his thumb, and I feel like we're back in university again. I feel like a confused 20-year-old who doesn't know how to tell the guy she likes how she feels. I feel like I'm going to melt into Jack and stay there forever, quietly, secretly wishing we could be more.

So I slip my hand out from his and pull it back. He blinks at me as if he's surprised, and then he clears his throat and sits up straighter in his chair. I can feel tears stinging my eyes so I open them wider and try not to blink for a second, hoping they'll go away. I look to the side so that he can't see, and take in a deep breath. Once I'm sure the tears have gone, I turn back to him. He's still looking at me like I'm a lost puppy.

"We can't lose touch this time," I say, a slight crack in my words.

"No, definitely not. I didn't go eight years of not being your friend just to lose you again six months later."

"Yeah," I say slowly. Even though nothing can ever happen between us, it feels nice to hear him say that. It's nice to feel like you mean something to somebody. "And you have to take pictures of all the landscapes and send them to me," I add, trying to steer the conversation into a bit of a different direction.

"I promise I will."

I smile at him and finish the last of my sandwich.

"Aspen, I'm sorry," Jack says once he's done his food.

"For what? For following your dream?"

"No. For what happened in university. For telling you that I needed space and then-"

"Jack, it's fine," I say, cutting him off. "You don't have to apologize for that, especially now."

"But you never let me explain before."

"Because I didn't need you to."

"But I didn't want you to think that I just immediately jumped into a relationship with her. After what happened with us, I swear I wanted-"

"Jack, it's fine. It was a long time ago, and I completely understood."

"Did you, though?"

"Yes. You don't need to explain what happened, because I figured out what happened on my own."

He cringes a little. "But I want to explain why I did it. That I didn't do it to hurt you."

"I know you didn't do it to hurt me."

"But I did anyway."

I can feel the tears coming on again and I look up, taking another deep breath.

"Aspen," he says quietly.

"It's fine, Jack," I say, shaking my head. "It doesn't matter if I got hurt. People get hurt over things. It happens. No one intentionally tried to hurt anyone and you were going through a lot, and it's fine. It was fine then, and it's fine now. We were always just friends anyway." This time I don't say that with a snark, and I feel like I'm telling the truth.

Jack looks down at the table for a few seconds and then slowly looks back up at me. "Were we, though?" His voice is almost a whisper.

"Yes," I say shortly. "We were always just friends."

"I just…" he sighs and licks his lips before continuing. "I knew that I had most likely hurt you, and you never let me explain when I tried. I was afraid that I'd made you feel like you weren't important to me."

"Oh."

"But you were," he adds. "You were always important to me."

I swallow and take a second to compose myself before I answer him. "You were important to me, too."

We walk across the street together and back to the Mars Group building. Jack smiles at me as we approach the doors, and then stops.

"Do you want to come see my office?" I ask.

"Oh. A doctor's office."

"Not an exam room, silly, my actual office. I have a desk and a rollie chair."

"Oh, well if there's a rollie chair."

I smile at him and he follows me to the main staircase.

"Elevators aren't working?" he asks.

"Yes, they're working, but it's only two flights of stairs. I like the exercise."

"Touché."

We walk beside each other up the curving stairs, and then he follows me down the hall to the stairwell where we can finish going up the last flight. Our shoes squeak on the floor and I giggle a little, which makes him smile and shake his head.

I open the door to my office and almost squeal because Shannon is sitting in my chair, and she immediately turns around in it to face us, a huge smile across her face.

"Holy shit," I say, putting my hands to my mouth. "What are you doing in here?"

"Sorry, I was waiting for you. I didn't know you were going to be with a friend."

"Sorry, Jack, this is Shannon. Shannon, this is Jack."

Shannon smiles so wide I swear the corners of her lips are going to crack. "Excellent to meet you, Jack." She turns her attention back to me. "I was just in here because I wanted to talk to you about… Um, well about, you know, the David thing."

"What David thing?" Jack asks.

"Nothing," I say quickly, trying to get Shannon to get out of my chair. "Shannon, I'll talk to you later, okay? Don't you have a patient?"

"I don't, actually, I'm free for the rest of the afternoon."

"Then don't you have some paperwork to fill out? Referrals and consults and such?"

"No, I have nothing."

"Shannon. Why are you so bad at taking a hint?"

"I'm not, I'm actually excellent at taking hints, I'm just bad at responding to them."

"Why?"

"Because it's fun to watch you panic."

"Oh god."

She smiles again and stands up. "Lock the door if you guys don't want anyone to walk in on you."

"Oh my god, Shannon! We're not- we aren't- just go? Please?"

She's still smiling like she's proud of herself, and leaves without a word, shutting the door behind her.

"Sorry about that," I say, hoping my face isn't as red as it feels.

"No worries," he says with a bit of a laugh. "She seems like fun."

"Yeah. She usually is."

"So have you told her about me or something?"

"Not really."

"So you've told her a little about me."

"Not really. She was asking about you today when she saw you in the lobby, but I didn't want to tell her the whole story."

"There's a whole story?" he asks.

"Y- yes. I mean… yes?"

He smirks and tilts his head to the side a bit. "You don't sound too sure about that."

"There's… a story. We both know there's a story. You just tried to explain your side of the story at lunch, so…"

"Yeah, and you wouldn't let me," he says, stepping a little closer to me.

"I told you, I don't need you to."

"But if you told Shannon the whole story, you would have made me sound like a bad guy, right?"

"No. No, I wouldn't have. I would have said exactly what happened, which doesn't need an explanation, and no one's a bad guy. I just didn't have time. You were waiting for me."

"Right."

We stare at each other for a couple seconds, and then he clears his throat again. "So this is your office."

"Yeah." I raise my arms up at my sides, in a sort of show off. "This is my office."

"It's pretty nice. You've got a nice window." He walks over to it and looks outside.

"Yeah, nice view. The forest in the back is nice."

"Yeah, it is." He taps his fingers on the windowsill and then turns back to me.

I imagine stepping across the room and jumping into his arms. I imagine us kissing. I imagine him pulling my shirt off and me unbuttoning his pants.

"I should probably get going," he says, pulling me back to reality.

"Yeah. I have a patient soon anyway."
"Yeah. Thanks for showing me. And for having lunch with me."
"Of course. It was fun."
"Yeah. We should do it again."

CHAPTER 18
(THEN)

I got into medical school. It was almost the end of my fourth year, and I matched with the program at my current university, so I could stay and do my rotation at the hospital there once that part of medical school started.

My mom was on a video call with me; she's the one who opened my letter for me. My address at school wasn't my permanent address, and I was worried I might get my letter after I had already gone home after graduation.

My mom jumped up and down and screamed with me, and then she started to cry.

"Mom, why are you crying?"

"I'm just so happy for you," she said between literal sobs.

"It sounds like you're having a breakdown. Are you sure you're happy?"

"Yes, I'm very happy for my daughter who's about to graduate from university and then continue to stay away from home to go to medical school."

"Mom."

"I said I'm happy!"

"Okay," I said slowly. "Maybe I should let you go."

"Okay." My mom nodded and sobbed more. "I love you." And then she disconnected the call.

Well that was weird.

But oh my god! I got into medical school! I had to tell Brianna! But she wasn't home! No one was home!

"I got into medical school!" I shouted, throwing my arms up in the air. It wasn't enough. I needed to tell a real live person. So I threw on my shoes and ran across the street to Jack's apartment. I didn't even text him first to make sure he was home or was okay with me coming over.

I buzzed his apartment and someone let me in right away, so I ran to the elevator and bounced on my toes as I waited for it to open. I ran in, as if that would make it go faster, and then bounced around inside as it went up to the 9th floor. I couldn't stop smiling, or moving, for that matter. Once the doors opened, I ran down the hallway to Jack's apartment and knocked a bunch of times in a row.

"Hey," Jack said as he opened the door. "What's up?"

"I got into medical school!" I shouted.

"Whaaat! That's amazing! Congratulations! Are you going here?"

"Yes!"

"That's incredible! Because I'm going to teacher's college here too!"

"You got into teacher's college!?"

"Of course I did! I just got my letter today."

"Ah! We're both so amazing!"

"You're more amazing, because I'm sure medical school is much harder to get into."

"We're both amazing!" I shouted, jumping up and down.

Jack grabbed onto my hands and jumped up and down with me. He finally pulled me into his apartment so we could shut the door, and we continued to scream and jump up and down. But all I could think about was his hands on mine. How I wanted them other places on me, too.

Once we calmed down, we laughed a little, both of us out of breath. I looked up at him and he looked down at me, and suddenly I wasn't worried about what would happen if I did anything about my feelings. I wasn't worried about him not feeling the same way and it ruining our friendship, I wasn't worried about the fact that he always called me his best friend. I just wanted to kiss him, so I did.

I felt him tense for half a second, and I almost pulled away from him. I almost turned and walked out of his apartment, too embarrassed to even say sorry, but then he took in a breath through his nose, and his entire body relaxed into mine. He put his hands on my lower back and pulled me into him so that we were pressed together, and he kissed me back.

He kissed me back.

We stood in the entryway of his apartment for an unnecessary length of time I was sure, just kissing. He pulled me closer to his body and opened his mouth against mine, slowly, gently. His tongue was like satin and his hands against my hips were like a cozy fire.

He finally brought his hands up to my face and cupped my cheeks, his thumbs softly caressing my skin. He pulled his mouth away from mine but pressed our foreheads together.

"You have no idea how long I've wanted to do that," he whispered.

I let out a bit of a breathy laugh because I had no idea what to say in return. I wanted to say something hot, or romantic, but I knew anything that came out of my mouth would sound stupid. I brought my hands up to his and he laughed too, and then kissed my nose. I lifted my face up higher so I could kiss him again, and he pulled back a little, smiling at me.

"Hey," I said playfully.

"Hey." Only he said it like he hadn't seen me in years and felt relieved to finally be this close to me. I looked into his dark eyes and I could feel him looking into mine.

"Hey," I said again.

I guess this was new for us, and taking a bit of time to adjust was normal. Everything he did felt right, though. Even his little 'hey' made me melt, made me feel like I was the only one for him.

"Can we keep kissing?" I finally asked him.

"What a silly question." He smiled against my lips and then kissed them, and I kissed him back, and his hands left my face for my back, my hips, my butt. We explored each other's bodies over our clothes, and he pressed my back against the door, his kisses trailing to my jaw and down my neck. He brought his mouth back up to mine for a few minutes, and then he pulled back, but I leaned forward and stood up higher on my toes, not letting him stop. He laughed and let me kiss him again.

I kissed him deeper and started walking him towards his room. He walked backwards for a few steps and then he grabbed onto my thighs and lifted me up, so I wrapped my legs around his waist and let him carry me to his room. He set me down on his bed and I lay on my back, letting him lower himself on top of me.

"Are you okay?" he whispered, putting some of his weight on me.

"Yeah," I said, kissing him again.

"I can't believe this is happening."

"Me neither." I chuckled a little and pressed my lips against his.

He kissed me back and then he kissed my jaw, my neck, under my ear. He moved his lips back to mine and whispered into my mouth, "I want to kiss you forever. You were so worth the wait."

I wish I had something as equally amazing to say to him, but I wasn't good at any of that stuff, so I just smiled and pulled him closer to me.

He slipped his hand under the hem of my shirt, sliding his hand up my side, and then running his fingers over my ribs. "Can I take your shirt off?" he asked.

I nodded and sat up a bit so he could pull it over my head. I had never felt so comfortable being vulnerable in front of someone before. I wanted to take his shirt off too, and there was no anxiety in me telling me not to. There was no voice in my head telling me not to move further, or not to let him touch me. I knew if I took his shirt off, we would just be closer, and everything would be amazing.

I started to lift his t-shirt and he finished taking it off for me, before lowering himself on top of me again.

"You're beautiful," he said, before kissing me again. He only kissed me for a second and then pulled back. "You know that, right?"

"Well, I do now," I laughed.

"I'm sorry I never told you before. I should have told you."

"It's okay. You're telling me now." I sat up, forcing him to sit up too, and I crawled into his lap, straddling his waist. "I think you're beautiful, too."

He smiled, tucked some hair behind my ear, and kissed me again. His hands reached behind me and he unhooked my bra. I shrugged it off my shoulders and threw it to the side, pressing myself into his chest. I felt like I couldn't get close enough to him. Our bare chests were pressed against each other, and I still needed to be closer.

He started to undo my belt and I got up on my knees, my legs on either side of him, and reached for his belt too. I fumbled and couldn't get his undone, and we both laughed quietly.

"It's okay, I got it," he said, doing it himself and then unzipping his pants.

"Wait," I said.

"What's wrong?"

"Nothing." I pressed myself against him and kissed him, but he pulled back.

"Is this too fast?" he asked.

"No," I whispered. "I just feel a little…" I trailed off and bit my bottom lip.

"A little what?"

"I want to touch you," I finally said. "But I don't know how you want me to do it."

He grinned and whispered, "I'll show you." He kissed me, and guided my hand towards him.

Jack and I moved our hands together at first, and after a little while, he gently pushed me back into the bed and put his weight on me again, his hand sliding under my pants.

I gasped into his mouth and I felt him smile against my lips.

"I feel like I still need to be closer to you," I breathed.

"Should I get a condom?"

I nodded. "Yes."

He sat up and grabbed one from his nightstand and I watched as he climbed out of his pants and pulled his boxers down. This was actually happening. I was going to have sex with Jack. Jack and I were going to have sex. I felt weird still having my jeans on so I shimmied them off, and then Jack lowered himself over me.

"Just go slow," I said. "I… Uh, I haven't done this before."

"Wait, really?"

I bit my bottom lip. "Yeah. Have you?"

"Yeah, I had a girlfriend in high school."

"Oh. How many times did you do it?"

He laughed and lowered his face into the crook of my neck. "I didn't keep track, Aspen."

"Right." I laughed a little too, and then trailed my fingers up and down his bare back.

"Are you nervous?" he asked, looking at me.

"I don't know. Maybe a little."

"I know it isn't something you can help, but you have no reason to be nervous with me. We don't have to keep doing this."

"No, no, I want to. I do, I swear. I'm just a little overwhelmed?"

"We don't have to jump right into this, Aspen. There are so many other things that we can do and work our way up to it."

"Like what we were doing earlier?"

"Yeah. And other things."

"But isn't this stupid?" I asked.

"Isn't what stupid?"

"I'm 21 and I've never had sex."

"So?"

"So? Haven't most people my age had sex by now?"

"Yeah, probably. But a lot of people also haven't. I don't see why it matters when someone loses their virginity."

"I don't know, for some reason I thought you were like me. I mean you don't really go to parties or hang out with other girls, so I thought… I thought maybe this would be your first time doing this too."

"It's true that I don't go to parties or hang out with other girls."

"But you have sex with them?"

He laughed and rolled us over so that he was on his back and I was sort of on top of him. He readjusted us and put his arm around me, letting me cuddle into his side.

"No, I don't have sex with them," he said. "I haven't had sex in a long time."

"Why not?"

"I don't know. I guess I don't like having sex with people unless I really like them. And I haven't liked anyone at school."

"Oh."

He kissed my forehead and rubbed the back of my arm. "Except for you."

I smiled and closed my eyes, relaxing into his warm skin. "Why didn't you say anything, then?"

"About liking you?"

"Yeah."

He shrugged. "Well at first, we were just friends. I mean I just thought of you as a friend, because it takes a while for me to really like a girl like that. And once I started really liking you, we were really good friends. I didn't want to make you uncomfortable. Plus I really liked being your friend and I didn't want to ruin that if you didn't feel the same way."

"Same," I said with a sigh.

"We're ridiculous."

"You called me your best friend so many times, I was sure you didn't like me like that."

"You are my best friend. I'm just also in love with you."

My eyes snapped open and I took in a sharp breath. "You're-you're in love with me?"

"Yes." He slid out from beside me and climbed on top of me again, his hands on either side of me. "I'm in love with you, Aspen. I've wanted to say it for so long but I was afraid that if I did, I would ruin something already amazing. I guess since we're both in bed naked together and we've touched each other's private parts, adding that I'm in love with you won't make much of a difference. Also, I'm sorry for saying private parts, it sounded better in my head and now that I've heard it, it sounds very childish and silly and not at all romantic. But yeah. I'm in love with you."

I felt a smile forming on my lips and couldn't stop it.

"You're in love with me too, aren't you?" he asked.

"Yes. I'm in love with you, too."

He smiled even more than he already was and then he lowered his face to mine and kissed me. I brought my hands around his back and pulled him closer to me.

"Let's work our way up to it," I whispered.

He nodded and trailed his hand down my side and over my thigh.

"Just tell me if anything is too much," he said.

All I could do was nod.

Jack and I explored each other's bodies with our hands, slowly and gently, and whispered to each other between kisses. Sometimes our movements were less calm and it was harder to only whisper, but everything was amazing. Nothing was awkward. Nothing made me nervous. Sometimes we laughed, and sometimes I sighed into his mouth. Everything he did felt incredible.

His roommate was gone to some party, so he ran to the kitchen wearing nothing but his socks, and came back with grapes and a bag of chips. We watched a movie in his bed, naked, while eating snacks.

I fell asleep on his shoulder and I woke up a little when I felt him get out of bed to turn the light off. He crawled back under the covers and wrapped his arms around me, breathing in my hair. I turned around so that I could nuzzle my face into his chest.

"I love you," I whispered.

"I love you too."

We slept in pretty late, but to be fair, we were up pretty late. Jack kissed the back of my neck, pulling me into him, his arms wrapped around my chest.

"Good morning, beautiful," he said.

"Good morning."

"Do you want breakfast?"

"You wanna go somewhere?" I asked.

"No, I want to make you something."

"I will allow that."

He chuckled and got out of bed. He pulled on a pair of track pants and whistled on his way out his bedroom. I yawned and closed my eyes, letting myself fall back asleep. I loved Jack's bed. It was so warm and cozy, and smelled like Jack. I never wanted to leave.

"Hey sleepyhead." Jack's voice by my ear woke me up, but it was nice to be woken up by him. I wished I could be woken up by him every morning.

"Hi," I murmured.

"I made French Toast."

"Oh wow." I sat up in bed, and shivered as the comforter fell from my shoulders.

"Here," Jack said, handing me one of his hoodies. I pulled it over my head and pulled the sleeve cuffs over my hands, bringing them to my face so I could smell them.

"Are you smelling my sweater?" he asked.

"Yeah, so? You smelled my hair."

"Okay, fair."

He handed me a plate of French toast smothered in maple syrup, whipped cream, and icing sugar. I balanced it on my lap and cut into it right away. It was amazing. I nodded at him as I shoved more in my mouth, and he smiled, digging into his own breakfast. He turned the TV on and we watched the first episode of a new space themed Netflix show.

When we were done eating, Jack kissed my temple and took our plates away. I wanted to follow him and help him, but I didn't know where my underwear was. What if his roommate walked in and saw me only wearing one of Jack's hoodies and nothing else? I decided to get up and try to find them on the floor, but by the time I did, Jack was back, and shutting the door behind him.

"Hi," he said, walking closer to me.

"Hi."

My underwear was in my hand, and I saw him looking down at it. "Don't put those back on," he said.

"Why not?"

"Okay, sorry, you can if you want. I mean, of course, put your underwear on. I just sort of wanted to…" he trailed off, and I smiled.

"You were just going to take them off anyway?" I asked.

"Only if you want me to."

I smiled at him and stepped into my underwear, pulling them up over my hips. He stood back and grinned at me, and I kept my eye on him the whole time. I walked closer to him and then stood on my toes so I could kiss him.

"I want you to take them off," I whispered.

I swear I felt him melt against me. We explored each other's bodies again, and eventually we were back to where we were the night before.

"You should put a condom on," I said.

"Are you sure?"

"Yes."

"Because we can wait longer. Do more of this."

"I don't want to wait," I said. "Unless you want to wait."

He smiled and shook his head. "I don't want to wait. I just wanted to make sure-"

"Jack," I said, cutting him off.

"Sorry. Yeah. Neither of us wants to wait." His smile grew and I couldn't help but grin in response. He grabbed a new condom and I watched him put it on again. "Are you okay?" he asked, bringing himself closer.

"Yeah," I breathed. "Are you?"

"I'm perfect."

I ran to the bathroom to pee after, once Jack made sure that Brad wasn't home. I washed my hands and gargled some cold water, and then went back to his bed.

"I really liked doing that with you," he said.

"So did I."

"We could have been doing that for the last two and a half years."

I laughed a little. "What's wrong with us?"

"Everything, apparently. Instead, we were studying and pretending that feelings didn't exist."

"Maybe it wouldn't have been as good if we did it earlier. Maybe because we know each other so well, that's what made it amazing."

"Yeah, you're probably right."

"Can we stay in bed all day?" I asked.

"All day? How 'bout all weekend?"

"Yeah, that sounds better."

Jack grinned at me. "Can we be naked the whole time?"

"As long as you keep me warm when I get cold."

"Are you cold now?"

"No, I'm okay now."

"Okay," he said with a smirk. "I see how it is."

"I'll let you know when I need warming up," I said.

He nuzzled his face into my neck and I curled my fingers between the twists in his hair. He breathed deeply and I breathed deeply to match, and we fell asleep.

The entire weekend was a blur of sleeping, eating, and having some sort of sex. It was like we were making up for lost time, only none of it felt rushed, or like that was what we were actually doing. We were just so in awe of how much we loved each other, and how amazing it was to express it this way. At least that's how I felt, and it somehow felt like he was experiencing the same thing. Like we were going through it together.

Jack took pictures of me from in bed. He held the camera against his pillow and aimed the lens at me, my face half buried in the blankets. He arranged the sheets so that I was covered, and took pictures of me while I curled up on my side. He gave me one of his t-shirts and took pictures of me from above, standing on his mattress with his feet on either side of my ribs. He waited until I giggled and then I would hear the shutter, or he waited until I was looking at something else, always trying to catch me in real life. He took a few pictures of me looking out the window, or sitting up in bed with his comforter wrapped around me like a shawl. And then he made me laugh by taking close up photos of me eating grapes, or scooping peanut butter out of the jar with my finger.

His smile was so soft as he looked at the previews on the back of the camera, and when he moved his eyes back to me for a second before putting the viewfinder back up to his face, it felt like we were the only two people in the world. I would smile and blush at him and he would tell me how to sit, or where to look.

"Why aren't you taking any pictures?" I asked, sitting cross-legged on his bed in a pair of his boxers and one of his t-shirts. He was looking through his camera but I hadn't heard the shutter click in a few minutes.

"I am," he said with a chuckle.

"But you're not. You finger hasn't pressed the shutter button in forever."

"I'm just waiting."

"For what?"

And then the shutter went. I laughed and leaned forward a little.

"Really?" I said. "You wanted a picture of me with that confused look?"

He shrugged and I laughed again, and he took another picture.

"That's what I wanted," he said, smiling at me over the camera.

I tried to take a few pictures of him, but just glancing at the previews on the screen showed me that he had a talent that I didn't. His photos were framed so elegantly, and the lighting was always perfect, with a steak of light coming in from the window cutting the picture in the most artistic way, or putting half of me in a mysterious shadow. I had no idea how he did it.

On Sunday afternoon, Jack's phone rang, and he ignored it. He ignored it to pull me on top of him and run his hands down my back. I kissed him and moved my body over his, sighing every time he moved his hands to a new spot on me. I kissed his neck below his ear, and then tugged on his earlobe a little with my teeth.

"Should you get that?" I asked.

"No. I'm busy." He rolled us over and kissed me a little deeper.

His phone stopped ringing and we kissed until he started to trail his lips down my chest.

His phone rang again and it woke us both up.

"You should probably get that," I said.

He looked at the screen and tossed it back onto his nightstand. "It's just my mom," he said.

"Just your mom? What if it's important?"

He sighed and grabbed his phone again, but it stopped ringing. It notified us to let him know there was a voicemail.

"I'm hungry. Do you want something to eat?" he asked. "I'll check her message later."

"Sure."

Jack and I made pizza rolls and watched the TV that Brad was watching from the kitchen while we waited for them to cook. He didn't say much to us, and I felt a little embarrassed for some reason. We brought the pizza rolls back to his room and after Jack popped a few in his mouth, he grabbed his phone to check the message from his mom. I started to eat my lunch while he listened to the message, but after about thirty seconds, his hand snapped to my wrist, gripping it tightly. I looked over at him as I finished chewing my pizza roll, and he had tears in his eyes. His grip tightened on my wrist, and it was starting to hurt, but it looked like he had no idea that he was doing it.

"Jack," I said quietly. "What is it?"

His phone was still to his ear, but it didn't sound like the message was playing anymore.

"Jack?"

He turned to me slowly, and when his eyes found mine, he let go of my wrist. "My mom has cancer."

Tears spilled out of his eyes and rolled down his face, and he didn't even sob or anything, they just came out like an overflowing glass of water. I didn't know what to do, so I grabbed onto his hand, and said nothing. What was I supposed to say?

"I have to call her back," he said, wiping his face with his sleeve.

"Okay," I said. He dialed her number and put the phone to his ear. I could tell he was trying to hold in sobs as it rang.

"Mom?" he choked out when I assumed she answered. "I'm sorry I didn't answer my phone, I was with a friend."

He paused and listened to his mom talk and then he started crying. Full on sobbing. I didn't know if he wanted me there or if I should just quietly get up and leave. But then his grip tightened on my hand, so I stayed.

"Okay," he said into the phone. "Can I come home tomorrow? Okay. I'll take the bus, then. Okay I love you. Bye." He put the phone down on his bed and stared ahead of him, almost emotionless. Tears were still steaming down his face but the sobs had stopped.

"Jack," I finally said.

He jerked a bit, as if he forgot that I was there, and then slowly looked at me. "My mom's going to die."

"You don't know that."

"I do know that. My mom's going to die, Aspen." And then he started to sob again, and he buried his face in my shoulder. I held him, and we eventually fell back onto his mattress and he fell asleep. I didn't fall asleep. I listened to him breathe and I gently played with his hair, and he slept like a rock. I didn't know what to do. What was I supposed to do?

I guess I finally fell asleep at some point. Jack woke me by shaking my shoulder.

"Hey," he said when I opened my eyes and looked at him. He looked horrible. His eyes were bloodshot and his face and eyelids were puffy from crying.

"Hey," I whispered.

"I didn't know if you needed to get home. Since you have class in the morning."

"What time is it?" I asked.

"1am."

"Oh shit."

"Yeah."

"I mean, I can stay. If you want me to. I can set my alarm a little earlier than normal and just go home to get ready in the morning. If you want."

He smiled a little and nodded. "Okay. Stay."

He nuzzled back into me and I wrapped my arms around him, and together we went back to sleep.

CHAPTER 19 (NOW)

"I'm sorry, he apologized to you for getting a girlfriend ten years ago, and then he also told you that you were important to him?" Shannon asks after we're done with our patients for the day and I fill her in on our lunch. "Yeah, he's in love with you."

"You think?"

"What do you mean 'you think'? Of course I think!"

"But I told him that I'm single," I say. "He didn't go back on what he said, about not feeling anything more than friendship."

"Because he's in love with you! He's not going to jump you the second he hears that you're single. He wants to make sure that you're okay first. Probably make sure you know that it means something."

"Well by the time I'm okay, he'll be on Mars! And if it wasn't for stupid David, I'd have been there when he landed! And we wouldn't have to deal with this stupid mess!"

"So follow him."

"What?"

"You already know the Mars Group wanted you there, so just apply again. And tell Jack that's what you're doing."

"Ugh, this is so confusing."

"It's not confusing, Aspen. It's very clear. You're just a chicken."

"I'm not a chicken." Except that I am. Of course I am.

"You're totally a chicken," Shannon says with a hint of playfulness in her voice.

"Ugh." I throw my arms up in the air and turn around to grab the office door handle.

"What are you doing? Are you going to call Jack?"

"No. I'm going to David's so I can punch him in the throat."

"Oh! Wait for me!"

Shannon and I head down to the parking lot with a fervour I don't think I've seen in the two of us before. If anyone was in our path, I'm sure they would see us coming and quickly get out of our way. We look that focused and driven. I start to walk towards my car but Shannon grabs onto my elbow and steers me towards her parking spot.

"What are you doing?" I ask.

"I'm driving. You're in no shape to drive right now."

"And then you'll drive me back here to get my car after I punch David?"

"No, I'll take you home. You really won't be in a state to drive after punching your asshole ex. I'll pick you up in the morning."

"Oh. Okay. That sounds good."

"Of course it sounds good. I'm a genius."

We get into her car and I start to fume a little more. Everything about what David did is settling in more, hitting me. I mean I knew that David was a dick, but I never thought that he would do this. If he didn't want to go to Mars, why didn't he just tell me? But to sabotage my chance at going and be an ass to me for the next three years? Uncalled for.

I notice too late that Shannon is driving towards my apartment.

"This isn't the way to David's," I say.

"I know. I'm taking you to your place."

"I can't punch David at my place."

"Do you really want to punch David in the face?"

"Yes."

"Why don't you just go home, and call him instead?" She turns onto my street and looks at me briefly. "Then you can still tell him how mad you are at him, but there's no chance of assaulting him this way."

I roll my eyes and am about to say something, but Shannon keeps talking.

"Or you don't have to call him at all." She says it almost like a question. She pulls into a parking spot near the entrance of my building and turns to look at me. "Do you want me to come in with you?"

"No. Thanks, though. See you in the morning."

"Okay. See ya."

I undo my seatbelt and get out of the car. After I grab my stuff from in front of my seat, but before I shut the door, Shannon says, "Make good choices!" like she's my mom, so I mock laugh at her and shut the door.

She waves to me through the windshield and I head into my building. Although my apartment itself is fairly nice, the building is a complete shithole. It doesn't have an elevator even though it's four floors, and the hallways have old, browning and fraying carpets down the middle. You're not allowed to smoke in the building, but it always smells like cigarettes in the entrance, and more so near some apartment doors.

I walk up to the third floor where my apartment is and drop my stuff on my bed once I get inside. I immediately pull my phone out of my back pocket and bring up David in my contacts.

What the hell David???? I almost hit send but I think of a better message and erase it.

Did you sabotage my chance at going to Mars, you coward?

Nah. Backspace. I can come up with something better.

Why are you such a fucking scrotum?

I delete that too. I take in a breath and then pull up my contacts list again. I scroll until I see Jack's name, and I hit call.

"Hello?" He answers it on the second ring.

"Hey. It's Aspen. Can you come over?"

"To your place?" he asks.

"Yeah."

"Of course. Um, are you okay?"

"Please just come over." I'm afraid if I talk about it before he's here, I'll get even more worked up and explode.

"Okay," he says. "What's your address?"

It only takes Jack fifteen minutes to show up at my apartment. I buzz him in on my cell phone, and I imagine him running up the stairs two at a time to get here as fast as he can. I open the door to the hallway in anticipation of seeing him come through the stairwell door, and when he does, I almost collapse with relief. Seeing him walking down the hall somehow covers me in a sort of calming bubble. Well, almost. I'm not quite calm, just feeling slightly better now that he's here.

"Are you okay?" he asks, coming closer to me. "What's wrong?"

"You have to convince me not to go over to David's and punch him in the neck." I can feel my fists tightening at my sides, and Jack grabs onto my shoulders and gently guides me into my apartment. He looks around briefly and raises his eyebrows for a second, probably surprised at how tiny it is, and how open it is, with my bed right in the living room.

"Whoa," he says, looking back at me. "What's going on?"

"He ruined my chance at going to Mars!"

"What do you mean?"

"Well apparently, I was going to go to Mars!" I'm raising my voice much more than is probably acceptable but I can't help it. "They look at your applications before the deadline, you know? They weed people out so there's less work for them to do when everything's all final. And we all know that some of those jobs have opportunities on Earth. So there's a checkbox for those ones!" I make a checkmark in the air with my finger and Jack watches me intently, just listening.

"Do you want to work on Mars?" I continue. "And I checked yes! Yes, I did want to work on Mars! That's why I applied!" Now I'm starting to cry. I'm yelling and I'm crying and Jack can see my unmade bed behind me, covered in the stuff I brought home from work.

"What does David have to do with this?" Jack asks.

"He said he was okay with it! Spouses and families can join after six months; we were only going to be apart for six months!" I take in a deep breath, trying to calm myself, but it doesn't work. "He said he was excited," I cry. "He said he would live anywhere with me, but he lied."

"I'm really sorry, but I'm not following."

"He changed my application, Jack. He logged into my account right before the deadline, and he said no to Mars. I thought that I was just placed here because that's what they chose for me. But they chose me for Mars! I would have gotten those exciting questionnaires shortly after like you did, but I didn't. Because David ruined it."

Jack slumps a little, looking at me as if he totally understands how I feel. He takes a step towards me, but still keeps space between us.

"I could have been on Mars this whole time," I say through a crack in my voice.

It's quiet for a minute, and Jack and I just stare at each other. I look away a couple times and wipe away my tears, but mostly it's just quiet and we're just looking at each other.

"Aspen, I am really sorry that he did that to you," Jack finally says. "But I don't think that you should punch him. I don't even think that you should reach out to him."

"Why not?"

"What good would it do?"

I scoff. "It would let him know how much of an ass he is."

"I'm sure he knows he's an ass. And if he doesn't, confronting him about it isn't going to convince him that he is. Calling him to yell at him isn't going to make any of this better."

"But I'm so mad!" Tears spill out again and drip off my chin.

"I know," he says gently. "I know you are. And you have every right to be mad. But you guys have already been broken up for a little while already, right? What's the point in calling him out on something he did a few years ago?"

I want to say something. I want to say that he's right, but I don't want to admit it. I want David to feel bad for what he did. I want him to know that I know.

"Why don't you reapply?" Jack asks. "Or since you're already employed by them, maybe you can just request a transfer."

"What?" I know what he said. But for some reason it isn't registering the way that it should.

"Well you still want to go to Mars, don't you?"

"Yeah."

"So try again. There's no one holding you back this time."

I'm not sure why, but having both Shannon and Jack suggest trying to go to Mars again scares me. I was upset when I didn't get accepted before, of course I was. And I'm even more upset about it now that I know what happened, but thinking about uprooting my life again after I just worked up the courage to break up with David and move out on my own, is scary. My life will have to change again, really soon, and in the most drastic way possible. I was prepared for it before. All I ever wanted ever since hearing about The Mars Group was to be a doctor on Mars. It's all I dreamed of. For so long, it was all I ever wanted, especially after what happened with Jack. And when I applied for it, I had been with David for just under a year. We weren't living together yet, and moving to Mars together would have been our first big step.

We talked about it a lot before I applied. I told him that I was waiting to finish my residency before applying because I wanted a job on Mars as a doctor. I had told him that if I was single I wouldn't have thought twice about it. He smiled and said that Mars sounded like an adventure. He was planning on asking me to move in with him soon anyway, so this was even better. I remember laughing and rolling over in bed, letting him grab onto my hips and pull me on top of him.

"Really?" I had asked, looking down at him.

His smile was so contagious. This was when I still felt safe with him. Before I realized a lot of what he did was manipulative.

"Really," he said. "I can't think of anything better. Going to Mars with you sounds amazing. Even if I have to stay here without you for six months first."

"Oh, but it'll be so exciting! We'll be spending that whole time planning for you to get there, and I'll video chat with you and show you the apartment, and where I work, and I'll show you around the compound."

"You have to take me out on Mars walks too. In your cute little space suit."

"Oh, I'll definitely do that."

Was he just lying to me that entire time? All our conversations about it, was he pretending?

"Okay fine, you don't have to say anything," Jack says, pulling me from my memories and bringing me back to the present. "You can think about it and do whatever's best for you. But you know what we should do right now?"

"What?" I ask.

"Go to the bookstore."

"Really?"

"Yes, really. Like you said before, it's a good escape. We can buy books about badass chicks kicking people's asses."

"Why, so I don't feel the need to kick someone's ass myself?"

"Of course."

I smile at him, and he chuckles a little.

"Come on," he says, "I'll drive."

The drive to the bookstore is a bit longer from my new apartment than it was when I was living with David. We're pretty quiet as Jack drives us, but then he speaks up when we're almost there.

"I have a question."

"Okay," I say slowly.

"If David had told you that he didn't want to go to Mars, would you have gone anyway? Or would you have let it hold you back?"

"You think I've been held back by not being on Mars?"

"I didn't say that," he says, looking at me for half a second. "You wanted to go to Mars. That's all we ever talked about in school. You're not being held back as a person by staying here, but you're being held back in your life's ambitions."

"Right."

"So what would you have done?"

"I don't know," I say honestly.

"Hmm."

"Hmm?" I ask. "Why 'hmm'?"

"I don't know," he says, checking his blind spot and then turning into the bookstore parking lot. "I just feel like maybe Mars isn't as important to you as you once thought. When it was just talk, it was easy to be excited about and plan for it, but once it becomes real, it can be a lot."

"Of course it can be a lot. But I wanted it, Jack. I was devastated when I was placed here. I… I cried. And I'm upset about it now."

"Are you upset that you were stopped from going to Mars, or upset that David broke your trust?"

"Both."

"Okay." He nods and turns the car off, but doesn't make any other move to get out. "So if he told you that he didn't want to go with you, would you have gone anyway?"

"I told you I don't know. Why is this important?"

He shrugs. "Anna never wanted to go to Mars. And I thought I loved her. I mean, I did love her, but I thought I loved her more than Mars. I thought that being with her was enough."

"She wasn't?" I ask quietly.

"She would have been, if she had a real reason not to go other than she didn't want to. It was that I wasn't enough for her. I wasn't enough for her to want to follow me to Mars. And that's what ultimately ended our relationship. If she couldn't go to Mars because of physical or family limitations, something, anything other than she didn't want to, I would have stayed gladly. And I did at first, because I thought that she loved me the same way that I loved her. I didn't want to stay, but I stayed for her. She wouldn't have done the same for me, and it showed. She didn't even want to try."

"Jack, I'm sorry."

He shakes his head a little. "It's fine. It's okay. I didn't mean to tell you all that." He lets out a bit of a laugh that sounds a little forced, and undoes his seatbelt.

"I think I would have done the same," I finally say, making him stop with his hand on the door handle.

"And what's that?"

"I would have thought that he was enough for me. I would have stayed to be with him, because I would have thought he was enough. And I would have been wrong."

"It sort of sucks that we ended up in relationships that lasted longer than they should have, with people who didn't deserve us."

I take in a deep breath. "Yeah."

"I guess it sort of makes sense for me, though."

"What do you mean?" I ask.

"I didn't really deserve Anna in the beginning. I guess she just gave it back to me in the end."

"Oh?"

"Yeah," he says with a sigh.

"Care to elaborate?"

"Aahh, not right now."

"Come on, you brought it up."

"Yeah. I was talking too much. I just felt weird saying that Anna didn't deserve me. It made me feel like a dick."

I laugh and undo my seatbelt. "Okay, sure. Let's go buy some books then."

CHAPTER 20 (THEN)

When the alarm on my phone went off, Jack started to cry. I pulled him into me and let him sniffle into my shirt.

"I don't have to go to class," I said. "I can go with you to the bus station. I can go with you on the bus."

"Aspen, I love you, but I don't think it's a good idea for you to come home with me right now."

"Neither do I. I just meant I would ride the bus with you. So that you didn't have to be alone."

"Then what would you do?"

I shrugged. "Take the bus back."

"I can't ask you to do that."

"You didn't."

He looked at me, his eyes still puffy but less red. "I…"

"It's okay, Jack. It was just a thought."

I crawled out of his bed and grabbed my jeans from the floor. I sat back down after putting them on so I could adjust my socks, and before I had a chance to get up again, Jack grabbed at me from behind. He pulled on my shirt and then gripped my arm, so I turned to face him.

"Don't go yet," he said.

"Okay."

"How long until you have to be in class?"

"I told you I don't have to go today."

"Are you sure?"

"Yes. You're more important."

"Don't say that. I'm not."

"You are."

"I'm not. Your school is important. I don't want you to miss anything."

"I can get notes from classmates. Notes will always be there, but you might not be. I want to make sure you're okay."

"Aspen, I'm not going to kill myself."

"I know. There's more to being okay than just that."

"Okay."

I smiled. "Okay."

"Will you come with me, then? On the bus?"

"Of course I will."

I texted Brianna to let her know what I was doing, and she requested details when I got back. I helped Jack pack, and then we took the city bus to the Greyhound station. We waited quietly in plastic chairs for our bus to show up, and then we put his bags in the compartment underneath, and walked down the cramped aisle to a seat that looked good to us. I turned to Jack behind me when we made it to a spot near the middle without anyone sitting there yet, and he nodded at me. I sat down first and he took the aisle seat next to me. It took about twenty minutes before the bus got going, and Jack was already asleep on my shoulder.

"Thanks for coming," he said about halfway through the three-hour journey.

"Of course. I would do anything for you."

"Why, because I told you I love you?"

"What? No. No, because I love you. Because I'm in love with you."

"Okay. Promise me you won't ever give the world to someone just because they tell you they love you."

"O-Okay," I stammered.

He nuzzled into my shoulder again and went back to sleep.

I rested my head on top of his, like how we did on our way back from the first Mars Send Off, only reversed. I put my arm around his waist and he wrapped his arm around me, too. I let myself fall asleep, and we stayed like that until the bus stopped at the station in his town.

"I don't know if my parents are here yet," Jack said, looking past me out the window.

"Have you texted them?"

"No. I will now."

I watched as he pulled his phone out of his pocket and went through his contacts with shaking fingers. I tried to pretend that I didn't notice, but he winced at me a little after sending his message, as if he was afraid that I saw.

He got up from his seat and I followed him off the bus. Jack found his two bags in the pile of luggage on the pavement and I carried one of them into the station for him. I looked around at the departure times and locations at each terminal, trying to gauge when I could get home.

"Is your bus going back right now?" he asked, noticing me look around.

"Oh. I don't think so."

"Do you need to go get a ticket to be sure?"

"I can wait."

"Are you sure?"

"Yeah." I walked over to the seating area and tried to get comfortable. Jack stayed standing in front of me, his hands in his pockets and his bag at his feet.

"Oh, there's my dad," Jack said, looking past me.

I turned around a little to see a man even taller than Jack coming towards us. His skin was a bit darker than Jack's but he looked just like him. He gave Jack a weak smile as he approached, and they hugged while I sat awkwardly in my plastic orange chair.

"Oh, dad, this is Aspen," Jack said when he pulled away from his dad and looked down at me briefly, as if he had forgotten I was there.

"Aspen. Hello." His dad nodded at me, but I could tell he wasn't sure what to make of me being there.

"I'm going home," I said quickly. "I just came for moral support."

"Oh. Would you like to come over for dinner first?"

"Oh that's nice of you," I said. "Thank you very much. But I think I should probably go. I don't want to get back too late. It is three hours away, after all."

"Well thank you very much for keeping my son company."

"Any time."

"Dad, I'll be right back, okay?" Jack said to his dad, before grabbing onto my hand and pulling me to my feet.

"Okay. I'll be right here."

Jack pulled me away from his dad and past the next few terminals. He kept a hold of my hand the whole time, and I squeezed his gently, smiling inside when he squeezed back. We finally stopped walking and Jack looked back, maybe to see if it was obvious if his dad could see us.

"I'm sorry this is happening," he said, turning back to me.

"Why are you sorry?" I asked. "I'm sorry."

"I just hate that we finally did something about our feelings and now it's basically being ripped away from us."

"Nothing has to be ripped away from us just because we're going to be apart for a little while."

He nodded and looked back towards his dad. "Right."

"Jack. Hey."

He looked back at me, his eyes suddenly filled with tears. "I'm scared, Aspen."

"That's allowed. I would be scared too."

"I don't know what I'm going to do if she dies."

"Don't think about that yet. Maybe she won't."

"It's really bad, Aspen. Like it's…" Tears fell down his face and he looked up, as if trying to stop them. "It's really bad."

I held out my arms to him and he stepped into me. I wrapped my arms around his back and let him breathe me in. He squeezed me tight and rocked me a little, and we stayed like that for a few minutes.

"Your dad's waiting," I whispered. "Go be with your mom."

"Okay." He pulled away but then grabbed onto my face and kissed me. I kissed him back, slowly and gently, and when we stopped, he kept his forehead pressed to mine. "I love you."

"I love you too," I said.

"I'm sorry it took me so long to say it."

"Me too."

He kissed my forehead and I leaned into his lips a little, and then he stepped away and walked towards his dad without looking back. I watched him hug his dad again, and then the two of them picked up his bags and left through the main doors. I stood there by myself for a little while, trying to figure out how to move my legs. I was so overwhelmed all of a sudden. I had just spent the entire weekend with Jack, doing a lot of things for the first time with him, telling him that I loved him, hearing him say that he loved me, and then he was going away, just like that. Should I have gone with him? Was it okay that I suggested that? I wasn't giving the world to him because he told me he loved me, was I? No. Even if the past weekend hadn't happened, I still would have gone with him. I wouldn't have even thought about it. No question, I would have been right there beside him.

So I wasn't giving him the world because he loved me. I was giving it to him because that's what he deserved. I shook my head a little and took in a deep breath before making my way over to the ticket counter for my bus ride home.

Turns out the next bus home wasn't for another two hours, so I had some time to kill. I looked at my watch. It was only 2:30, but I was starving. I guess I hadn't eaten yet, so suddenly 2:30 seemed very late. I stepped out into the sun and looked around for somewhere to eat. There was a Burger King across the street, so I made my way over. I ordered a Junior Whopper and a poutine, and ate my meal in the corner, away from the few other people who were in there eating.

My phone went off and I opened it immediately, thinking it might be Jack, but it was Brianna.

Where are you? Are you on your way back yet? her message read.

Not yet. It doesn't leave until 5:20 so I'm killing time.

What are you doing?

I'm eating a poutine at Burger King.

Fancy. Let me know when you're on your way home!

I will.

I contemplated texting Jack, but he literally just got in. He needed to spend time with his family. I finished my poutine and then refilled my cup with Frutopia before walking back over to the bus station. I was glad that I came with Jack. I was happy that I could be there for him. But in those two hours waiting for my bus home, I had never felt so lonely.

Brianna and Carly met me at the Greyhound station, which was really nice. They both hugged me when I got off the bus, making me feel like I had been gone on some long vacation, or like I was an old friend they hadn't seen in a long time. We got on the city bus together without saying much, but Carly ended up getting off a few stops before us to go see her new boyfriend. Brianna put her arm around my shoulder and I leaned my head against hers.

"Thanks for coming to get me," I said.

"Any time. Thanks for being there for Jack. That was really nice of you."

"Yeah, I guess."

"I hope he's doing okay."

"Me too."

"So what were you guys doing all weekend, anyway? Midterms are over."

I chuckled nervously, and she raised her eyebrows at me.

"What does that mean?" she asked.

"Let's talk about it at home."

"Aspen! Oh my god!"

"Shh," I whispered, not wanting everyone else on the bus to hear.

"Shut up," she said quietly.

"I'm trying to."

She shoved me in the shoulder and I laughed.

I pressed the button on the handrail for our stop, and when the bus pulled over, Brianna practically pushed me off the bus. We giggled and ran in to our building.

"Tell me everything!" she said in the elevator.

"Oh my god, I don't even know where to start."

"Tell me, tell me, tell me!"

"I don't know! I just went over to tell him I got into medical school and-"

"You got into medical school!?"

"Oh my god, I forgot I haven't been home all weekend to tell you! Yeah!"

"That's amazing! Congratulations!"

"Thanks!"

The elevator doors pinged open and we practically skipped down the hall to our apartment.

"So then what happened?" she asked, practically tripping over the Ryan Reynolds cut out. "Oh my god why is this in front of the door!?"

"Why isn't it just always in her room!?" I shouted.

"And why does she still have it!? She's had it since the beginning of second year!"

I picked it up and carried it to Carly's room but her door was locked, so I set it down right in front. But then he was just staring at me, with this half smile on his face, one that told me he was up to no good and that he also knew how incredibly sexy he was, so I turned him around so that he was facing the door. "There," I said. "That's better."

"Come to my room," Brianna said.

I sat down on her bed and told her about the weekend, from our first kiss, to what he said when I told him I'd never had sex before, to all the things we did after. Brianna squealed into her pillow and I laughed at her. But then it got serious when I told her about the phone call from his mom, and how our magical weekend turned into something devastating.

"That really sucks," she said.

"Yeah. It does."

"Have you talked to him since he got home?"

"No, I wanted to give him some space."

"Makes sense. But don't give him too much. You don't want him to think that he's something you don't want to have to deal with."

"Oh my god, do you think he would think that?"

She shrugged. "I don't know, he might. Is he an over-thinker?"

"I guess he is a little."

"Text him tomorrow."

"Okay."

And I did. I texted him the next morning and asked how he was doing. It took him a while to respond, and when he did, he just said that he was okay.

Let me know if I can do anything to help I said.

Okay. I will.

I opened the emoji keyboard and found the red heart, but I was a little nervous to send it. Was it appropriate to send a heart to the guy you just confessed your love to and had sex with, but also didn't discuss the specifics of your relationship before he went home to see his probably dying mother?

Probably not.

I waited about ten minutes and then I sent it. I couldn't help it.

He sent one back.

We texted a little over the next week, but not much. It was mostly me asking how he was doing, and him saying that he was okay. He asked me how school was and I said okay. I asked him if he was going to have to redo his last semester and he said he was figuring it out. When he didn't elaborate, I figured he was doing something online, but I wasn't sure.

The next week, he suggested that we watch a movie over the phone together. We planned it for Saturday night, and it was going to be my study break, but about two hours before we were going to start watching it, he messaged me and said that his mom was being rushed to the hospital and he would need to postpone. I told him that I was thinking of him and I hoped everything would be okay. He replied with a heart, but nothing else.

He texted me a few days later to say that his mom ended up being okay, but that it's really hard to deal with.

Is it okay if you give me some space for a little while? he asked.

Yes of course if that's what you need.

I don't want you to take it the wrong way. It's not that I don't want to talk to you, because I do. I just don't think that I can right now. I don't even know how to talk to my own family let alone you, who isn't even in the same room as me.

It's okay I get it.

It's not okay but I'm glad you get it. I thought I could do this. I thought I could be here for my family and also talk to you every night about normal things but I can't.

You don't have to talk to me about 'normal things' I replied. **You can talk to me about your mom if you want to.**

I don't want to. I don't want to talk to anyone about it. It's too hard.

Okay.

I'm sorry, Aspen. And then he sent a heart and that emoji that people use for both heartbreak and tears of cuteness.

Don't be sorry. You can message me whenever you feel ready. I'll be here.

Thanks. Another heart emoji.

I sent a heart emoji back, and then I turned off my phone.

And he didn't text me for a month. I didn't want to be the first to text to him when he asked me for space. He needed to be the one to reach out. When he did, he just said hi, and I said hi back.

I miss you he said.

I miss you too.

We didn't say anything else.

Finals came and went, pretty sure I aced them all, and then I packed up my apartment. Carly and Brianna weren't coming back for any kind of post-grad schooling, so we wouldn't be seeing as much of each other after this. They were both moving back to their home towns to find jobs, and I would be coming back here by myself in the fall. Unless Jack came back by then.

My parents helped me load all my stuff into a moving van and I stood in the empty living room for a while before we left, trying not to cry. Both Carly and Brianna left the night before, and it was sad then, but standing in the bare apartment three years after moving in was a little surreal. I had lived with the two of them since second year, and now it was all ending.

"How's your friend Jack doing?" My mom asked on the drive home. My dad was driving the truck in front of us.

"Oh. I didn't tell you. His mom has stage 4 cancer. Um, pancreatic, I think. So he left early to go be with his family."

"Oh no, that's terrible."

"Yeah, it's pretty sad. Especially because they like, just found out and it's already so progressed."

"Aw, sweety. I'm sorry."

"Me too."

I decided to text Jack after I had been back home for a few days. I was applying to live in Residence again because it was about half the price of a one bedroom apartment, and I wasn't sure if I wanted to live in a single or double that had shared bathrooms and kitchens on each floor, or if I wanted to live in a suite with three other people. It was tough.

Hey I started with. **Just checking in.**

Hey he replied.

I'm living in res next semester.

Oh yeah? Which dorm?

Not sure yet. I'm trying to decide what to put on my application. I get to pick three buildings.

Go for suites. It's so much easier sharing a kitchen with 3 people than with an entire floor.

How would you know the difference? I asked.

I lived in a dorm first year and Brad was in a suite. I was so jealous of him.

Oh for some reason I thought you and Brad were roommates in first year.

No we had a couple classes together.

Oh cool.

You and Brianna were roommates in first year, right? he asked.

Yeah. And Carly lived on our floor.

Go for a suite he said. **Definitely.**

But what if I get roomed with a bunch of first years and they're all partiers?

I think they try to put same year students together.

How many post-grads do you know staying in dorms?

At least one. He added the winking emoji.

Well it's way cheaper than an apartment. Hopefully I'll make friends once school starts and can split another two or three-bedroom with them for the rest of med school.

I have no doubt that you'll make new friends.

I replied with a smiley face and waited to see if he would tell me anything about his mom. I didn't want to bring it up and upset him, but I also didn't want to make it seem like I didn't care.

How's your mom doing? I finally asked.

Not great. She sleeps a lot.

I'm sorry.

He didn't reply.

When I was going to bed a few hours later, I texted goodnight to him, and he still hadn't replied by the time I fell asleep.

I woke up at 7:00 for work and saw that he said goodnight to me at 2:04am.

We still texted every now and then, but it became less and less conversational as the summer went by. I would try to talk about fun things, about happy things, even about Mars, or Infinity Pool, or new sci-fi movies, and Jack would be responsive for a few minutes and then our conversation would fizzle out. I tried to keep the conversation going, tried to ask him questions, get him talking, but he never did. Sometimes he wouldn't answer me for hours.

I still said goodnight to him most nights, and most nights he would reply well after I fell asleep.

In August I got a letter from the school that said I was accepted into one of the suites. The letter had the email address of the three other girls I would be staying with, but I didn't send them anything right away. Three days later I got an email from one of them, Becca, asking what kitchen things each of us would bring. She had a toaster. I replied and said that I could bring pots, pans, and cutlery, and about an hour later, the other two girls replied saying they would bring tea towels, dishes, and an electric kettle. I wondered if our suite came with a microwave.

This was my first time not being excited for school. Every year I was happy to leave home and go back to studying and getting up early for classes, because my friends were there. Even though Carly wasn't the best, she was okay sometimes, and I had fun with her and Brianna. I had fun with Jack. It was cozy going back to school knowing they would all be there. But this time I was going to be alone, with people I didn't know.

I texted goodnight to Jack as I got into bed a week before going back to school, and there was no response from him when I woke up. I didn't want to say anything else to him, since we hadn't said anything else to each other for almost a month straight. Our string of texts was literally just:

Goodnight

Goodnight

Goodnight

Goodnight

Goodnight

Goodnight

for so long. You could scroll up through our messages for over a minute and it would look the same. So I couldn't say anything else to him. If he wanted to talk, he would. I couldn't even pretend that I knew what he was going through, so I didn't want to push or pry. I wanted him to deal with what he was going through in whatever way he knew how.

I was scrolling through Facebook the next morning and saw a post that Jack was tagged in. His mom passed away the night before. I started to cry right there at the table, and my dad came running into the kitchen to ask what was wrong.

I didn't even know her, and I was devastated. I was so devastated for Jack. He must have been hurting so much. My dad grabbed another chair at the table and dragged it over to me so that he could sit with his arms around me. I cried into his shoulder and he rubbed my back.

"This is so silly," I said. "I didn't even know her."

"It's not silly," my dad said.

I waited to text Jack about it. I didn't want to be a part of the people who were probably bombarding him with condolences. It must have been hard to deal with. I waited until I got back to school and my stuff was unpacked into my room in the suite. We didn't have to take much because the suite came with furniture. Ugly dorm furniture, but furniture nonetheless. I sat on my new comforter that my mom bought me, crossed my legs under me and opened my text conversation with Jack.

Would it be better to call him? Would sending him a text about how sorry I am for his loss be too impersonal? But we had hardly texted at all in the last month and a half, let alone talked on the phone, so maybe it would be weird.

Hi jack. I heard about your mom and I want to say that I'm so sorry. It must be so hard. I just wanted you to know that I love you – I thought about it for a second and then I erased the last three words. **I'm here for you. If you ever need anything, even if it's a friend to travel with on the bus, I'll be there. Let me know and I'll be there. Take care.**

The little speech bubble with three dots popped up and I held my breath. The bubble went away. But then it came back. And then it went away again. I gave up and went to the cafeteria to get some supper since my roommates hadn't moved in yet and I didn't have any food or plates to eat off of. I walked the familiar path that Jack and I took pictures on, that we walked along to get to class or go to the library, and found my way to the caf.

I was eating a burnt burger and fries by myself when my phone went off. I flipped it over to see a reply from Jack.

Thanks.

That's all it said. Thanks. Not even a heart.

CHAPTER 21
(NOW)

Jack and I have separated. I made my way over to the manga section, and hadn't even realized that Jack wasn't with me. I look around, past the shelving and into the rest of the store but I can't see him, so I shrug and continue looking for the next volume of *Spy Family*. What do I have at home? 1-7? Shit, now I can't even remember. I sigh and wander over to the fantasy section, where I find Jack eyeing a big hardcover.

"I thought I lost you," I say, nudging him in the arm.

"Don't worry, I knew where you were," he says without taking his eyes off the book in his hand.

"But I didn't know where you were."

"Really?" He looks at me now. "You didn't know that I would be in the fantasy section? I'm hurt, Aspen."

I shove him playfully and he laughs.

"Thanks for taking me here," I say.

"Any time. Has it helped?"

"Yeah."

"Good. I'm glad."

We wander around the store together for another hour and then make our way to the café. I get my usual iced coffee with no sugar and Jack gets a coffee with two milks. Instead of finding a table to sit at, Jack heads back into the store.

"Where are you going?" I ask.

"Did you see me buy any books?"

"Well… no."

"Then isn't it obvious? I can't go to the bookstore and leave without a book."

I smile and follow him, and we stay browsing books until the store starts closing. Jack and I each get VE Schwab's newest book with the intention of reading them at the same time.

Jack drives me home and he gently grabs onto my wrist when I move to get out of the car.

"I'm really sorry you're dealing with this," he says to me.

"Thanks."

"And I'm really sorry for university."

"Jack. I said you didn't have to do that."

"You told me I didn't have to explain, you never said that I didn't have to apologize, and I would like to apologize."

"But you didn't do anything wrong. Unless you ghosted me and then got a girlfriend on purpose?"

He sighs and smiles a little. "Okay, I didn't ghost you. And no, I didn't do it on purpose."

"Then it's fine. It was a long time ago, anyway."

"I'm still sorry."

"I already forgave you."

"Okay."

"Do you want to come in for a little bit?" I ask.

"No, I should go. I have to work in the morning."

"Right. So do I."

"Have a good night, then."

Shannon comes to get me for work the next morning and she's smiling before I even get in the car.

"You're in a good mood," I say, doing up my seat belt.

"The Infinity Pool concert is only ten weeks away!"

"Oh my god, you're ridiculous," I laugh, leaning my head back on the headrest. "You realize that's more than two months, right?"

"Yes! That's so soon! It's going to be the greatest night of our lives!"

"Okay, I don't think I would go so far as to say that, but it is going to be excellent."

"The most excellent night of our lives!"

I laugh and Shannon hits the gas, driving a little too quickly out of the parking lot.

She parks next to my car and we walk into the building together. We say hi to the receptionist and she smiles at us, and we walk side by side up the main staircase.

"So Jack came over last night," I tell her when we get to the floor with our offices and the exam rooms.

"Oh? Did something happen?"

"No, nothing happened. I was going to call David to yell at him, but I ended up calling Jack instead. He came over and calmed me down. We went to the bookstore for a few hours."

"Oh, that's sweet. Did he buy you a book?"

"Um. No, he didn't. But we did buy copies of the same book so we could read it together."

"What! That's the cutest thing I've ever heard. Do people actually do that?"

"Yes?" I unlock the door to my office and Shannon follows me in, immediately sitting in my desk chair.

"You don't sound too sure of that answer," she says.

"Yes. People do do that. I just said it like a question because I thought it was obvious."

"Well I don't know, I don't read. Did you guys do anything else?"

"No. But he asked me about David, basically about how I felt about him when we were together. And he told me a little about his ex, and then he apologized again."

"For getting a girlfriend ten years ago?"

"Yeah."

"Girl, he's so in love with you."

"Or he just wants to be my friend, with no hard feelings."

"No, he's in love with you."

My tablet beeps at me so I open the Mars Group Med app and check to see what room my first patient is in.

"I gotta go," I say.

"I want to talk more about this later," she says, leaving my office.

"There's nothing to talk about." I put my coat on and head down the hall to see my first patient.

Jack texts me a little later in the day and says that we should go to the bookstore again next Thursday. I tell him that sounds like a fun idea, and he replies with a smiley face emoji. Shannon's going to eat this up. I also realize as I head down to the lobby to meet her for lunch, that I didn't tell her about Jack telling me to request a transfer to Mars. If she knows that he said that, she wouldn't let me tell her that he just wants to be friends. But she wasn't there when we were friends in school. And okay okay, I know that we were both in love with each other the whole time and just didn't say or do anything about it, but we were still friends. Neither of us wanted to do anything to ruin it because being friends was important to us. We were important to each other, and if it meant staying friends instead of possibly ruining what we had, then we wanted to stay friends. That's why it took us forever to do anything about it. If I hadn't gotten into medical school, I'm not sure that I would have done anything at all. We still would have lost touch, only this time he wouldn't feel the need to explain him getting a girlfriend to me.

Becoming friends again now would have been easier if that weekend never happened.

"Whatcha thinking about?" Shannon asks.

"What?"

"You look spaced out."

"Oh. Sorry. Yeah."

She raises her eyebrows at me in a sort of question.

"What?" I ask again.

"What were you thinking about?"

"Oh. Nothing."

"You were thinking about Jack, weren't you?"

"No. Maybe."

"Aspen, you have to talk to him about this."

"About what?"

"About your obvious feelings."

"I don't have feelings. I just broke up with David."

"So? You can still have feelings. And I think you wanted to break up with David for a while, you just didn't have the guts to leave."

"Excuse me?"

"No, sorry, I don't mean that in a bad way," she says quickly. "I just mean that I know how hard it is to leave a relationship especially when you don't really have anywhere to go. Even if you know that leaving is the best thing for you."

"I didn't want to break up with him for a while. I wanted him to stop being a dick. I didn't want to end things; I just wanted him to grow up. I wanted it to be like it was when we first started dating."

"Okay."

"But now that I think about it, he was a dick when we first started dating, too. He just also had sweet moments. He told me that he loved me."

Shannon doesn't say anything, she just looks at me like she feels sorry for me.

"He had sweet moments the whole time we dated," I add. "He was really good at them. He just always did them after making me cry. So any time I thought about how I deserved better, he would come in with some romantic date night, or he would tell me I'm beautiful, and I would think, 'oh, he does love me,' or 'he must realize what he said hurt me and he won't do it again' and the cycle would repeat."

"I'll bet Jack never did that to you."

"But Jack and I were never actually a thing. We were best friends for almost three years and then we had an incredible weekend, and then… his mom died."

CHAPTER 22
(THEN)

My roommates were all in medical school too, which I was happy about, because we studied together and went to class together, and didn't party.

I thought about texting Jack a few times but never did. I would lie on my bed with my phone in my hands, our last conversation up on the screen, and I would stare at it, but I would never type anything. I wanted to ask him if he was doing okay, but obviously he wasn't doing okay. I wanted to text goodnight to him again, to see if he would at least do that with me, but I didn't want him to feel like I was trying to cling to him.

He never texted me either, and I wondered if he stopped texting all his friends, or if it was just me. I almost sent a friend request to Brad so I could ask him if he knew how Jack was doing, but I knew that was silly. Jack was my best friend. If I wanted to know how he was doing, there was nothing wrong with asking myself.

One night a few days before going home for Christmas, I finally sent him a text.

Thinking about you.

He replied a few minutes later and I practically jumped out of bed with excitement.

That's nice he said, along with a smiley face.

How are you doing? I asked.

Okay.

Are you coming back to school?

Yeah.

That's great. Are you coming after Christmas or waiting to start back in the fall?

In the fall.

Oh cool. Still kind of far away, but I'm excited to see you when you get back.

Me too.

I didn't know what else to say to him, so I didn't say anything else. I was a little nervous about saying anything because I didn't know if how he felt about me last semester still stood. I didn't know if everything that happened with his mom made our weekend feel like a fluke, and that we would just end up back where we were before, as best friends and nothing else. I had no idea if he fell out of love with me while he was away. If he would continue to fall out of love with me over the next several months. What if we finally saw each other again and he didn't even want to be my friend at all?

I tried not to think about Jack while I was at home for Christmas break. I texted him Merry Christmas after my family and I opened our presents, and he replied with the same two words, but nothing else was said.

Were we even friends anymore?

"Hey, is everything okay?" my sister asked me, shoving her elbow into my arm.

"Yeah." I forced a smile. "Everything's great."

Jack texted me a happy new year message with a champagne glass emoji, and I replied with the same thing, only I added a few exclamation points. He replied with a toothy grin emoji, so I replied with a blushing smiley emoji.

When I got back to school, I spent most of my free time (which wasn't much) trying to stalk him on social media before sending him messages. I wanted to try and get a feel for how he was doing before asking him anything about… well, us. He didn't post on Facebook ever, so that wasn't any help, and his Instagram page had very few new photos, with only hashtags in the descriptions. His photos were really good, but also had a very sad feel to them. They weren't all in black and white, but the atmosphere of them and the way the lighting and colours were presented in the photos felt very dark and depressing. I figured he wasn't doing too great, and I wanted to text him but felt strange asking how he was doing again. That was almost always the first thing I sent to him when I texted him. Why was I forgetting how to be his friend?

I decided to text him goodnight once, and he replied almost immediately. It made me smile, and I was able to fall asleep really easily.

He texted goodnight to me the next night, and I squealed with delight, replying right away.

We texted goodnight to each other for about a week, and then it stopped.

I waited for him to do it when I had initiated it the night before, but he didn't. I waited the next night for him to text, and he didn't.

I waited a week, and neither of us sent the other a goodnight text.

I lay in bed one April night, staring at our string of goodnight texts from a few months prior. Neither of us had said anything else since then. He liked a couple of my Instagram pictures, but that's it. He was going to be coming back to school in the fall, and it was like we weren't even friends at all anymore. I was getting nervous thinking about sending him another text and that's when I realized that I shouldn't be nervous to text a friend. Talking to a friend or asking how they're doing shouldn't give you anxiety. I was too afraid of him not answering, or of him telling me he'd moved on or didn't want to be my friend anymore. So I didn't text him. I stared at our text conversation for far too long, but I didn't add to it.

I ended up staying in res for second year, too. My roommates and I thought it was a good idea because we could get a meal plan with the cafeteria and not have to worry about cooking if we got too busy. The cafeteria usually had some healthy options too, so we decided to apply to live together in a suite again, and we got accepted.

We were all in our new suite a week before classes started, so we decided to go out and have fun before we couldn't again for the rest of the year. We all got ready together, having a few drinks while we put our makeup on. I was a little sad that I wasn't going out with Carly and Brianna, but I was still excited that I had new friends to go out with.

Once we walked through the doors of the campus pub and into the nice air conditioning, my heart stopped. Jack was standing at the bar. He was here! Jack was here!

I turned to my roommates. "A really good friend I haven't seen in a long time is over at the bar. I'm just going to go say hi, but I won't be long."

"Okay, we're going to get a table."

I nodded and smiled, and made my way over to the bar. Jack turned towards the entrance, where I was coming from, and I could tell that he saw me right away. He smiled and nodded a little. I walked faster. Why wasn't he meeting me in the middle? Was he not as excited about seeing me again as I was about seeing him?

"Jack!" I called as I got closer. His smile grew, but still he stayed in the same place, just waiting for me to come to him. We finally met at the bar and I put my arms around him without even thinking about it. He hugged me back, but not very tightly, almost as if he was uncomfortable. I pulled away sooner than I would have liked to, and took a step back to look at him.

"It's so good to see you," I said.

"You too."

Someone cleared their throat rather loudly and I looked to my right to see a pretty girl with bronze skin and dark, wavy hair staring at us.

"Can we help you?" I asked.

"Oh, um, sorry," Jack said. "Aspen, this is Anna. My girlfriend."

I couldn't even focus on the fact that it seemed like Jack was afraid to introduce her to me. His voice shook as he said those last two words. *My girlfriend.* It was something I noticed, but I couldn't focus on it because my heart felt like it was going to rip out of my chest. I tried to blink back the tears that were stinging my eyes, but I couldn't. All I could focus on was the fact that Jack and his new girlfriend were going to see me cry. His girlfriend would immediately hate me because she would know that I was obviously in love with him, otherwise why would I cry when I found out he had a girlfriend? Also my heart. My heart was pounding. My chest was closing in on itself and I couldn't breathe. Was I about to have a panic attack? Over my best friend getting a girlfriend? I had to stop saying girlfriend.

"Jack, I'm so happy for you," I managed to say before I promptly turned in the other direction to find my friends.

"Aspen, wait!" Jack called after me, but I didn't stop or slow down. I weaved through the crowd, hoping to lose him, but it really wasn't all that crowded. He grabbed onto my wrist and spun me around. "Aspen, can I explain?"

"Explain what?" I asked. "There's nothing to explain."

"Why are you crying, then?"

"I'm not crying. I'm fine. I'm better than fine."

"I swear I didn't mean for-"

"I said I was happy for you, Jack. I have to find my friends. I came here with my friends and I can't just ditch them."

He let go of my wrist and nodded. "We can still study together," he said quietly, sounding a little unsure of himself.

"Great." I turned around and found Becca at a table on her own, so I made my way over to her.

"Hey, where's Sara and Chelsea?" I asked.

"The washroom. Who was that?"

"Who was what?"

"That guy you were just talking to."

I let my gaze follow hers, back to the crowd where Jack was making his way back to the bar, where Anna was waiting for him. "Oh. No one."

"Didn't look like no one."

I just shrugged. "Let's get a drink."

I had a few drinks and got pleasantly tipsy, but stopped well before the other girls. They continued doing shots when I switched to water, and I just couldn't get my mind off of Jack. I kept looking back to see if I could spot him in the crowd, and a few times I did. He never caught me looking at him, at least I didn't think he did, and every time, he was smiling at his girlfriend as if she was Mars shining in the distance. I finally got up from our table and started to make my way into the middle of the pub.

"Where are you going?" Becca asked.

"To meet guys," I said with a shrug. "I've been waiting for someone for too long who wasn't waiting for me."

"Oh. Well, can I come?"

"Of course you can."

Chelsea and Sara came with us too, and we walked right up to a table of guys as if we weren't nervous at all. Well maybe they actually weren't nervous, but I was.

"We're all going to be doctors," Chelsea said to them.

Their conversation stopped and they all turned towards us, probably thinking we were weird.

"That's cool," one of the guys with a beer bottle in his hand said.

"My friend Aspen here needs cheering up," she continued.

I felt my eyes widen in horror and I immediately shook my head. "No I don't," I said. "We just wanted to come say hi."

"Why do you need cheering up?" A guy with fluffy blond hair asked me.

"I said I don't. I don't need cheering up."

"She thought a guy liked her but he doesn't," Chelsea said for me.

"Chelsea! Can you not?"

"Do you want to get a drink?" Fluffy Blond asked.

"She's already switched to water," Becca said.

"I can have one drink," I said. "But thanks for looking out for me, Becca."

She smiled at me and I looked back at her as I headed to the bar with Fluffy Blond guy. He leaned his elbows on the wooden bar top when we got there, so I did the same, feeling completely out of my comfort zone.

"I'm Alex, by the way," he said with a nice smile.

"Aspen."

"Yeah, your friend said."

"Right."

"What do you want to drink?"

I shrugged. I wanted an Alexander Keith's but I felt weird saying that after he just told me that his name was Alex. That's stupid, right? "Maybe a Caesar."

"Cool, I'll get one too."

He ordered us both a Caesar and when the bartender asked if we wanted them spicy, Alex said no before I had a chance to say anything. I just smiled and let him pay for the drinks.

"So you're going to be a doctor?" he asked.

"Yeah, I'm about to start my second year of medical school."

"That's really cool. I'm taking linguistics. About to start my final year."

"That's exciting. What are you going to do with it?"

"Probably be a speech therapist."

"Neat."

Our drinks came and I took a sip right away. It would have been better if it was spicier, but there was still a tiny bit of heat to it, so it was good. I licked some of the rimmer off the edge of the glass and took another sip. Two stools freed up next to us and he nodded at them so I pulled myself onto one while he got on the other.

"Thanks for buying me a drink," I finally said. I didn't know why I thought this would be a good idea. I didn't want to meet guys randomly at the campus pub. I wanted to get to know someone slowly, fall in love with them over time. Be comfortable with them. Like how it happened with Jack.

"No problem," he said, smiling at me over his glass. And then his hand was on my thigh and I didn't know what to do. Maybe if I let him keep it there it wouldn't be so bad. Maybe I just had to let myself experience things. I had been holding back for far too long. So I took a long drink of my Caesar, downing about half of it, and then I put my hand on top of his.

"I'm glad you came over to say hi to us," he said, leaning a little closer to me.

"Yeah," I said, still feeling a little unsure of myself. "Me too."

I looked down at my hand on top of his, and when I looked back up, he was already staring into my eyes. I felt his fingers grip my leg a little so I wrapped mine around his hand, making him ease up a bit. But then he flipped his hand over and linked his fingers through mine, and I sighed a little in relief. I liked that better. I was much more comfortable with holding his hand than I was with him holding my thigh.

"So you're probably a little older than me," he said with a chuckle.

"Maybe. I just turned 23."

"I'm 21."

"So I'm not that much older."

He shrugged. "Not that much, no. You are really hot, though."

"Oh. You think I'm hot?"

He just smiled and nodded.

"Thanks." I didn't know what else to say.

"Can I kiss you?"

Did I want to kiss him? I didn't think I wanted to kiss him, but I didn't know what I wanted at all. Maybe once we started kissing, I would like it, and I would be glad that I told him he could kiss me.

"No thank you," I said quietly.

"Oh. Sorry."

"It's okay. I didn't really want to be pulled away from my friends. I shouldn't have come over here with you."

He scrunched his eyebrows at me and frowned a little. "Oh."

"Yeah." I slid off my bar stool and started to make my way back to my friends, and Alex followed me, but kept a bit of a distance.

"Is everything okay?" Becca asked me when we got back to their table.

"Yeah," I shrugged. "I think I'm going to go home."

"Are you sure? Do you want me to come with you?"

"No, it's okay. I kind of want to be alone."

She gave me a bit of a sad look but nodded. "Okay. Text me if you need me."

"I will."

I turned to head out of the pub and almost walked right into Jack and his girlfriend.

"Oh. Hi again," Jack said with a warm smile that made me weak in the knees. His dimple was coming out in full force and I had to look away so I didn't start crying.

"Hi," I said as I pushed past.

"Are you okay?" I felt him start to follow me, but just as I decided to turn around and answer him, his girlfriend - Anna, was it? – told him to leave it.

"Just leave it, Jack," she said to him. "Why are you so concerned about her?"

I stopped walking at that point, but I didn't turn to face them. I wasn't sure if they were still looking at me or if they were looking at each other, if they could even see me out of the corner of their eye, but I stayed put, my feet planted on the floor, listening to them.

"Because she's my friend," Jack replied.

"She's obviously jealous of me."

Jack snorted and laughed, and I felt the back of my neck start to burn.

"I haven't talked to her in like, a year, Anna," I heard him continue.

"So? She clearly has feelings for you."

"We're just friends," he said. "It doesn't matter if she feels anything, because we've never been anything more than that, okay?"

I knew he was saying that to calm her nerves, but it still hurt. Or maybe he was telling her the truth, and our weekend actually meant nothing to him. Even though we said we loved each other. But I guess Anna was his everything now. We were friends for longer than we weren't, and now that's all we were again. All we ever would be.

That's when I decided to turn around. I walked past them again, brushing my shoulder against Anna's on my way, and marched back over to my friends who were still with the guys we met earlier.

"Hey, you change your mind?" Becca asked.

"Yeah. I did." I took a deep breath and grabbed onto Alex's arm. I could feel Jack watching me from across the room, so I leaned a little closer and said, "You still want that kiss?"

Alex's lips immediately curled into a huge grin and he nodded. "Fuck yeah."

I stood on my toes, closed my eyes, and pressed my mouth to his. I wanted to see if Jack or Anna were watching me, but I also didn't want to be any more obvious than I probably already was. Alex wrapped his arms around my back and then slid his hands down to my hips. I ran my fingers through his hair and let him slip his tongue into my mouth.

I didn't like it. I didn't like any of it, and I wanted to stop, but I also wanted Jack and Anna to see. I wanted Anna to think that I wasn't jealous of her, but I wanted Jack to be jealous of me. I couldn't believe that Jack stopped talking to me and then got a girlfriend. That he would tell me he loved me, that I was beautiful, that he would have a weekend full of sex with me and then get a girlfriend instead of having anything to do with me.

Someone at our table cheered and it made me pull back. "Sorry," I said. "That was rude to do that right here in front of everyone."

"I don't care," one of Alex's friends said.

"I see you're feeling better," Becca said with a smile.

I laughed, but I wasn't feeling better at all. I couldn't believe that I just made out with someone I didn't even know. It was not fun.

"Can I give you my number?" Alex whispered to me.

"Uh. Sure."

Alex texted me almost immediately. He said that he loved kissing me and he wanted to do it again. I did not want to do it again. I had no idea how people did stuff like that. Just letting people put their tongues in their mouths or touch them without having any feelings for them. It made no sense to me. I needed to talk to someone about it, and even though my new med school friends were pretty cool and we were pretty comfortable with each other by that point, they weren't the same as Brianna. I needed to talk to Brianna.

"I can't believe him," Brianna said to me after I called her and told her about seeing Jack at the pub.

"Yeah," I sighed.

"I mean, I guess you guys haven't talked for a long time, but still. He should've kept talking to you instead of getting to know someone else. You guys were already in love and stuff."

"Yeah," I said again.

"Ugh. I'm so mad at him. Do you want me to punch him?"

"No, don't do that," I laughed.

"Do you think you guys will still be friends?"

"I don't know."

"What about this Alex guy? Do you like him?"

"No. I mean, I don't even know him. I just kissed him hoping that Jack would see and get jealous. I actually didn't like kissing him at all. It made me feel all creepy crawly."

"That's not good. Maybe it's just because you don't know him well enough. What if you guys hung out more?"

I shrugged. "I dunno. Maybe."

"Well either way, you can't lead him on. If you don't want to kiss him again, you need to tell him."

"Yeah, you're right."

My phone buzzed and I pulled it away from my ear to see who was texting me. It was Jack!

"Oh my god, Jack just texted me," I said.

"Oh my god, what did he say?"

I pulled the notification bar down and opened his message.

I put my phone on speaker and read his text out loud. **It was good seeing you tonight. Study session when school starts?**

"What are you going to do?" Brianna asked.

"I don't know."

I couldn't believe that I was meeting Jack at the library. We hadn't hung out since before his mom died, and now he had a girlfriend and I was meeting him to study.

He was already inside at our usual table when I got there, and he immediately smiled and put a hand in the air so that I would see him. Not that I didn't see him as soon as I stepped through the doors. He stood up when I got to the table, and I didn't know what to do. I wanted to give him a hug but I didn't know if I should.

"Hey," I said. I wanted to die.

"Hey." He smiled and sat back down, so I sat in the chair across the table from him.

"How's it going?"

"Pretty decent," he replied. "Do you have flashcards for me?"

"Of course I do." I grinned at him and pulled them out of my bag.

"Oh, these ones are fancy," he said, shuffling through them. "Colour coded and laminated."

"Yeah," I said with a bit of a nervous laugh. "I've upped my game."

"You sure have."

"I sort of want to always have these ones. This is stuff that will be helpful for a long time."

"Makes sense."

I wanted to ask him about Anna. About how long they'd been together. If they were sharing an apartment. But I was afraid that if we talked about her, I would cry. After having a few weeks to think about it and process it, I guess I wasn't mad at him for getting a girlfriend. I was mad at the situation, and mad that we weren't able to stay in touch while he was away, but it's not like he could just push someone away because he told a girl he no longer talked to that he loved her however long ago. Being mad at him for that was silly.

"Listen," Jack said after he'd been quizzing me for about an hour. "About Anna."

I shook my head. "It's okay," I said.

"Really?"

"Yeah. If you're happy, I'm happy."

He smiled. "Okay."

But the next time that we hung out, it was in my suite on res, in my room, with the door closed. I so badly wanted to crawl across my bed and get into his lap as he sat on my computer chair, but I didn't. I thought about it, and I distracted myself over it, but I didn't do it.

"I know you said everything was okay," Jack said with a sigh, sort of startling me. "But I want to explain."

"You don't need to explain anything," I said.

"I think I do, though. It's not what you think. Anna and me, we were-"

"Jack, it's fine. We were never a thing. We had a weekend… that was, um, fantastic. But then everything happened and we drifted apart and it's fine."

"Yeah, but when we-"

"You don't need to explain yourself, Jack. In fact, I don't want you to. I just want to go back to the way things were before."

"You mean before we said we loved each other, and saw each other naked."

I felt my entire face heat up, and all I could do was nod.

"Okay. Yeah. I want that too," he said quietly.

"Good."

CHAPTER 23 (NOW)

I'm not totally sure how to go about requesting a transfer with The Mars Group, but I start on the application part of the website to see if there's any information about it. When I don't find anything, I head to my profile on The Mars Group site and look through all the tabs, trying to find anything that resembles transfers, applications, or even jobs. The closest thing I can find is my benefits package, so I open my email and draft something up to the Mars Group Director.

Hello Dr Pershing,

I was hoping you could provide me with information on how to request a transfer to Mars. I've been working here at the Earth offices as a physician for the last three and a half years and would love the opportunity to work in the compound on Mars. I know from applying previously that there are mixed positions and would feel incredibly grateful if I were able to help out in new areas.

Thank you so much for your time,

Dr Aspen Robitaille

I'm surprised when I get a reply less than twenty minutes later. But my heart drops a little when I see what it says.

Dr. Robitaille,

Thanks for your inquiry. You can apply for a Mars position on the official Mars Group application found on our site.

Dr Pershing

Well. I guess that's it then. I just have to apply like everyone else. I know it's silly, but I kind of thought I would be able to just press a button and then have people decide whether or not they wanted me to move and work for them instead. I get the application started right away and then sneak over to Shannon's office so she can do my physical for me.

"No way! Are you serious?" she practically screeches.

"Yes. Now be quiet. I don't want anyone to know."

"Why not?"

"I don't know. I feel weird about it."

"That's silly. When's your next patient? Can I help you fill out your application?"

"I have a patient in forty minutes, and I'm fine, I can fill it out myself. I'll work on it tonight."

She grins at me and we speed through my appointment so we can add the results to my application right away.

Jack texts me halfway through the day a week after our first impromptu bookstore date to ask if I'm still interested in going again. I tell him that I am, and he says he'll meet me there at six. I try to keep my mind off it for the rest of the work day, but it's hard.

"Why do you look so depressed?" Shannon asks me at lunch.

"What?" I look up at her from my sandwich. "I look depressed?"

"I don't know, maybe not depressed, but you don't look good. What's up?"

I shrug and put my sandwich down. "I'm going out with Jack tonight. I dunno, I'm nervous about it."

"Is this a date?"

"No, I don't think so. But I feel weird about it, I don't know. Last week he took me to cheer me up and I feel like he's just judging me or something."

"Aspen, he is not judging you. What would he be judging you about?"

"About being with David for so long."

Shannon tilts her head to the side and gives me a wry smile.

I get to the bookstore before Jack and I want to wait near the front for him, but I feel awkward just standing in the middle, like I'm in everyone's way. I start to browse the tables and then end up finding my way over to the sci-fi and fantasy section. I pick up a few books and read the backs, but put them all back on the shelf. I check my phone to see if I've missed any texts from Jack, but I haven't. Where is he? I stand on my toes and look down the aisles, and then I make my way back to the front of the store. I finally see him coming out of the café with a drink in each hand. He smiles and nods as he walks towards me.

"Hey!" he says.

"Hey. I thought you weren't coming."

"Oh shit, sorry, am I that late?"

"I dunno, maybe I was early."

"Maybe it was a bit of both. I got you a non-sweet iced coffee."

"Thanks," I say as I take it from him.

We browse together and I buy a new Manga and he buys some giant hardcover fantasy that looks incredibly intimidating.

"Have you started reading the book we both bought last week?" he asks me as we head to the parking lot.

"No, I was waiting for you," I say.

"Do you want to start reading it this weekend? How many pages do you normally read a day?"

"I don't know, I guess it depends on how much I like it."

"Fair. We'll just let each other know what page or chapter we're on and we can talk about it if we're at the same part."

"Yeah, that sounds like fun."

We part ways without even really saying anything; I think we just instinctively go to our own cars without thinking about it. I stop when I realize we've separated, and look back to find him at his car across the lot.

"Jack!" I call.

He looks around and then finds me and raises his chin at me.

"Have a good night," I say.

"Oh. Uh, yeah. You too." He sounds a little disappointed, and I wonder if he thought I was going to ask him back to my place or something. And the truth is, I would love for him to come back to my apartment, but it would only hurt me more if he did. If we did anything about our feelings, or well, about my feelings at least, and then he went to live on a different planet, I would be even more devastated than I know I already will be. I can't let myself fall for him even more than I already am. I can't act on it or tell him about it because it will be terrible when he leaves.

I smile at him and then get in my car.

He texts me on Saturday afternoon. **What page are you on?**

98 I reply.

Do you love it as much as I do?

Probably. I can't put it down. I literally haven't put it down since I picked it up to start reading it.

Same. I'm on page 130. It gets intense.

DON'T TELL ME ANYTHING I type quickly.

I would never. But you have to text me when you get to that part because OH MY GOD

Okay okay, let me keep reading then.

Okay.

I find myself smiling and when I realize it, I shake my head and try to wipe it away. No. I will not let this happen to me. I will not fall in love with Jack Duncan again. I will not.

And then I get to page 130 and I try my hardest not to text Jack about it, but I can't not. I pull my phone out from under my blankets and send him a message.

OH MY GOD

Page 130? he replies.

YES

RIGHT!? My jaw was literally on the floor. Well, it was figuratively on the floor. But my jaw! Dropped!

Jack and I end up going to the bookstore the next Thursday as well, and we pick out a new book to read together because we both devoured the other one before the end of the weekend. We part ways in the parking lot just like we did last week, although our cars are parked closer together this time.

We read our new book before our next bookstore date, and we meet again the next Thursday to get another one. Every week it's the same. We meet at the store, one of us gets the other our drinks, we look for a new book to read, and then make jokes and act silly until the store closes, and then we separate in the parking lot. We text each other about the book we're reading, and then we do it all again the next week. Neither of us invites the other to our apartment, we don't go out for dinner, and we don't have any lunch dates. It's just book shopping and buddy reading. Sometimes we sit in the café and chat, but that's it. And I'm really enjoying it. It feels just like it did when we were in university, and it's making me all nostalgic. Jack really is a good friend.

After five or six weeks of this, Jack nudges my arm with his as we stand side by side in front of the New and Hot section.

"You wanna come over after this?" he asks.

"Oh." I swallow, thinking about why he might be asking. He never went back on his statement about not feeling more than friendship with me, but we also don't have the best reputation for communicating well.

"Don't worry, Aspen, I won't try to kiss you."

I feel my eyes bulge out a bit and I can tell that I'm blushing. My whole face is on fire.

"Unless you want me to," he adds with a smirk.

"No," I say, shaking my head. "No, I don't want you to."

"Oh. Okay, well good, because I wasn't going to anyway. I just thought it would be fun to hang out more, that's all."

"Jack, you're going to Mars."

"I'm aware. I don't see what that has to do with anything."

"I can't… I can't…" I look down at my feet and let out a deep breath. "I can't let myself feel anything for you. If you weren't going, then maybe-"

But he cuts me off and says, "Who said anything about feelings?"

"Well, you were kind of flirting- I mean, I was- I mean when you said that-"

"You're adorable when you stammer. But I literally just wanted to hang out as friends. I didn't mean to flirt with you, I swear. It's just so easy with you sometimes. Being myself, I mean."

"It's easy with you, too," I manage to say.

"Cool. Come hang out at my place, then."

Jack's apartment is exactly how I expected it. It's tidy but not pristine. There's a balled up blanket on the couch, and an empty mug on the coffee table, some dishes in the sink, but his bed is made - I can see past his bedroom door from the living room – and his bathroom looks like it's been cleaned recently. His recycling bins are half full but there's a small cardboard box from a set of earbuds lying next to the bins on the floor as if he tossed it and missed, but didn't feel like getting up to fix it.

"Your apartment is really nice," I say.

"Thanks."

"Much bigger than mine," I laugh.

He shrugs and moves to sit on the couch. "Nothing wrong with having a small apartment."

"It gets cluttered so easily," I say, sitting next to him.

"Yeah, that makes sense, I guess. Have you heard anything from The Mars Group?"

"About transferring? No."

"That sucks. I really thought you would have heard something by now."

"Me too. But I had to apply the same way, so maybe they have to put me through the same process as everyone else, too."

"Maybe."

"And the deadline isn't for another two months anyway."

He nods and we're quiet for a minute or so, and then Jack asks if I want to play Mario Kart.

"Fuck yes I do," I say, getting up and grabbing a controller that I see on his TV stand.

We play through most of the tracks before my eyes start to burn and I realize how late it is.

"I should go," I whisper to him.

"Yeah. I have to work in the morning, and I'm sure you do too."

"I definitely do."

We both stand up from the couch and stretch, and it feels comfortable but awkward at the same time. I didn't think that could be possible, but here we are.

"Thanks for coming over," Jack says. "We should watch something next time."

I walk towards the door. "Yeah, we should. There's a documentary on Pluto I've been meaning to check out."

"That sounds perfect."

The next week, Jack comes to my place after the bookstore and we sit on the couch to watch the Pluto docuseries. We make microwave popcorn and pour extra butter on top, and we chat a little throughout the show. He comes over the next week to watch the rest of the series, and we get burgers from Harvey's on the way. He makes fun of me for having to specify twice that I want two pickles on my burger and I hit him the shoulder.

"Any time I just say pickles without saying an amount, they always only ever put one!" I say. "Who puts one pickle on a burger? Like, come on."

"But you didn't have to say it twice."

"I didn't say it twice. I said it once, and then I asked if that's what they did."

He just raises an eyebrow at me.

"I can't see them putting the stuff on the burger when we go through the drive thru! Stop judging!" I hit him in the shoulder and we both laugh.

We take our burgers out in front of the TV and silently watch the show together. When it's over, I look at him and he smiles.

"What?" he asks.

"I just realized that we came here in my car but we met at the bookstore."

"You only just realized that?"

"You knew what we were doing?"

"Yes. It was very obvious."

"But now I'm going to have to drive you back to your car."

"Oh no. The horror."

"Shut up," I laugh. "But I do have to work in the morning so is it okay if I take you back now?"

"Yes, that's okay."

It feels like he's walking closer to me than he normally does as we head down the stairs to the main floor, but I try to ignore it. He told me a few weeks ago that he just wanted to hang out as friends, so there's no point in imagining him wanting more. But then he nudges my shoulder with his as we walk across the parking lot.

"What was that for?" I ask.

"Nothing. I just like hanging out with you. I'm going to miss you when I leave."

"I'll miss you too."

"You've always been my favourite person to hang out with."

How am I supposed to respond to that? Instead of saying anything, I get in the car and hope the conversation deviates.

"Thanks for driving me back to my car," he says once his seatbelt is done up.

"No problem. Thanks for always book shopping with me."

"Oh, the pleasure is all mine."

Instead of talking during the drive, we listen to music and I smile when he softly sings along to most of the songs. I turn the volume up when an Infinity Pool song comes on and we both belt out the lyrics, laughing a little when the song ends.

We get back to the bookstore and I pull up next to his car and he smiles at me before getting out. He waves through his window once he starts his own car, and then he pulls out of his spot and drives out of the parking lot.

The next week, we go to Jack's apartment to play Mario Kart and he nudges my arm with his elbow a lot. I look over at him every time he does it and he just smiles and shrugs, so I keep playing. We finish a race set and neither of us does anything to select a new set of tracks, we just sit there with our controllers in our hands, staring at the TV. I finally turn my gaze to him and he looks at me. I let out a deep breath and try to think of something to say, but I've got nothing. Is this more than friendship that's been happening these past four weeks? Are we really going to go down that road again right before he leaves for Mars? No. We can't. Absolutely not.

But then Jack starts to lean in to me, just slightly, like he's waiting to see what I do. So I turn away and say, "I should probably go."

He nods. "Yeah, it's getting late."

"Plus you promised that you weren't going to kiss me."

"You're right, I did promise that."

"It's just… better," I say slowly.

"Yeah." He swallows and straightens up a bit on the couch. "Yeah, of course. Makes total sense."

"Thanks for being my friend, though."

"Likewise."

It's one month away from the next Mars application deadline, and one month and three days away from the Mars Send Off. I can't stop stressing over whether or not I'm going to move forward in the interview process, and Shannon can't stop bouncing off the walls. Her reasons for not being able to sit still are different from mine, though. The Infinity Pool concert is tonight and there's no way she's going to make it to the end of the day. I jump up and down with her whenever she gets a random burst of excitement but it doesn't help her calm down in any way, and doesn't help take my mind off the launch.

"When's your last appointment again?" Shannon asks me after lunch. Her hair is purple now, and it's very bright, so she must have done it last night, for the concert.

"3:30."

"Good, okay, me too. So we should both be done by four."

"Yes."

"Can you rush yours?" she asks.

"I... Can try?"

"Okay," she says with a nod. "Me too. I can rush mine."

"The concert doesn't start until nine, Shannon, and it's less than an hour away."

"I know, but I'm just so excited!" She squeals again, so I squeal with her and we jump up and down together. Again.

We get changed in our offices when our appointments are done, and Shannon drives us to the concert. We stop for dinner on the way, and arrive at the stadium more than two hours early. But the lineup outside is huge, and by the time we get through the doors, we're less than an hour from the concert starting. It's crowded everywhere and so many people are screaming and squealing, but Shannon and I push past mobs as best as we can and make it down to the floor. We're not as close to the stage as we'd like to be, but if we try hard enough, maybe we can push our way through eventually. There's a small band opening for them, and they're really good, but we start to get antsy when they're still playing by the time it's almost 10pm. They finally finish their set and while we're waiting for Infinity Pool to come out, people start cheering and whooing, and people start chanting IN-FIN-IT-Y, IN-FIN-IT-Y, and when the five members come out on stage, everyone cheers and goes wild. Shannon and I throw our hands up and cheer with everyone else, and I'm so excited that I almost cry.

We don't manage to get any closer to the stage, but it's still amazing. They play all our favourite songs and we yell and sing to them and sway our arms in the air. Even though I have never been to an Infinity Pool concert before, I feel like I'm in university. A part of me is a little sad that I'm not here with Brianna, or even Becca, and an even bigger part of me is sad that I'm not here with Jack. We didn't bond over music as much as we did over space and science fiction, but if we're not going to get to go to Mars together, it would have been nice if I at least got to experience this concert with him. I guess singing in my car together is the closest I'll get.

I have fun with Shannon. And Shannon's a good friend, who tries her best to be there for me. And having her next to me while we jump up and down to the music and scream the lyrics at the top of our lungs is close to everything that I need right now. We smile over at each other every now and then, and sometimes we scream the song lyrics to each other instead of towards the band on stage.

When the concert is over, I feel an emptiness inside of me that I wasn't expecting. I wish it could go on forever. Shannon and I sort of frown at each other as we squeeze our way through the crowd, but before we get out into the main part of the arena, I lose her. Shit.

I'm completely wired and my ears are ringing, and looking around for her is making me panic. There are so many people everywhere and I have no idea how we got separated so easily. She was right there; we were right next to each other and now I'm alone. I pull my phone out of my back pocket, but of course it's dead, so I sigh, and decide to head to the washrooms. Maybe she's waiting for me there. The lineup at the washroom is of course a mile long, so I decide to see if the men's room has a shorter line. There's no one even in there! Do men not pee? I look around and decide to go in quickly before anyone notices. I grab a stall and shut the door as fast as I can, trying to get in and out before anyone else comes in. Two guys walk in just as I open the stall door to leave and they both freeze.

"Sorry," I say. "I had to go really bad and the women's washroom had a huge line."

"Okay," they both say, nodding.

"Sorry. I'm leaving." I wash my hands and then turn to leave, but I bump into someone coming in.

"Oof, sorry," he says, and I realize before I see his face that it's Jack. Jack is here? Jack was here the whole time, while I was sort of wishing he was here? "Aspen?" he asks, pulling away from me a little.

"Surprise!" I laugh. Because I of course can't say anything intelligent.

"Surprise?"

"I don't know why I said that. I had to pee. And now I have to find Shannon."

"Wait, hang on," he says, following me out of the bathroom.

I stop and turn towards him. "Yeah?"

"I don't know, actually." He lets out what sounds like a nervous laugh, and then looks away for a second. "It just caught me off guard seeing you here and I felt like we needed to talk."

"Oh. Yeah. But I mean, it's Infinity Pool, they've been my favourite band since they released their first single."

"Yeah, of course, I knew that. I just wasn't expecting to run into you."

"I wasn't expecting to run into you either. Are you here with anyone?"

"Yeah, I'm here with my buddy." He pauses for a second before he says, "Uh, Brad."

"You're still friends with Brad?"

"Yeah. He's married to Carly now."

"Wait, are you serious? Did you go to their wedding?"

He laughs a little. "I did. I was in the wedding."

"No way!"

"Yeah. I can't believe you didn't know they got married."

"Hey, Brad was your friend, not mine."

"Yeah, but Carly was your friend, wasn't she?"

"Yeah. I haven't talked to her since we graduated, though."

"Oh really?"

"Yeah," I say with a nod. "I still talk to Brianna, though."

"That's nice."

"Is Carly here too?" I ask.

"No, it's just me and Brad."

"Cool. Well do you think you could help me find Shannon?"

"Yeah, I think I can do that."

"Do you remember what she looks like?" I ask.

He laughs and nods. "Yes, I remember what she looks like."

"Hey, I was just checking, you've only met her once. Plus her hair is purple now."

"Was it not purple before?"

"No, it was pink."

"Okay, but the rest of her is the same?"

"Yes, of course."

"Okay good," he says. "I was worried for a second that because her hair was a different colour, she would look completely different and I wouldn't be able to recognize her if I saw her."

"Oh, shut up," I say playfully.

I can't believe he was here the whole time tonight.

"Aspen!" I hear from behind me. I turn around and breathe a sigh of relief when I see Shannon coming towards us. "Where did you go!?"

"I didn't go anywhere, you were just gone!"

"I was not! You disappeared on me!" But then she notices Jack and smiles up at him. "Well, hello. I wasn't expecting to see you here."

"Likewise. I should probably go, though, and find my friend."

"Apparently this is where friends go to get lost, so I understand," Shannon says to him. "Good luck."

Jack smiles and nods at her and then he reaches out and squeezes my elbow. "It was good seeing you," he says. And then he disappears into the crowd.

"What was that?" Shannon asks, clearly interested.

"What was what?"

"He just squeezed your arm!"

"So?"

"What do you mean 'so'!? Are you sure you guys don't have sex after your weekly bookstore dates?"

"I'm sure, Shannon! We buy books and then sometimes we go back to his place and play video games, or go to my place and watch space documentaries."

"Excuse me? When did that start?"

The crowd is thinning now, and it's easier for us to hear each other and also for us to stick together. We walk out to the parking lot and I'm hit with a wall of humidity that should have started disappearing two weeks ago. I forgot how hot it was outside, even with the amount of people inside making it harder for the air conditioning to work.

"Ugh, it's so gross out," Shannon says before I have a chance to answer her question.

"Yeah. Hopefully the fall weather starts coming around soon. It's the middle of September. Like, come on."

"That would be nice. I love sweater weather."

I notice someone a few parking spaces away from us raise his hand in the air. He calls my name, but I don't know who it is, so I don't say anything. Maybe he's not talking to me. But Shannon's car is parked sort of close to his, so we end up getting close enough for me to recognize Brad. As if Jack is still friends with him.

"Oh, hey Brad," I say. Jack comes into view after shutting the trunk, and I suddenly feel out of my element.

"It's good to see you," Brad says.

"Yeah." I don't really know what to say. We didn't know each other that well. "You too."

"I'm glad you and Jack reconnected. Carly and I were sad that you guys stopped hanging out."

And as if out of all the people he could have stayed in contact with, Carly was one of them. Carly, for crying out loud! He couldn't stay in touch with his best friend who he was apparently in love with, but he could get a random girlfriend and then stay in touch with Carly?

"Oh, that Carly," I say, forcing out a weird breathy laugh. I don't want to be here anymore. I don't want all the reminders that people I don't like are living a part of the life that I should have had.

"You should come by some time and we can hang out, the four of us. Like a double date!"

"Yeah, except Jack and I aren't dating. And he's leaving for Mars in a month, so."

"So all the more reason for us to get together! We can hang before he leaves."

"Sure, whatever." I say shortly. I notice Jack furrow his eyebrows at that, but I try to ignore it. "Anyway, we should get going."

"Right. Of course," he says. "Have a good night."

"Yeah. You too."

I turn my head a little and look back at them when we get to Shannon's car, and Jack is still looking over at us. I can't see his expression from here, but for some reason all I can picture is his face when he introduced me to Anna. I'm not sure why.

CHAPTER 24
(THEN)

Alex and I hung out a couple more times. I was going to tell him that I didn't want to keep kissing him, but every time I saw Jack with Anna, I got this rage of jealousy and I thought that maybe kissing Alex again wouldn't be so bad. I really thought that if we kissed more, I would start to like it, start to like him, but it didn't happen. I liked it when Jack and I kissed and did other things, and all I could think about most of the time was doing that again with him. But with Alex, it made me feel gross. I didn't let him take it any further than kissing; any time his hands started to wander, I would slap them away or move them somewhere else on my body, like my shoulder.

"You're not really into this, are you?" Alex said one night, as we both lied on top of my comforter.

"Of course I am." I grabbed at his face and tried to pull it towards me but he wouldn't budge.

"We've made out a lot, Aspen, and you still don't want me to touch you."

"So? I'm not comfortable with touching."

"Why not?"

Because I didn't like him. I mean, I liked him fine, he was fine. But I didn't have any feelings for him. And I was still in love with my best friend, and I felt like I would never get over him.

I sighed and looked away.

"Well, I don't really want to be a part of this if you don't want to," Alex said with a huff. He sat up and swung his legs over the side of the bed.

"I don't not want to," I said.

"What does that mean?"

"I don't know. I'm just not… a very physical person, I guess. And I thought that if we kissed more, maybe I would become more comfortable with it. But I'm not."

"You're not even comfortable with kissing?"

I shrugged. "It's okay. It's less weird now."

"What? Are you being serious right now?"

I didn't know what to say, so I just nodded.

"This is ridiculous," he said.

"I'm sorry."

"Yeah." He stood up and opened my bedroom door. "Me too." And then he left.

Fuck. I was a piece of shit.

I didn't know what to do. From all the movies I watched when I was younger, everything told me that in order to get over someone, I needed to find someone new. I needed a rebound guy, someone to make out with or sleep with, but it wasn't working. It always seemed fun in the movies but it wasn't fun for me, it was horrible. Was something wrong with me?

I didn't want anyone else, I only wanted Jack. And I knew that I couldn't have him, so the next best thing was to be his friend, but I didn't know how to be his friend when I knew that there was a time that we could have been more than that. That if Jack's life wasn't interrupted, mine wouldn't have been either. I wanted to still be his friend; not being his friend at all sounded awful, but being his friend while I was in love with him, and while he had a girlfriend, was also awful. Seeing him felt wonderful and soul crushing at the same time, and I didn't know what to do with any of these feelings. Did he feel anything for me anymore? Or was Anna the love of his life? Did Anna make him forget about me? Did she help him get over me?

Jack was sitting on the end of my single bed in my dorm, and I was curled up against the headboard with a fluffy pillow in my arms. We had only hung out a handful of times over the school year, mostly because I was always busy, but also because he had a girlfriend and I guess we both felt like we weren't allowed to hang out in the same way. But it was the beginning of April and there was a Mars Send Off party in two days. I wanted to ask Jack to go with me, but I was afraid of him saying no, or asking if he could invite Anna. If he asked, I would probably tell him that yes of course she could come, but I would be miserable the whole time. Who the hell was I kidding, I was miserable all the time already. I wasn't mad at Jack for getting a girlfriend after we drifted apart, but I was still hurt. And I was jealous as fuck.

"Are you going to the Send Off on Friday?" I finally got the nerve to ask.

"Oh, I forgot that was happening. Sounds fun. Is anyone else going?"

"I haven't asked anyone else," I said with a shrug.

"We should get your roommates to come. And Anna will probably come. She's not into the Mars stuff like we are, but the Send Offs are fun."

I sighed. "Cool."

"Are you okay?"

"Yeah." I swallowed, trying to be honest with him instead of burying my feelings about everything. "I just thought it might be fun if we went just us two, like we did before."

"Oh yeah, that was fun. But I don't think Anna would approve."

"She has to approve of you hanging out with your friend?"

"No, I'm hanging out with you now, aren't I?" He raised his shoulders.

"Yeah. But you just said that Anna doesn't even like all the Mars stuff, so why wouldn't she approve of you doing something with me that she doesn't want to do?"

"I never said that she wouldn't want to do it. The Send Off just seems a little like a date, I guess."

"Does it?" It wasn't a date when we went before, I wanted to say. Why was it a date now?

"Yeah, kind of. Why don't you bring that Alex guy?"

"Alex and I haven't hung out in months."

"Oh. Sorry."

"Yeah. Anyway, I'm tired. I think I need to get ready for bed."

He stood up pretty quickly and looked taken aback. "Right. Of course. See you later."

"See you later."

Becca and I went to the Mars Send Off together, and I couldn't help but look around for Jack the whole time that we were there. I wondered if he told Anna about it. I wondered if he asked her to go and if she said she didn't want to. Becca and I got a few drinks and butted our way into conversations, trying to sound smart and sophisticated.

"But we are smart and sophisticated," Becca said to me as we left a circle of people and made our way back to the bar. "There's no trying involved, Aspen, we already are."

"I'm not," I said.

"Sure you are. We're in medical school, for crying out loud!"

"There are some dumb people in medical school."

Becca snorted and hit me in the shoulder. "Well those people obviously aren't going to do well. We are both doing excellently, therefore we are already smart and sophisticated."

"Okay. Whatever you say."

"Aspen!" I turned around at the person who called my name to see Jack and Anna standing in line for drinks, just a few people behind us.

"Oh. Hey." I smiled at him and turned back to Becca, who gave me a look. "What?" I asked her.

"Go say hi," she said.

"I did."

Becca knew a little bit of our story, but not in as much detail as say, Brianna did. I told her the short version of what happened after we ran into each other at the campus pub, and then filled her in a little bit more each time Jack and I hung out in my room.

"You want to be his friend, don't you?"

"Yes," I sighed.

"Then go be his friend." She nudged me a little and I huffed before stepping out of line to meet them.

"Hey," I said, feeling unsure of myself.

"Hey," Jack said.

"Nice to see you, Anna," I managed to say.

She smiled at me but it looked bitchy.

"It's cool that you came to this," I added, trying to sound cool with her, even though she clearly hated me and I obviously hated her back. "I know this isn't really your thing, so I'm sure Jack is over the moon that you came to it with him."

"Who said it wasn't my thing?" she asked, her eyes narrowed.

"Well. Jack," I said quietly, wondering if I made a mistake mentioning that. Maybe she shouldn't know that Jack and I had talked about her a little bit during our study sessions. "Not in a bad way," I added quickly. "It just came up in conversation."

"Well, anything that Jack loves, I love," she said with another bitchy smile. Or maybe it was just a regular smile and I hated her so I saw it as a bitchy smile.

"Right. Well anyway, I'm going to go back to my friend."

"Don't be a stranger," Jack said to me before I turned away. "Come say hi to us later."

"You could also come say hi to me."

He nodded a little. "You're right, we could."

I gave him a weak smile and headed back to my spot in line with Becca.

"That looked super awkward," she said to me.

"It was. It was terrible. I'm pretty sure our friendship is doomed."

"It's not doomed. You guys will find your groove."

I sighed and looked back at them in the line. Anna's smile with him was definitely different. She seemed at ease. Happy. Something Jack said made her laugh and she put her hand on his chest and threw her head back a little. He pulled her into him and she kissed his nose.

I wanted to scream.

Jack was very drunk. He found Becca and me at a standing table and practically fell into it. He righted himself on the edge of the table and laughed.

"Hey!" he said quite enthusiastically.

"Hey. Where's your girlfriend?"

"Anna?"

"Do you have more than one?" I asked.

"No. I'm just very drunk and my brain is not working as well as it should. Anna went home."

"Why did she go home?" Becca asked.

He shrugged and leaned his shoulder into me a little. "She wasn't having fun. But she told me to stay! So now we can hang out!"

"You should probably go home and be with her," I said.

"Really?" He sounded surprised.

"Yes, Jack."

"But we never get to see each other anymore."

"Whose fault is that?"

I noticed Becca's eyes widen when I said that, and I gulped, suddenly nervous for Jack's reaction.

"What? It's no one's fault, Aspen. It's just hard keeping in touch with everyone when things start changing." Almost every single word in his sentence slurred together, but I got what he said.

"You should really go home and be with Anna," I said again. "She's probably upset that you didn't go with her."

"No, she said that she wasn't." He shook his head pretty aggressively and leaned into me more, which I would have liked under different circumstances, but it wasn't appropriate, so I moved away, which made him fall. He grabbed onto the table to catch himself, but that just made him bring the table down with him, and as if everything happened in slow motion, I watched in horror as it crashed to the floor. The sound of the glasses breaking seemed to silence the party, and everyone stopped at looked at us. I had stepped back on instinct, but booze still covered my shoes and splashes of it sprinkled my pants. I tried to ignore everyone's stares and think of something to say, but I was so embarrassed, I didn't know what to do. I cleared my throat and carefully stepped over the broken glass to make sure Jack was okay.

"Sorry!" Becca shouted out to everyone as I leaned down and grabbed onto Jack's arms, helping him up. Shit, he was heavy.

"Jack, what's wrong with you?" I asked.

"I didn't do it on purpose!"

"Now we're going to miss the countdown," I said.

"No we won't, we can still stay."

"No we can't, Jack. We've just embarrassed ourselves in front of everyone and might get charged with destruction of property." I eyed a security guard looking at us with his arms crossed, and then a different security guard started walking towards us.

"It was an accident," Jack huffed, getting to his feet with my help.

"Is everything okay?" the security guard asked.

"Yeah, sorry, he just lost his balance. We can pay for the broken glasses."

"Not necessary. We'll get someone to clean this up."

"Okay. Sorry, again."

"I still think we should go," Becca said.

"But they have weird sparklers this year," Jack whined.

"I will get you a weird sparkler and we can turn them on when we leave. Can you walk?"

"Of course I can walk."

Becca grabbed three sparklers for us as we headed out the door and together the three of us walked to the bus stop.

"Where do you live?" I asked Jack.

"You know where I live."

"I do not," I said flatly. "We've always met at my place or the library."

"Oh shit, you're right. It's because Anna's at my place."

"Of course it is."

Mine and Becca's bus came by so we got on and Jack followed us up the steps and down the aisle to a seat in the back.

It was quiet for a few minutes, all of us just looking up the aisle or out the window, and listening to the engine of the bus every time it started moving again after a stop.

"I love her, you know," Jack said quietly.

I took a minute to answer, but finally I turned to look at him, and simply said, "I know."

"She's not the bad guy. I know you're having trouble liking her, but she's really great. She just knows our history and she's threatened by you. That's why we can't hang out as much."

"I would never do anything to get between you guys. And if she doesn't trust you, then-" I stopped myself before I said more. I closed my eyes and shook my head a little, decided to try again. "She needs to get over herself." That wasn't much better.

"She's allowed to have insecurities," he argued.

"You're right. She is. And I'm allowed to be hurt. You were supposed to be with me and instead you're with some girl you just met."

"I didn't just meet her," he said defensively. "I've known her since high school." Anna wasn't his high school girlfriend, was she? No, she couldn't be. There was no way.

"Well, you were still supposed to be with me."

"I know. Sometimes I think I fucked up."

I couldn't believe he was saying all this to me. I realized that I had been looking at my knees or my feet for most of this conversation, so I looked up and saw Becca watching me from the seat facing us, her jaw practically on the floor. I guess she couldn't believe he was saying all this either.

"What makes you think you fucked up?" I asked him after a minute or so of silence.

He shrugged and rested his head on the window. I watched his breath fog it up every time he breathed.

"Jack." I nudged him in the arm and he grunted. "What makes you think you fucked up?"

"I only think that sometimes. Like when I saw you in the pub in the fall. I thought it then. I thought, 'Oh Jack, you done fucked up real good.' Because you were better."

"I was better?" I asked. "Than Anna?" My heart was pounding so hard and my mouth was dry as cotton.

"Yeah. But I love her now. I'm in love with her. I like being with her."

"That's good. You should definitely like being with your girlfriend."

"I'm sorry. I didn't mean to fuck everything up. It just sort of happened."

"I know."

Becca let out a sigh and her face told me that she felt sorry for the two of us. Or maybe she just felt sorry for me.

"I mean, we weren't talking anymore, and I thought you didn't even want to be my friend," he added.

"Why would you think that?"

He didn't answer, and I moved closer to see if he had fallen asleep or something. He was fast asleep with his face pressed against the window, his mouth slightly open.

"That was fast," Becca said.

"And also somehow not fast at all."

"Are you okay?" she asked.

"Yeah," I said slowly. "I think so."

We helped Jack stumble into our dorm and we put him in my bed. I took his shoes off and pulled my comforter over him. I put a glass of water beside the bed so he had something to drink when he woke up incredibly hungover, and then I grabbed two of the sparklers that we took from the Send Off. I put them next to the water, with a note on them that said *light these with Anna.* Although I guess these weren't the kind of sparklers you lit. I didn't really know how they worked, to be honest, but I knew you didn't light them on fire. Oh well, he would know what the note meant. I turned the light off and curled up in bed with Becca.

When we woke up in the morning, Jack was gone, and so were the sparklers. He had written on the note I left for him, and I turned my head to the side to read it without picking it up from the nightstand.

Sorry if I said or did anything embarrassing. I hope I didn't ruin your night.

Jack

So he definitely didn't remember telling me all the stuff he said on the bus. He probably didn't even remember knocking the table over. I figured he wouldn't remember anyway, and a part of me was relieved that he didn't. But another part of me was sad. Another part of me was sad that he wouldn't remember the hurt in his own voice when he told me that he fucked up. When he told me that I was better than Anna.

But I guess it was better for him not to remember that.

CHAPTER 25
(NOW)

I cancel on my bookstore date with Jack the following Thursday because I feel weird about it. We haven't talked since seeing each other at the concert, and I'm not mad at him, but I'm a little hurt. I feel like I'm in med school all over again. He thought that someone was better than me to keep in his life. And that someone wasn't even a good person. I was a good person, wasn't I? Aren't I? If I go hang out with him, I'll just cry or yell at him or say something stupid. So I tell him that I have to stay late at work to catch up on paperwork.

And you have to do it tonight? Jack texts to me. **You can't do it some other day?**

No I have to be done it by tomorrow. Sorry.

Okay.

I ask Shannon if she wants to come over to watch movies and she looks at me with furrowed eyebrows.

"Don't you go to the bookstore with Jack on Thursdays?"

I shrug. "Yeah, I told him I couldn't today."

"Why?"

"I'm just confused."

"I will watch movies with you any time, you know that. But I want to make sure that you're not just avoiding Jack because he's leaving soon."

"I'm not avoiding him because he's leaving soon. I'm avoiding him because I'm upset with him."

"What did he do?"

I wait until we're at my apartment after work, and tell Shannon more details of our story, and how it's annoying that he's still in touch with Carly of all people. She tries to tell me that it has nothing to do with me, but when I cry about it like a stupid child, she shushes me and presses my head to her shoulder. We watch an old sci-fi movie and then turn on a medical drama so we can laugh at all the stuff that they get wrong.

"Have you heard anything about your application?" Shannon asks me after a little while of watching TV.

"Nope, nothing," I say.

"You did submit it, right?"

"Yeah, of course I did."

"Have you followed up?"

"No. Should I?"

"Yes, of course you should!" Shannon says. "Maybe they think you aren't serious. Especially after backing out at the last minute the first time you applied."

"But that wasn't me!"

"They don't know that."

"Ugh, you're right."

"You've wanted this for so long, Aspen. Don't let this chance slip away again."

"I wanted it a long time ago," I tell her honestly. "But I've lived with the fact that I wasn't going to Mars for so long, I got used to it. I got comfortable here."

"I know that the possibility of moving to another planet is scary, but don't let the comfort pull you in. It's not real! It just feels safe because it's a routine that you know."

"Why don't you go to Mars?" I ask.

She laughs. "No way."

"Why not?"

"I wouldn't last three seconds out there. I need my seasons to change. I need to go running under the morning sun in the middle of June. I need concerts. I need airplanes and cruise ships. I need to make snow angels. I need my family close by."

"You don't need me?"

She shakes her head. "I love you. But I don't need you. I want you," she laughs. "I wish I could continue to see you every day and bug you while you're supposed to be working, and make fun of medical dramas with you. But I'll be okay if you go to Mars. I'll be happy for you. And we can video chat and you can tell me all about your amazing adventures that I could never be a part of and actually be happy about it."

I smile at her. "Okay."

"You don't need me, do you?"

"I guess not," I say. "But I'll miss you."

The next day at work I decide to stop in on my boss, who's on the hiring committee. She's been on the hiring committee every year since I was hired, and while she's definitely nice, I find her quite intimidating. I ball my hand into a tight fist before knocking on her door. I don't want her to notice me shaking.

She opens the door with a warm smile and steps aside so that I can join her in her office.

"What's up, Aspen?" she asks me.

"Oh." I ring my hands out and crack my knuckles as a distraction from myself, but I notice her eyeing me, so I try to stop. "I'm just, I mean I was just—" I stop and take a breath. "I was just wondering if you, or if anyone else on the committee got my application submission."

"Yes."

That's it? Yes? "Oh," I say.

She gives me a quick, tight smile and I feel like I'm just supposed to leave now. But I can't. I can't just leave.

"Is it being reviewed?" I ask, hoping she can't hear my voice tremble.

"Yes."

I nod once and put a hand on the doorknob. "Um. Good."

"You're going through the same review process as everyone else applying."

"Right."

"Thanks for checking with me, though. It's good to see."

"Oh. Um. Yeah. Of course."

Her hand finds the doorknob even though I'm already holding it, so I snap my hand back and let her open the door. "Thanks for coming by," she says.

"Yeah. No problem."

I let out a deep breath and lean against the door as soon as she shuts it behind me. That was a lot. Why was she so closed off? She hardly said anything to me! It was like she was doing it on purpose to throw me off!

I decide that night to go home and rewatch all the Mars Group documentaries that Jack and I watched in university to remember why I wanted to live there. I don't want to be applying to work on Mars just because Jack is going to be there. I wasn't friends with Jack for over eight years and I was fine. I was fine without him and I'll continue to be fine without him.

But if I can be with him, don't I want to? If I can be with Jack and live on Mars, isn't that the best outcome? I was crushed when I was placed on Earth, and Jack wasn't even in my life then. I wanted to live on Mars for me, not for some guy. Maybe this is just the thing that's pushing me to try again, but not necessarily my whole reason for doing it.

I cry throughout the entirety of the first docuseries. I wanted this so badly when I was younger, and as I watch it, I can remember what it felt like to experience these shows for the first time. What it felt like to learn about how the compound works, and how life is on Mars. I wanted to go there so badly, and I realize now that I still do. I don't want to go just because of Jack, I want to go for me. But I don't want to risk taking things further with Jack if I'm not going.

CHAPTER 26
(THEN)

Med school had been incredibly busy. Becca, Chelsea, Sara and I got an apartment together as soon as second year was done, and we started our rotations at the hospital in the middle of the summer. Our apartment building didn't have air conditioning, so we loved being in the cool air of the hospital more often than being at home. We were always exhausted, though. When Jack came back to school in the fall to do his second year of teacher's college, we didn't even get a chance to meet up. We texted a little bit here and there, and I told him about some really cool cases I got to work on, but we never actually got to see each other. Becca asked about him every now and then, and I always said that there was nothing to tell. He had a girlfriend and I was too busy to think about him much anyway.

"But you do still think about him?" she asked. We were both assigned to the ER, and there was a quiet chunk to talk during a night shift.

"Not really," I said quickly. "I mean obviously I think about him enough to remember to text him sometimes."

One of the residents we'd gotten to know pretty well, Ryan, came up behind us and asked what we were talking about.

"Nothing," Becca sighed. "Unrequited love."

"Aw that's sad. Do you need someone to requite some love for you?" Ryan asked in a mock serious tone. "I could requite some love."

"Gross," Becca said. "I need someone to teach me something, actually."

"Yeah, I agree. I want someone to teach me something too."

"Fine come with me, I'll find you something to learn."

"As long as you don't try to requite love on us," I said.

"I will refrain from requiting love on you."

Becca smiled at me as we walked behind them, and I twisted my eyebrows in response. She pointed to our resident and I shook my head. She mouthed 'why not?' and I mouthed 'because they're our resident!' and she gave me a questioning look, probably because she had no idea what I said.

Ryan turned around but kept walking backwards so they could talk to us. "I have two options for learning," they said. And then they walked into a supply cart and half stumbled to the ground.

Becca and I tried not to laugh but it was hard. Ryan wiped their pants off and righted themself as casually as possible.

"That was not one of the options," they said, their face turning red.

I laughed. "But I learned such fantastic information."

"Yeah, don't walk backwards in the hospital," Becca added.

I wanted to text Jack about Ryan stumbling over the cart, but I figured he probably wouldn't appreciate a text waking him up at 3am, and neither would Anna. She would probably get jealous if she found out that it was from me, too. So I pocketed my phone and found something else to do for the rest of the unusually quiet night.

Christmas came and went, and I didn't even get a chance to give Jack the present I had gotten him. I wasn't sure if he was going to get me anything; I was actually pretty positive that he wasn't, so I almost didn't get him anything either. But I saw this cute Mars Bar keychain that actually looked like a real mini chocolate bar, with a shiny wrapper and everything. I wasn't sure what it was made out of, but the wrapper was hard and shiny. It was kind of stupid, because it's not even like it was his favourite chocolate bar or anything, but it reminded me of our dream to go to Mars. So I got it for him and I kept it in my sock drawer so I wouldn't lose it or be tempted to use it myself. I would give it to him when the opportunity presented itself.

Jack sent me a happy new year text at midnight, but I was working a rotation in the ER again and I only had time to look at it. I told myself I would respond before I went to bed, but I was so exhausted that I didn't even change my clothes before getting under my covers when I got home at 6am.

It snowed for the next week straight, and the power went out for a couple of hours when I was home with Becca. We lit candles and wrapped ourselves in blankets. That would have been a good time to text Jack back, to ask how he was doing, even ask him if he had power at his apartment. But I didn't. I thought about it, but it hurt to picture Anna sitting beside him while he opened the text from me. It hurt to imagine her smiling at him, asking who he was talking to. It hurt to hear him in my head, telling her that he wasn't talking to anyone important, or saying something like '*Just* Aspen." So Becca and I sat by the candles and quizzed each other with my laminated flashcards instead.

I saw Anna at the hospital on my way to my Oncology rotation. The snow had just started melting, but I knew it would come back again in a couple of weeks. Everyone was wearing hoodies or jean jackets, some people still wearing their winter boots. I noticed that Anna was wearing a pair of tattered Chucks, and the fabric looked like it was soaked through to her socks. I almost didn't say hi to her; I mean we weren't friends, and I was pretty sure she hated me, but then she saw me and I couldn't just ignore her.

"Hey," I said, a little unsure, but trying to sound confident anyway. Like maybe I cared, and actually wanted to say hi.

"Oh, hi," she replied. She sounded unsure of herself. "What are you doing here?"

"I'm doing a med school rotation here."

"Oh." She nodded and looked down the hall, then back at me. "Sorry, where are you doing it?"

"Oncology."

"Oh good," she said with a bit of a sigh.

I scrunched my eyebrows a little in confusion, but before I got a chance to say anything, she started talking again.

"I mean not good," she corrected. "Cancer sucks. I just meant good for you. It must be interesting work."

"Um. Yeah. Is everything okay?"

"Yeah. Everything's fine. Do me a favour? Don't tell Jack that you saw me here."

"Why? What's up?"

"Nothing's up. I was just meeting a friend."

"In Oncology?" I looked past her at the signs pointing the way, and at the signs for OB that directed people around the next corner.

"Yeah," she said quickly, sounding a little relieved. "She's helping me do research."

"On?"

"It's none of your business."

"Right," I said slowly. It was beginning to dawn on me that maybe she was lying about meeting a friend in Oncology and was actually on her way to or from OB. "And it's also not Jack's business?"

"No, Aspen, it isn't. So I would appreciate it if you didn't tell him."

"Yeah, sure, it's not my place to say anything. Not that I would know what to say anyway."

"You're not going to tell him anything."

"But you're also not going to tell him anything? I mean, if you're really here to, um, meet a friend in Oncology, I think you should probably tell Jack about it."

"It's also not your place to say anything to me about this," she said sharply.

I nodded once. "Right. Whatever."

"Look, I get that you guys had some little thing a couple years ago, but he's with me now. He chose me, okay? So back off."

"Back off? I'm not doing anything. I literally just said hi to you."

"Right. Sure."

"I don't understand what's happening," I said. "I was just trying to be nice."

And then she gave me this bitchy smile and walked away! What the hell? I wondered what other things she kept from Jack, if my suspicions were right and she was hiding a pregnancy from him. No matter what she decided to do about it, she should still tell him, no? I also couldn't imagine going through that and not having the person I love with me by my side for it.

But Anna was right, it wasn't my place to say anything to him about it. I made a mental note to text him later, but not be specific about Anna.

I didn't text Jack later. I had no idea what to even say to him, but I was formulating a plan while I was in the grocery store. So I planned to text him, maybe not that night, but soon, but I ran into him instead while I was heading for the checkout.

"Aspen!" he called, making me turn around to find him in the crowd.

"Oh, hey." I walked over to him and we moved to one side of the aisle, out of the weekend rush of people.

"I feel like I haven't seen you in forever."

"Because you haven't," I said with a laugh. "I've been so busy it's not even funny. And when I'm not busy, I'm sleeping because I'm exhausted. *All* the time."

"That sucks. Are you busy now? Once you're done here, I mean?"

"I was going to go home and sleep, to be honest."

"Oh."

"But we should hang out. Um. I don't really have any money to go out or anything. Do you want to come over? You can watch me meal prep."

"I'll do you one better and I'll help you meal prep."

"Really?"

"Yeah. And we can catch up at the same time."

I felt a smile so genuine on my face that I suddenly wasn't tired anymore. Any time I wasn't with Jack but thought about being with him or talking to him, it made me not want to be with Jack. I could never get Anna out of my head, or Jack telling her that we had always just been friends. Even though I knew now that she knew we technically weren't, him saying that just always seemed to repeat in my head. But here I was, talking to Jack for the first time in months, as if we had been hanging out just the day before. It felt like no time had passed at all, and standing in the grocery store with him, I wasn't thinking about Anna, or about the fact that he didn't love me. I was just hanging out with Jack as if nothing was wrong. And in that moment, I felt silly for ever thinking it was.

Jack came back to my apartment on the bus with me, and one of my roommates, Sara, was home. Chelsea and Becca were doing rotations at the hospital and wouldn't be back until 7am. Sara was in the living room watching TV and she waved to us when we came in but didn't get up to greet us or anything.

"Do you remember Jack?" I asked.

"Yeah, I think so," she said. "Hey."

"Yeah, we might've met once or twice," Jack said with a nod.

"We haven't seen each other in a while, so we're catching up," I added.

She gave me a thumbs up and went back to watching TV. I peeked around the corner of the kitchen at her a couple times as we made my food, and she was asleep before we were even halfway done.

I tried to ask Jack about Anna and her so-called 'friend in oncology that's around the corner from OB', but I didn't know how to do it without being obvious or giving away that I saw her at the hospital.

"So how's Anna doing?" I asked.

"She's good, thanks. You have a boyfriend yet?"

"I don't have time for a boyfriend, are you kidding me?"

"Yeah, sorry, I guess you're right. I just thought maybe you'd meet someone in med school or something."

I shook my head. "So did you say you knew Anna before? You went to school together?"

"Yeah, we went to the same high school. We weren't really friends in high school, but we were friendly?"

"Acquaintances?" I clarified.

"Yeah. Acquaintances."

"So you weren't super close in school, then." I didn't know how I was going to go from them knowing each other in high school to asking if he knew whether or not she was pregnant, but I was trying.

He raised an eyebrow at me. "No. Why?"

I shrugged. "I was just curious."

"Yeah, but why?"

"For no reason other than wanting to know. I just wanted to know if you guys had this big, romantic reunion."

He laughed. "It was not romantic. We just became friends, really."

"Right." I was doing a terrible job at getting to the bottom of Anna being or not being pregnant, and her telling or not telling Jack about it, so I gave up. It didn't matter anyway. She would tell him or not, and I would have no impact on it whatsoever. Plus I was afraid he was going to get into details about how they fell in love, so I changed the subject. "I saw someone the other day with a tumor so big they had to carry it."

"I'm sorry, they had to what?" he asked.

"Yeah, it was growing from their abdomen and it was protruding so much, and was so heavy that they had to keep their hands under it when they walked."

"That's brutal."

"Yeah."

Jack texted me the next day that we shouldn't let that much time pass again before we hang out the next time. I agreed, but of course that much time passed, and more.

CHAPTER 27 (NOW)

I text Jack less throughout the next week, and I feel bad, but mostly I'm just trying to figure out what to say to him. I know it's probably silly to be upset about the Carly thing, but I can't help but feel like I'm never good enough for anybody. And why would I be? I'm not confident, I can't open up about my feelings if it involves anyone else, and I'm probably annoying. Of course I'm annoying.

Bookstore tonight? Jack texts me at lunch on Thursday.

Yeah I reply.

"Is that Jack?" Shannon asks when she sees me looking at my phone.

"Yeah," I sigh.

"Why haven't you guys done anything about your feelings yet? You're obviously both in love with each other."

"Because he's going to Mars!"

"But you also might be going to Mars!"

"What if I don't get accepted? I can't, Shannon. If I get accepted, I'll see him again in six months."

"What if he gets a girlfriend by then? Six months is a long time to get a girlfriend! And then you'll be heartbroken all over again."

"No, I will just still be heartbroken. Plus I'm not heartbroken. Stop making me say things that aren't true!"

Shannon laughs and puts her hands up in surrender. "You're the one who agreed with me!"

"Not on purpose! I'm not heartbroken. I'm just…" I sigh and look away. "I don't know what I am. But if I end up going to Mars and he has a girlfriend, then we were obviously never meant to be together."

"Right."

"You don't think he would get a girlfriend in six months, do you?"

Shannon shrugs.

"Fuck."

"You have to talk to him about this or you'll hate yourself for it," she says. "Especially if he does end up getting a girlfriend."

"Ugghh."

Jack and I have been at the bookstore for about fifteen minutes, and I have no idea what to say to him. I want to talk to him about Carly more than anything, about how he made me feel like I wasn't important to him. But I guess I should say something about my feelings? No. I can't. If he feels the same way about me - which I'm pretty sure he does, or he wouldn't have tried to kiss me before - we're probably going to have sex, and I can't have sex with someone before he goes to Mars forever.

"Are you okay?" Jack asks, probably sensing my apprehension.

"Hmm? Oh. Yeah, I'm fine." I sigh and head to the YA section to look for a fun fantasy read.

I can feel Jack following me, but he doesn't say anything. He ends up beside me as I stop in front of one of the bookcases to read the spines that are facing me.

"Why are you lying to me?" he asks.

"I'm not lying."

"You're totally lying. Something's wrong."

I huff and look at him. "I don't know, Jack. I'm just." I shake my head and pull a book down off the shelf. "I don't know."

"You don't know what? Can I help you figure it out?"

"You're still in touch with Carly."

"What?"

"You lost touch with me twice and you're still friends with Carly?"

"I wouldn't really say that we're friends…" The end of his sentence hangs in the air as if he's going to add to it, but he doesn't.

"Why didn't you stay in touch with me?" I dare to ask.

"Can we not do this here?"

"Do what? We're just having a conversation."

"I know, but I don't feel comfortable talking about this here. Can we go back to my place or something?"

"And do what? Argue about things that happened ten years ago?"

He shrugs and I notice that his eyes are a little red. Holding back tears? "If that's what you want."

"What's that supposed to mean?" I scrunch my eyebrows at him and shove the book I've been holding back onto the shelf.

"It means we can argue about stuff that happened ten years ago if it'll help."

"I don't want to argue because I think it'll help, Jack. I don't want to argue at all! But I can't…" I trail off and start to walk past him.

"You can't what?" he asks, gently grabbing onto my arm to stop me.

"I can't deal with this!" I shake his hand off and head out of the store.

"Aspen, wait!" He follows me but I beeline it to my car. "Aspen, talk to me!"

"I can't, I have to go." I'm fighting off tears myself at this point, and I fumble with my car keys, but Jack catches up to me and presses himself in between me and my car.

"Why are you doing this!? Maybe this is why we never kept in touch! Because you're always leaving!"

"What!?" I can feel my eyes burning into him and I want to scream. "I'm always leaving?" I half shout. "How am I always leaving? You're the one who told me you loved me and then fucking ghosted me!"

"Oh, so this is what it's about? You've been mad at me this whole time, have you?"

"I wasn't mad, Jack, but I was fucking hurt! And then you did it again and I find out that you're still in touch with Carly!"

"Because she's married to my best friend! And I didn't do it again, you were just as much a part of us drifting apart as I was! Don't you put that on me."

"Well it was all you the first time, wasn't it?"

"When my mom died? Excuse me for not knowing how to deal with my feelings, Aspen, but I was barely 22! I didn't know how to handle any of that shit, let alone the person I couldn't get out of my head!"

"What? Are you talking about me?"

"Of course I am!"

"So it's my fault that you were thinking about me?"

"No, Jesus, don't put words in my mouth. I was just…" he scrubs his hand over his face and lets out a deep breath. "I was in love with you, and I missed you, but my mom was dying. I don't know, okay?"

"But then you went and fell in love with Anna even though you missed me! You were supposed to be with me!"

"Yeah, because she was there for me!"

I take in a sharp breath and feel a tear escape. I close my eyes and shake my head. "You lived three hours away, Jack!" I say, snapping my eyes back open and letting more tears fall.

"You could have come to see me! No one came to see me." He says that last sentence quietly, like he's hurting. "You rode the bus with me so I didn't have to go home alone, and then you went back by yourself, and that was it!"

"I tried to have movie nights with you and you kept cancelling! And then you said you needed space! What was I supposed to do!?"

"I don't know! Talk to me like you used to? Instead of just sending empty condolences?"

"I tried! You hardly responded to me! And I was supposed to take that to mean that you wanted me to come visit you?"

Jack is crying now too, and a couple people in the parking lot are watching us. I feel self conscious about it but I don't think either of us are in a good state to drive right now. I want to get this out anyway, even if it's in the parking lot of a bookstore.

"I thought you would have, I don't know!" Jacks half shouts. "And so I thought that you didn't want to be my friend anymore! I thought that my shit was too much to deal with."

"Why on Earth would you think that?"

"Because you did so much without asking before that, and then you just… stopped."

"I didn't, though. I tried, Jack. I didn't know what I was supposed to do."

He chuckles a little, but it sounds frustrated. "Neither did I. And…" he takes a deep breath and looks away briefly. Grabs at the back of his neck. "And Anna…" he drops his arm back to his side and looks at me. "I knew Anna from high school. We hadn't seen each other since graduation, and when my mom died…" He covers his face with his hands and sobs a little. I want to hug him. I want to step into him and wrap him up in my arms but I don't know if I should. He takes a deep breath and uncovers his face before I make up my mind. "Anna was always there. Sometimes we wouldn't even say anything, we would just lie in bed and stare at the ceiling together. But she never let me be alone. I mean, she did, she wasn't with me all the time, but she was… there. And you weren't."

My tears are falling again because I'm so frustrated. "I was at school," I say shortly. "Stop saying that like I was next door and refused to see you."

He lets out a slow breath. "I really did think that you didn't think I was worth it. But I also meant that I fell for her because she was, um, the person who happened to be there."

My eyes widen a little and he shakes his head quickly.

"That sounds bad," he says. "That sounds so bad. I don't mean that I only got together with her because I felt like I had no other option. That wasn't it at all. It was just that… I was so broken, Aspen. I didn't know how to even begin picking up the pieces. They were everywhere, and I didn't know how to fit you in. I wanted to, but I didn't know how to even try. It was like each piece weighed fifty pounds so just picking up one or two was too much. And then I felt like a piece of shit because I didn't answer you as much as I wanted to, but I also didn't know how to talk to you anymore. I didn't know how to talk to anyone. And with Anna, we didn't need to talk, and she made me feel safe, and things just sort of … happened."

I wipe the tears off my face with my whole hand and nod at him because I don't know what else to do.

"It was slow," he adds. "Nothing even happened until, like, after Halloween. And I didn't mean to start anything with her. And I don't want to make it sound like I only got together with her because I had no one else, because that's not it. But I guess I needed someone? And she just happened to be that someone. The first time we kissed I felt like-"

"I don't need to hear about you two kissing," I say, interrupting him.

"Right. Yeah. Sorry. I just don't want you to think that I hurt you on purpose. I was hurting too. And there was no point in trying to stay in touch with you once we started drifting apart again. You and I both know that we were always more than friends. Even before anything happened between us, we were more than friends. And trying to only be friends wouldn't have gone well for anyone. I was with Anna, and you needed to move on."

I nod again and reach for my car door handle. "Right."

He puts his hand on mine, stopping me from pulling the door open. "But I'm not with Anna anymore," he half whispers.

I look up at him and my heart starts to hammer. "No," I say quietly. "But you're going to Mars."

He lets out a breath and closes his eyes. "Why can we never get this right?"

"Do you want to?" I can hear my voice shaking. I hope he can't hear my voice shaking.

"I've always wanted to get it right. I hated myself sometimes for not getting it right."

"Even when you were with Anna?"

He huffs and then swallows, as if he's afraid to answer me. "Yes," he finally says.

"And instead of doing something about it, you stayed with her for almost ten years."

He shrugs. "You say that as if you and I were friends that whole time. We weren't friends for like, eight of those years, Aspen. I didn't stay with someone for ten years wishing I was with someone else the entire time, what kind of a person do you think I am?"

"Sorry. Yeah, you're right." I swallow and open the car door, making him step back a little.

"Can we please talk more about this?" he asks.

"I can't, Jack. I'm sorry. I can't do this again."

"You can't do what again?"

"Fall in love with you and then lose you before I even really get to have you."

The muscles in his jaw clench and he nods. He lets me get in the car and I watch him in my mirror as he walks to his own car. I wait until he's inside before I let myself sob.

CHAPTER 28 (THEN)

Jack graduated from teacher's college and invited me to a party at his and Anna's apartment. I was working, but I told him I would try to stop by on my way in. I wished that Becca was working the same rotation as me so we could go to the party together, but alas, I was alone. I didn't know why I was nervous to go alone; it's not like I didn't know Jack, but I guess I was afraid of Anna a little bit. Afraid of how she made me feel. I wasn't jealous of her really, not anymore, but when I saw them together it still made me feel weird. I was pretty sure there would always be a part of me that loved Jack, and it felt stronger every time I saw them together. Or any time I saw Jack at all, really. But it was worse when he was with Anna.

Nothing ever came of her maybe pregnancy, so either she wasn't pregnant, or whatever decision she made out about it, Jack wasn't a part of it. Or he was, and he just didn't tell me. We didn't tell each other a lot of things anymore, so even though the thought hurt, it made sense if he just didn't happen to fill me in on any details. A part of me wished that he didn't tell me about it because Anna did keep it a secret from him. If Anna kept that big of a thing from him, then that meant they weren't right for each other. That she wasn't good enough for him. That maybe they wouldn't last.

I felt weird showing up to the party in my scrubs, but I tried to ignore everyone looking at me. I wished I had Becca's confidence, who would have flat out told everyone that she was a doctor. I saw Jack before he saw me. He was with Anna, of course, and they looked so at ease with each other. Comfortable. A pinch of sadness I was hoping I wouldn't feel, bit at me while I watched them. His arm was wrapped loosely around her waist and her hand rested on his chest as they stared at each other, all smiles. They were really in love, weren't they?

Before I really stepped into the apartment though, Jack saw me and slipped away from Anna after whispering something into her hair. She smiled but also rolled her eyes, and Jack came over to me with a big grin on his face. I brought his Mars Bar keychain, but something was stopping me from giving it to him. It was a stupid gift.

"I'm so glad you came!" he said, giving me a hug.

"Me too. Sorry I can't stay long."

"Oh no worries, I get it. You've got lives to save."

"Well. I've got to learn how to save people's lives."

"Yeah, I feel like that's more important. You can't save people's lives if you don't know how."

I smiled at him and stepped further into his apartment, looking around and realizing I'd actually never been in here before. It was pretty nice; the kitchen looked new, but the furniture in the living room could do with some slipcovers or something. The fabric on the armrests looked like they had been scratched by a cat, and the cushions looked a little worn.

"Are you a doctor?" someone asked, walking up to me.

"A med student," I said.

"Oh, lame."

Jack and I gave each other a look and then laughed.

I followed him into the kitchen where we leaned against the counter behind us, and I drank a Diet Coke while he drank a beer. We laughed and caught each other up on our lives, and the rest of the party seemed to be quiet around us. It was like we were the main characters in a movie, and the rest of the party was just made up of background actors, pretending to talk so that our conversation could be heard on camera. Our arms brushed against each other every now and then and I wished that I could lean my shoulder against his.

The alarm on my phone finally went off, telling me that I needed to get to the hospital, so Jack walked me down to the lobby of his building.

"Don't be a stranger," he said to me.

"You neither," I said.

"I'll try my best."

"Same."

"Well, have a good shift."

"Thanks. Have a good party."

"Thanks," he said with a smile.

"And congrats."

"Thanks. You too."

"Me too?"

He shrugged. "For the whole med school thing. For doing it. I'm really proud of you."

"Oh." I felt my eyes sting with tears so I nodded and forced a smile. "Thanks."

We just stood in the apartment vestibule staring at each other like we wanted to kiss but were each afraid to make the first move. I knew that he didn't actually want to kiss me, but I wanted to kiss him. I wanted to kiss him so badly.

"Okay, well, see ya," I said, reaching for the door.

"Bye." He smiled and gave a little wave as I stepped out into the parking lot.

I walked across the tarmac without looking back, and I wished I had a car I could get into because I needed to cry. I needed to cry big, heaving sobs of sadness, but I had to get on a bus with other people, so instead I had to hold it in. It physically hurt to not allow myself to sob, and the few tears and sniffles that escaped on the bus were not enough to make that pain go away.

It hurt me so much to realize how much Jack and I had grown apart. We were still comfortable with each other whenever we were together, but it was too easy for us to go months and months apart without either of us questioning it. And I couldn't stop picturing him and Anna together. She never seemed like a bitch unless I was talking to her. She always seemed pleasant from the outside. Probably because she was pleasant. Jack wouldn't have been with her if she wasn't.

But still, the fact that he wasn't with me, the fact that nothing had driven them apart, the fact that Jack hadn't realized he made a mistake after all this time, meant that we were never going to be together. That Jack probably never thought about me as a possibility, or as something he shouldn't have let slip away. The things he said while he was drunk after the Send Off the year before, were not things he thought about anymore, I felt that much. And here I was still pining for him. Still wishing that he would change his mind. And he wouldn't.

How did I let us drift so far away from each other?

I couldn't focus at all throughout my rotation that night, and my resident actually had to ask me if I was okay. I managed to make it through but once I got home, I finally let myself cry. Loudly. Jack and I were supposed to go to Mars together. And instead he was with someone who didn't even like going to Mars Send Off parties. But he was also with someone who didn't like going to Mars Send Off parties but went to them anyway, because *he* wanted to.

I was so mad at myself for still being in love with him, and I was mad at him for being in love with Anna. I was mad at both of us for not really being friends anymore. If being friends was all we could be, then that's what we had wanted, and we couldn't even do that right.

When I finally got it all out of me, I was stuffy and lightheaded, and my heart was still aching. I knew I would be okay, and I knew I would eventually stop loving him. But that time hadn't come yet. And I think this was my first time fully accepting that nothing would ever happen between us. That we would never again be friends in the same way. So I was allowed to ache over it. So I let myself ache over it, just for a while.

Jack and Anna moved to a different part of town a few months later and we never got the chance to see each other again. We still texted a little bit, and each time hurt a little less, but they were fewer and farther between, until eventually I had my life, he had his, and they never intertwined.

Until I met him in my exam room eight years later.

CHAPTER 29
(NOW)

Jack calls me as soon as I get home. I'm not even all the way up the stairs yet when my phone goes off.

"Hello?" I sniffle into it.

"Are you okay?"

"No."

"Why not?"

"Because you're going to Mars."

"You've known this for months, Aspen."

"I know, but now it's happening." I open the big stairwell door and make my way down the hall to my apartment.

"Not for another two weeks."

"It doesn't matter. That's basically tomorrow."

"Do you want me to come over?"

"No," I cry. "It'll only make it harder. I told you, I can't do this again."

"Yeah," he sighs. It's quiet for a minute, and then he just says, "yeah," again.

"Thanks for calling."

"Hey Aspen," he says, before I can hang up.

"Yeah?" I unlock my apartment and make my way inside.

"You might be going to Mars too."

"Yeah, might. I might be going to Mars."

He sighs again. "Yeah. Okay. I get it. I can still come over if you want, though. Just friends."

"No. Thanks, though. I'll see you next week at the bookstore, though?"

"Absolutely."

Jack texts me the next day to say that he can't make our bookstore date because he has Mars Group meetings that day and he was told they usually run late.

But maybe I can come visit you in your office he says.

Yeah, that would be nice.

Jack knocks on my open door at 3pm the next Thursday and steps into my office with a smile on his face.

"Hey," I say, spinning around in my chair.

"Are you terribly busy?" he asks.

"I'm never busy. How's your day going?"

"It's good. This is all starting to feel real."

"It didn't feel real before?'

He shakes his head. "Until today it felt like a dream, or like I was just daydreaming about it like we did back in school."

"Are you nervous?"

"No. Not yet, at least. But it feels weird."

"What are you going to do with all the books you've been buying over the last few months?"

Jack laughs and his hand finds the back of his neck for a quick second. "I'm still not sure what I want to do with all my stuff."

"What? You're leaving in a week, Jack!"

"I know," he groans, leaning on my desk and half sitting on it. "I can't decide if I want to get rid of most of my stuff or put it in storage."

"Are you planning on coming back?"

"I'm not sure. There's always a possibility."

"I don't think I would come back."

"Really? Not even to see family?"

I shrug. "It feels like a lot of work."

"That's harsh," Jack says with a chuckle.

"Mars is really far away," I say.

"Not as far as it used to be."

"Okay, that's a lie. It's the same distance from Earth as it's always been."

"But we can get there faster. It makes a difference."

"I would need to take 2 months off to come visit for a week."

"They're talking about giving Mars Group members two passes to Earth, with paid time off."

"Like, two total? For the rest of their lives?"

"Two that are paid for, at least."

"Interesting."

"Yeah."

"So how much stuff are you allowed to bring with you?" I ask.

"A fair amount, actually. They gave us each two tote bins that we can fill, and they're a pretty good size. I'm taking my favourite books, some clothes and shoes, my camera. My comforter."

"That's it?"

"No, I'm taking more," he says with a smile. "I didn't think you wanted me to list everything off."

"Right. Sorry." I shake my head and swivel in my chair a little. "What time are you done tonight?"

"Not until after eight, I think."

"Okay. Well, I have an appointment in a few minutes, so I should get ready for that."

"Aren't doctors always keeping their patients waiting?"

"Not me. I never make them wait."

"You're such a good doctor."

"I try."

I get up from my chair and he straightens up so that we're standing right in front of each other. He's so close that I can feel his breath on my lips.

"Um. Have a good appointment," he says quietly.

"You too."

"Me too? Am I coming with you?"

"Ha. I meant have a good day. A good rest of your day. With the Mars stuff. Have a good time with your Mars stuff."

His grin makes me want to kiss him. Instead I bite my bottom lip and step back.

"Thanks," he says. "I'll see you around."

"Yeah. See you around."

Jack leaves and I take a deep breath to collect myself. I don't have a chance to do anything else before Shannon comes into my office with her mouth open.

"Oh my god, this room is dripping in sexual tension!" she says.

"Oh, fuck off, Shannon."

She furrows her eyebrows and leans her head back a bit in surprise. I can feel myself starting to cry and I can't go examine a patient while that's happening so I sit back down and spin my chair away from her.

"Sorry," she says softly. "Are you okay?"

"I get it, Shannon! Okay?" I half-shout, spinning back around to face her. "I get it. I'm not just hiding my feelings from him because I'm afraid he's going to reject me. And I'm not hiding my feelings, by the way. We both know exactly how we feel about each other, and I can't do it. I can't bring myself to act on my feelings when he's literally going to be living on a different planet a week from now."

"Right. You're right, I'm sorry. I don't try to be pushy like that with you, but I know I am."

"It's hard enough as it is without you pointing it out all the time."

"I know. I'm really sorry."

I wipe the tears from my face and take in another breath. "Ugh, I have a patient."

"Do you want me to take it?" she asks.

"Don't you have a patient?"

"Not until 3:30. They can wait. And I can rush."

"Sure. Thanks." I transfer my patient to her on my tablet and Shannon smiles at me before leaving.

Jack and I hardly even text over the next week because he's so busy getting ready to leave. He's got meetings at The Mars Group, and I see him a few times in the building but we don't have time to chat. He tells me that he decided to get a storage unit for now, but he's spending any free time he has moving everything into it. I tell him I can help, but he's doing it with his dad and step-mom as a way to spend time with them before he leaves.

I hope you're doing more than just making them move all your shit as a way to say goodbye I text to him.

Har har. Of course I am.

You taking them out for dinner or something?

Yes, and also to the zoo.

That's cute.

I thought so. They love the zoo. The zebras are their favourite.

Why? I ask. **They're just stripey horses.**

Why not? They're stripey horses!

Ha.

What's your favourite animal at the zoo, then?

Capybaras. I text.

Why capybaras? They're just giant prairie dogs.

Excuse me sir, capybaras are more than giant prairie dogs. Also they're more like giant guinea pigs.

Sure.

Also Elephants.

What? he asks. **They are not like elephants.**

No haha, I also like the elephants. The African ones.

The week leading up to Jack leaving has gone by too fast. I'm getting ready for the Send Off and I feel like I'm going to barf. I can't believe I found Jack again and now I might never see him again for the rest of my life. Is it good that I didn't let anything happen between us? Yes, of course it is. Saying goodbye to him would hurt so much more if we had done anything physical. Plus being physical with him would have just made me more attached to him. And make saying goodbye even harder. Yes, it was best for us to just stay friends. Right?

I get to the Send Off early and make my way to my office. Being here after hours always makes me feel like I'm at school for a Christmas concert or parent-teacher interviews. I always got this feeling inside me when we had to be at my school in the evening, this feeling in my chest and my limbs, that was oddly comforting and a little awkward. Like something special was happening and even though I was at a place I didn't really like, it was okay for this event. The normal school stuff didn't happen, and people acted differently. Things in hallways sounded different, the lighting was different. I felt different.

Anyway, that's how I feel now, walking down the hall to my office so I can hide before the party gets started. Maybe hide throughout all of it.

Jack texts me about twenty minutes later asking when I'll be there, and I reply and say that I already am. He sends me a raised eyebrow emoji and I send him a shrugging emoji. A knock on my door comes less than five minutes later and my heart just about jumps out of my throat. I get up and open the door to find Jack standing in the hallway, wearing dark jeans and a white button down.

"You look nice," I say.

"Thanks. So do you."

I'm just wearing a loose fitting knitted sweater and black pants. Casual but yeah, nice, I guess.

"How come you're here so early?" I ask.

"I'm getting nervous. I thought maybe you could calm me down."

"That didn't answer my question."

"Right." He grins at me. "Um. We're in the barracks tonight and we all got here a few hours ago."

"Yes, that makes sense. You're out of your place by now."

"Yeah."

"And you're leaving tomorrow morning."

"Yeah."

"I don't know what I can do to calm you down," I say.

"Just talking to you is helping."

"Oh. Well that's good."

"Also you have to download the Mars Chat app, so we can talk."

"Right yes, I got it last night, but I don't know how to add you."

"Here, I can scan your phone."

I pull my phone out and open the app, and Jack touches a few things so that a QR code shows up on the screen and then he scans it with his own phone. It looks new, not like a phone I recognize. Both our phones ding and I look at my screen to see a little emoji person under the name Jack Duncan.

"Cool," I say.

"You can send texts, pictures, videos, and you can live video chat too. They said it can take a bit of time to connect, but once it does, it doesn't lag or anything. And now that I have you on my fancy new Mars phone, I can rest easy when I give them my old one."

"You have to give them your old phone? How is your Mars phone working here? When do you have to give them your phone?"

He laughs. "One question at a time, Aspen. I don't have to give them my old phone, but since they provide us with new ones, they give us the option to hand them in. They wipe them and give them to people who can't afford cell phones."

"Oh that's smart."

"Yeah. So I'm handing mine in at the party."

"So does your Mars phone work here, then? Can I send you a message now, or does one of us have to be on Mars?"

"I don't know." He looks at his phone and types something, and immediately my phone dings.

Hello there his message says.

I smile, remembering the message I sent to him when we first gave each other our phone numbers back in university.

"Did you read that in Ewan McGregor's voice?" he asks.

"Of course I did."

CHAPTER 30
(NOW)

We finally decide that we should join the party downstairs. We heard the music and chattering of people at least forty minutes ago, and it's been getting louder. We drag our feet down the hall and take a stairwell down to the main floor since we know the grand staircase is going to be roped off. I see Shannon almost immediately and she comes over to say hi and congratulations to Jack. He says thanks, and then four people come over and practically knock him over.

"Duncan! I can't believe you're leaving for Mars!" one of them says.

"Yeah, it's pretty weird," he replies.

"Come have a drink with us!" one of his other friends says. "It's your last night on Earth!"

Jack turns to me and puts a hand on my elbow. "I'll come find you later, okay?"

I nod, and he smiles, squeezes my elbow, and leaves with his friends.

"Are you okay?" Shannon asks.

"Not really. But I guess I have to be."

I look around at the growing crowd in the lobby and my heart stops for a second when I swear I see David. No. There's no way it's him. Why would he be here? Better yet, who would he be here with?

"What?" Shannon asks, looking in the direction I'm looking.

"David is over there," I say. "What the actual fuck."

"Oh my god."

I start to walk over to him, and Shannon grabs onto my arm. "Aspen, it's not worth it," she says.

"I think it is!"

I can feel Shannon trying to grab my arm again but I march over to David without even thinking about it. He's laughing with some pretty girl and the second he sees me I notice his face drop and his mouth open a little.

"What makes you think it's okay to be here?" I ask, tears already stinging my eyes.

"Aspen, lay off."

"Are you kidding me right now?"

"Aspen," Shannon says, coming up behind me. She stops and looks at David. "Hey dickhead- I mean David."

David rolls his eyes and Shannon tries to drag me away.

"Shannon, stop," I say. "I can't just walk away after what he did!"

"It doesn't matter anymore."

"It matters to me!" I can hear my voice crack and I feel completely stupid but I can't help it. I turn back to David. "Why did you change my application?"

"What?"

"For The Mars Group when I first applied! You logged into my account and changed my application!"

He shrugs and actually says, "I didn't want to go to Mars."

"But you told me you wanted to!" I quickly wipe a tear away from my cheek and try to steady my voice.

"I lied."

"Why didn't you just let me go without you, then?" I'm shaking at this point, but I have to get this out.

"I didn't want to be alone," he says easily. As if he's just admitting that to me right now.

"You're a pathetic excuse for a human, you know that? I feel sorry for whoever you're here with." I turn to the pretty girl he was laughing with earlier. "Is it you? Is he here with you? Do yourself a favour and get out now. He's a manipulative piece of shit."

She stares at me with her mouth half open and then David takes her by the arm, about to lead her away. But I'm not done yet.

"And as if you're here with someone after never coming with me!"

"Come on, let's go," David says to the girl, and together they leave, looking back at me once before getting lost in the crowd.

I wipe the tears from my face and sigh, not knowing what else to do.

"Do you feel better?" Shannon asks.

"No," I cry. "I didn't get to punch him."

The fact that David was here with someone else gets to me the most. It just reminds me of Jack and how I felt like I wasn't good enough for him. I never seem to be good enough for anyone. I'm not good enough to attend Mars Send Off parties with, I'm not good enough for someone to stay friends with me over long distance, or even explore a relationship after confessing their love for me. I'm just everyone's backup. I'm the person who's there for someone when they have no one else. I'm not the person people want to do things with. I'm the person people have to do things with, and if they can be avoided, they are. Anything they could do with me, they would rather not do, or do with someone else.

"Aspen, do you have a free few minutes?" I hear beside me.

I turn to see my boss smiling at me, so I smile back and nod. "Yeah, I mean, yes. Yes of course."

She nods her head towards a stairwell and I follow her down the hall and through the heavy door.

"Thank you so much for speaking with me."

"Oh. No problem," I say, swallowing a lump in my throat.

"I just wanted to touch base with you about your application."

"Oh?"

"I'm sorry I'm doing this here, but I've been so busy through the work day and haven't been able to catch you in your office. The other hiring committee members put a flag on your application."

"They did? Wh- why?" I grip my glass of sparkling water so tightly I'm afraid I might crack it.

"Because we can see your application history. They're worried that you're going to change your mind at the last minute again."

I can feel the walls spinning around me. "Oh."

She nods. "How serious are you about this?"

"Very serious," I say quickly. "Last time I didn't even-" I stop myself before I can say what actually happened. I don't want to come across as unprofessional or like I'm trying to put the blame on someone else. Or that I don't take internet security as seriously as I should. "Sorry, I mean, there were different circumstances last time. I had other things to consider, and I don't have those things now."

She narrows her eyes at me a little. "Okay."

"Okay?"

"If you can tell me with 100% certainty that this is what you want, then I will advocate for you."

"Really?"

"Yes, of course. I can't say if it will pull any weight, but I can try. But only if this is absolutely what you want. I don't want to be made a fool if you pull out again."

"You won't. I promise I want this. I've always wanted this."

"Okay. Enjoy the rest of the party." She leaves into the hall and I let the heavy steel door slam closed behind her.

I don't know what to do. Does this mean there's a big chance I might not be going to Mars? Am I going to have to apply again and again to prove to them that I want this? And I mean I always thought about the possibility that I might not get accepted. This entire time I wasn't doing anything with Jack for the sole reason that I might not get to follow him, but now that I've had this conversation, it feels even less likely that I'll get to go. Holy shit. I might not get to go to Mars.

I'm hit with a wall of panic. At first I wasn't letting anything progress past friendship with Jack because he was going to Mars and I wasn't, and then it was because I might not get to go Mars, and now I actually probably won't get to go to Mars and I've just let Jack slip through my fingers again! I tried to save myself from heartache but now my heart is aching so much that I can't breathe. I passed up being close with Jack for the last few months, and for what? For nothing. To just never be close with him at all, or ever again.

The stairwell door bangs against the wall behind it and I look up, only just now realizing that I've been sitting on the floor with my face buried in my knees. How long have I been in here?

"What are you doing in here?" Shannon asks. "I've been looking everywhere for you." Her eyes meet mine and she gasps, kneels down next to me. "What's wrong? What happened? Did David come be an ass to you again or something?"

"I might not be going to Mars," I cry.

"That's bullshit, of course you're going to Mars."

I shake my head. "No. Dr. Lena just talked to me."

"What? What did she say?"

"That my application change from last time is on record and they're afraid I'll do it again."

"Jesus Christ. I'm going to kill David."

"He isn't still here, is he?"

Shannon shakes her head. "No, I don't think so."

"I'm so sick of this, Shannon. I'm never anyone's first choice, for anything."

"You're my first choice!"

"Thanks."

"I know that's not what you want to hear, but you are! I love you."

"I love you too."

"Anyway, they're about to do the send off." She eyes me sheepishly as she takes two sparklers out of her back pocket and slowly hands me one.

"Shit, I'm not even going to get to say goodbye to him." I wipe my face and stand up, but Shannon grabs me by the shoulders before I can run off.

"Wait," she says.

I stand there as she carefully wipes under my eyes to make sure I don't have any mascara smears from crying. When she steps back and smiles, I take the sparkler from her and run out of the stairwell and down the hall.

I can hear the countdown as my shoes squeak on the floor. Ten! – Squeak – Nine! – Squeak – Eight! – Squeak. I run faster but I'm afraid of slipping and getting there even later. They're at two when I break into the main lobby, and I spot Jack in the crew of twenty-three people who are leaving. They have on their red Mars Group uniforms, and Jack is smiling, his eyes darting around, I hope trying to find me. His chin is raised in the air as he looks over the heads of all the strangers holding up their sparklers, lighting up the room and making it almost impossible to make out anyone's face.

"Jack!" I shout, but he can't hear me. Everyone's shouting and cheering and I'm lost within it. The group leaves through a back door and I chase after them, but someone stops me before I get to the door.

"This exit is for Mars Party Members only," the security guard says to me.

"Yes, but I work for The Mars Group. I'm a physician here."

"You're not a Party Member."

"This is ridiculous! I just want to say goodbye to my friend!"

"Why didn't you say goodbye earlier?"

"Because! He was saying goodbye to other people…" I trail off, the reminder hitting me in the face that I literally come last for everyone, in every situation.

No.

Stop it.

I got pulled away. I was hiding in a stairwell. Jack was probably looking for me.

He was looking for me. Right?

I turn around, frantic to find a way to the barracks, and I crash into Shannon.

"I can't let him leave," I say around a lump in my throat.

"It's okay, we won't."

"They won't let me out that way." I shake my head and wipe the tears from my face with my palms.

"Can't you just text him? It's not like they lock them in there; he can meet you outside."

"Right. My brain isn't working." I open the Mars Chat since that's the only way we can communicate now that he only has his new phone. I open his name, the only one in my contacts, and hit call. "It's ringing," I say to Shannon. She smiles and gives me a thumbs up.

It keeps ringing. Can you leave messages on this app? Does it have an answering machine service? After about twelve rings, I disconnect the call and send him a text message.

I never got to say bye I type.

I wait a few minutes for him to reply, but he doesn't. Why isn't he answering his phone?

I pocket my phone and run past Shannon, ignoring her shouts for me to wait. I get outside into the cool air and watch my breath puff out in clouds in front of me before running around to the back of the building and towards the path that leads to the barracks.

The path is stone, and laid in winding swirls through the forest, taking you on a five minute journey when it could have been three. The path goes around trees and down hills, there's even a little wooden bridge that takes you over a stream so small you could jump over it.

I make it to the barracks, nestled against a fence at the back of the small forest, and look up at the cabin-like structure. How do I even know what room he's in? How do I get him to come down? I know it's probably locked, but I try the main door anyway, and of course it doesn't budge.

"Jack!?" I yell, hoping someone has a window open. "Jack! Answer your phone!"

I notice someone peeking at me through the curtains of a ground level window so I run over to it and put my face up to it, but the window is completely covered.

"Hello?" I say against the glass. "Can you hear me? Do you know where Jack Duncan is?"

The curtain opens and a guy a little younger than me appears in the window. He slides it over so he can talk to me through the screen.

"I think his room is upstairs," he says to me. "But you're not allowed in."

"I know. Do you think anyone can get him to come down? I just never got to say goodbye to him."

"Is your name Aspen?" someone else asks, coming up behind the first guy.

"Um. Yes." My heart thumps against my chest. Was Jack talking about me?

"Jack was looking everywhere for you, he even went to your office. The poor guy was on the verge of tears."

"Really?"

He nods. "Yeah. And his chat app kept crashing, and we tried adding you on my phone but we couldn't find you on it. He was so upset I think he went to bed as soon as we got in."

"Will you let me in?" I ask frantically.

"Shoot, yeah."

"Thank you so much," I say, already heading back to the main doors.

He lets me in and I walk past him into the entryway.

"I don't know what his room number is, but I know it's upstairs."

I nod and smile at him, my nerves too strong to let me form any words. I walk up the wooden stairs and run my hand along the railing, trying to make sure it isn't shaking. I grip the railing tighter and take a deep breath before stepping across the hall and knocking on the first door.

Someone in a Mars Group housecoat answers the door and scrunches his face in confusion at me.

"Sorry," I say quietly, "you wouldn't happen to know what room Jack Duncan is in, would you?"

"Yeah, the one at the end. I don't think he's in there, though." I wonder where he is, if that other guy thought he went to bed right away.

"Oh. Would it be weird if I waited for him?"

He shrugs. "I don't care."

I nod and make my way down the hall. A young woman comes out of one of the washrooms wearing the same style Mars Group housecoat, and her hair in a towel. She smiles at me and I smile back, glad that she doesn't question my presence. I get to the door at the end and shake out my arms before knocking. Just in case he's actually in there. When he doesn't respond after a couple of minutes, I knock again, but louder this time. When he still doesn't answer, I sit on the floor next to his door. He'll see me when he gets back.

But he doesn't get back. Where is he? I check my phone to see if maybe his chat app started working again and he's replied to my message, but he hasn't. I send him another message just in case, and lean my head back against the wall behind me. He can't not come back, so this is the best way to make sure I can talk to him.

I end up falling asleep and wake up suddenly when I hear a door shut. I look up, hopeful that it'll be Jack, but it isn't. The person coming down the hall looks confused by me sitting in the hall and I'm feeling incredibly self conscious so I start to dig through my bag. I have the Mars Bar keychain in here, the same one I've been saving for him since med school. I pull it out and then look through my bag again for a pen and a Post-It, which I find. I scribble on it, stick half the Post-It to the keychain ring, and then stick it to the door with the other half. He better see this when he gets back. And he better find a way to text me.

I walk backwards down the hall for a few steps, wondering if I should have contemplated a little longer about what to write on the note, but I'm too nervous to go back and change it now. I need to get out of here before someone calls security on me.

The note will have to do. I keep my eye on it until I can't read it anymore, and then I start to run down the stairs, the image of my handwriting now burned into my mind.

I wish I was going with you

CHAPTER 31
(NOW)

"Aspen?"

I stop at the top of the stairs and my breath catches. I turn around to see Jack at the end of the hall, his room door open behind him, the keychain in his hands in front of him.

"I…" I stammer and take a few steps towards him.

"Sorry, I was sleeping," he says. "Did you knock?"

"Yeah."

"I tried looking for you. My phone wasn't working and no one knew where you were. I was…" he sighs and licks his lips. "I was really upset about not being able to say goodbye and I just went to sleep right away. I'm really sorry that your knocking didn't wake me up."

I walk slowly towards him, dragging my shoes on the wood floor. "It's okay, it's not your fault."

Jack nods and raises his shoulders as he takes in a deep breath. He looks down at the keychain and his fingers play with the Post-It note still on it.

I wish I was going with you

"I changed my mind," I say quickly.

"What?"

"I changed my mind," I say again, more clearly this time.

He narrows his eyes at me a little, and I can see the gears turning in his head, but he doesn't say anything.

"I don't want to wait and see if I get accepted. I know I've been saying that I can't lose you again after never really getting to have you, but not getting to have you at all will be worse. If you go to Mars, and I have to stay here, and we didn't get to spend at least one night together first, I'll lose myself."

I can see his lips starting to curl into a smile, but I'm not done, so I don't let his smile turn into words.

"The thing is, Jack, when I saw you six months ago in my exam room, something inside of me woke up. After getting over the shock of seeing you again so suddenly, it was like no time had passed. It was like we were back in my dorm room watching space documentaries, or studying with my flash cards. Something about you has always made me feel safe. And being your friend again ignited a kind of happiness in me I haven't felt in years.

And tonight I found out that the hiring committee isn't sure if they want to accept me because of backing out last time, and I freaked out. And it wasn't because my dream of getting to go to Mars might be shattered yet again, it was because it was suddenly a real possibility that I might never see you again. I always knew that was a possibility, but this just snapped something inside of me and I couldn't let you go without making it perfectly clear that I'm in love with you."

Jack chuckles a little. "Thanks for clarifying, but it's been clear."

"Um. I mean. I just."

"Aspen," he says, cutting off my stammering.

"Wait, I'm not done," I say.

"Oh."

"Wait, maybe I am. I can't remember if I said everything that I wanted to say. I didn't practice this or anything, and my brain is spinning at a hundred miles a minute right now. I'm never nervous with you but I'm nervous right now. Because I'm so in love with you and so afraid of losing you again."

Whatever Jack had to say before seems to be gone now, because he's just standing there with a little grin on his face. What kind of a grin is that? Is that an 'I'm in love with you too' grin? Or is it a 'you're dumb and I'm going to make fun of you to my friends later' kind of grin?

"Say something," I half whisper.

"I want to kiss you so badly right now."

I let out a sigh of relief and feel myself smiling. "Then kiss me."

I don't even remember closing the gap between us. I can't tell you if he runs to me, if I run to him, or if we meet in the middle. I just know that when our arms wrap around each other, it's like nothing in the world can touch us. His mouth is warm and soft, and it's everything that I remember, only more. Better. His hands cradle my face and then his fingers comb through my hair and I walk him backwards into his room, suddenly worried that he has a roommate. But there are only twenty-three people going in this group, surely there are enough rooms for them to bunk alone. Jack doesn't say anything so I assume it's fine, and we shut the door behind us.

I let him press my back into the wall and I open my mouth against his, tasting him. My hands wander over his chest and then I slide them under his shirt, pulling my face back a little from his.

"Hey," I say just above a whisper.

He grins at me. "Hey."

My hands are still on his chest under his shirt, and his are on my hips, and we're just standing, staring at each other. I feel at home under his touch.

"Hey," I say again.

One of his hands moves to my face and he caresses my cheekbone with his thumb. "Hey," he whispers, before pressing his mouth to mine. And then without warning, he grabs the back of my thighs and lifts me up, letting me wrap my legs around his waist. He sets me down on the empty desk that's next to his bed and I pull him closer to me. I can't get close enough to him, but I also don't want to rush this. I want it to last as long as possible.

"What time do you have to get up in the morning?" I whisper against his mouth.

"Doesn't matter," he says, before kissing me deeper.

I pull his shirt over his head and toss it on the floor, and he plays with the hem of my shirt, teasing me. He finally takes it off for me, and we take our time before moving on to the next piece of clothing, savouring each other. We move to the bed and crawl under the covers, letting our hands and mouths explore each other's exposed parts before continuing to undress. I don't want this to end. I finally lean off the bed and pull a condom out of my purse. I tear it open and give it to Jack, who puts it on under the covers.

"You have no idea how long I've been wanting to do this," he whispers.

"I'm going to guess six months," I say.

He kisses me and pulls me closer. "Something like that."

CHAPTER 32
(SIX MONTHS LATER)

All the documentaries I've watched over the years, all the pictures from Jack, never could have prepared me for this view. Coming in to land on Mars is the most breathtaking thing I've ever experienced. The red planet is illuminated by the sun, bouncing light off the edges of craters caked in orange dust. As we enter the thin atmosphere, I can make out the compound in the distance, all white and clear walls, somehow clean and pristine looking.

I look at the new friend I've made over the seventeen-day journey, and smile.

"It's incredible, isn't it?" I ask her.

She smiles at me and nods. "I can't believe we're actually here."

"Neither can I."

The moment we land, I start to cry. I've been waiting for this moment for far too long. To put on our bulky space suits and walk across the Mars surface to the compound. We stand in the exit bay together, our helmets sealed around our faces, and when the door opens, we all gasp. We have mics in our helmets and we can all hear each other's sounds of awe and excitement. None of us can fully grasp where we are. It's windy when we step out, and I almost put my arm up to shield my face, forgetting that my helmet will do that for me. Sand blows across the ground and swirls around us, but we can still see the compound in the distance. Some people talk and make jokes as we make the fifteen-minute walk but all I can do is take in my surroundings. I can hear everyone in my earpiece but I can't make out what they're saying. All I can pay attention to is the feel of the rough dirt beneath my boots, the wind blowing sand in front of me, the sun shining down on us with a lower intensity and scattering across the land in a way that comforts me like a warm blanket. It's easier to bounce as I walk, and I do a few times, letting the gravity change feel welcome. I think it would be more noticeable if we weren't wearing these heavy suits when we first landed, but I can still feel how much lighter I am. It's amazing. I wanted to be here so badly for so long, and then thought I never would be. And now I am.

We make it to the compound and I want nothing more than to keep walking until I feel like I can't anymore. But alas, we step into the airlock chamber instead. We shut the main door behind us before taking our helmets off and waiting for further instructions. I still can't bring myself to take part in any of the conversation that's happening around me. I'm so in awe that I can't even really think. We're ushered off to separate areas for our intake physical exams and to be fitted for our own personal space suits. Jack showed me his a few times and I can't wait to get the lightweight suit and go on excursions outside of the compound. The gravity inside the compound is the same as Earth, so that it doesn't have an affect on our hearts if we want to move back.

They give us a quick tour of the compound, showing us the apartments, a park, gym, restaurants, and bars, the school. I gulp and hold my breath as we pass the school, hoping and also dreading seeing Jack. We planned to meet at the bar once I got settled, and I would love to see him earlier, but I'm afraid of seeing him for the first time in six months in front of everyone I just spent seventeen days with, and possibly in front of people he's grown close with too. I breathe a sigh of relief when we pass it without seeing anyone come out of the building, and we make our way to the hospital. I'm excited to see the hospital because this is where I'll be working. Full time in the ER, instead of rotating between that and being a general physician. There are enough people here now that it's not unheard of to have a steady night in the ER. It's mostly unstressful things I'm told, but still enough that they needed another shift set up to help out with accidental bone breaks, stitches, or the occasional heart attack. I guess life doesn't stop just because you're on a different planet.

The tone in the compound is a lot lighter than I was expecting, which is good, because a part of me was afraid that it would feel like being in a simulation or a part of Pleasantville or something. Everyone seems to be happy, but not in a forced way. Everyone I talk to seems like they're tired of everyday life just like the next person from Earth, but in a more balanced way.

I finally make it to my apartment which is up a set of stairs and down the end of the balcony walkway. I take out the keycard they gave me and open the door. I step into a warm room with light grey walls, dark furniture, and a huge window that looks right out the big clear wall of the compound. I can see the sun setting in the distance, and it's like nothing I've ever seen before. The sun is close to the horizon, and it's much smaller than it looks from Earth. There are no pinks or reds painting the sky, but instead there's a bright and soft blue sky around the sun, fading out as it gets farther away from it and turning into a soft, greyish purple. It's subtle. Quiet. And I'm going to love watching this from my living room every night.

I stand in the shower for far too long. I'm so exhausted and it takes everything out of me to turn the water off and get dried. I'm going to be late meeting Jack at the bar. I don't even know how long it takes to walk there; our tour was kind of all over the place and even though I knew they were showing us where everything was, I wasn't really paying attention to that part. I look at my watch and remember that it probably won't work here. We still use 24-hour clocks on Mars but they've all been programmed to move slower, so technically a minute here is longer than it is on Earth. I don't even know what time it is. Did my apartment come with a clock? Is there one on the stove? I pad to the kitchen, leaving wet footprints behind me, and sure enough, there is, and apparently it's 8:41. I get dressed and immediately regret chopping most of my hair off before I left Earth. Normally I would throw it up in a ponytail since I'm so exhausted, but now I have to do something with it so the layers don't just dry like a poof ball. I blow dry it and carefully brush through it, letting my wavy layers curl around my ears. I put on a touch of makeup and make my way to town.

As I walk along the clean brick path, I remember that all the housing is on the perimeter with everything else in the middle, so that no matter where you live, you can walk to most amenities in about fifteen or twenty minutes. It seems my apartment is as far away as you can get, but it's worth it for the view. Some people get to look out their window and see another apartment complex.

I find myself smiling before I even get to town. This place is so comfortable. Safe. Literally my dream come true.

The bar is warm and humid when I step in, and it reminds me of home. The dark wood of the bartop extends to the lower half of the walls, making it feel cozy. I look around the small crowd, wondering if Jack is already here, but I don't see him. I make my way to the bar and grin when I see the person working. I recognize him from the night Jack left. He's the one who let me into the barracks.

"Hey! Fancy seeing you here," he says.

"Likewise."

"Did everything work out with Jack?"

"It did." I smile and he smirks at me, as if he already knew the answer.

"I'm glad. So are you getting anything to drink?"

"Yeah. Uh, what would you recommend for someone's first night on Mars?"

"First night, eh? When did you get in?"

"Oh boy, I don't even know. It's been a long day."

"I can imagine. I've been told the new groups always arrive at slightly different times so there's never a planned thing until the Friday after. I didn't even know you guys all came in today, I'm a little sad I missed it."

"Maybe you'll catch the next one," I say.

"Yeah. There's many more to come. And many more welcome parties," he adds with a smile.

"Right yeah, they said there'd be a welcome party of sorts."

"Of sorts." He chuckles. "They're better than the Send Off parties, I'll tell you that much."

"Oh. I'm looking forward to it, then."

"Good. Anyway, first night on Mars, you gotta have one of our Martian beers. You can't get them anywhere else."

"Sounds great. Is there more than one?"

"Of course there is!"

"Cool. I'll have whichever is your favourite."

His grin grows and he knocks on the table a little as he backs away. "Coming right up."

I turn around and lean against the bar behind me, keeping an eye out for Jack. I look at my watch again out of habit and then roll my eyes at myself. I mean, the time won't be too far off, the days here are only about forty minutes longer, so the minutes aren't much different when you think about it. But since my watch runs faster, I'm probably early. If I'm even here on time. What time did we plan on meeting? I pull my phone out to check our conversation again. I've been so frazzled and dazed by everything since before we landed, and then I was completely captivated by that delightfully calm sunset that I didn't think to check it earlier. I can't function properly as a new Martian, apparently. I mean I had trouble functioning before, so this isn't alarming to me.

"Here's your beer," the bartender says to me before I open my chat with Jack.

"Thanks," I say, turning around to take it and pay. "What's your name, by the way?"

"Oh, sorry, I'm Mike."

"Nice to meet you, Mike. I'm Aspen."

"Yeah, I remember. Enjoy your beer."

"Thanks."

"And Jack." He winks at me and I look at him a little confused, until I hear my name from behind me.

I spin around so fast that it almost makes me dizzy. There's Jack, standing not three feet away from me. His hair is longer, which I knew about since we've been video chatting the past six months, but now he's got it in twists.

"Hi," I say.

"Hey stranger."

I step into him for a hug and I already thought I was as happy as I was going to be for a long time, but this extends it so far beyond my reach. I'm going to be happy for a long time here.

He pulls out of the hug and I'm about to kiss him but before I can, he pushes back a little and says, "Wait. You're not stalking me, are you?"

I feel my eyes widen for half a second before I realize he's joking. I hit him in the arm and he squeals, rubbing his new sore spot with his whole hand.

"Jesus, Aspen," he laughs. "When did you get so strong?"

I shrug and press myself into him. "I'm going to kiss you now," I say into his mouth.

"In front of all these people?"

"Yes. I've waited too long; I can't wait anymore."

"Okay."

I close the gap between us and let his kiss take my breath away.

"I like your hair like that," I say, barely pulling away from him.

"Thanks, me too. I shaved it when Anna and I broke up, and I dunno, I missed it. Hey, your hair is different, too!"

"Yeah!"

"It's like how it was in university."

"Is that a good thing?" I ask.

"It being the way it was in university has no relevance. It looks nice."

I smile at him. "Thanks."

"Of course."

"So you want to see my apartment?" I ask.

"Before you drink your fancy Mars beer?"

"Is it fancy?"

"No, Aspen, I'm making fun of you."

I pull back a little but he slips his hands into mine, and they stay between us, our fingers loosely locked together.

"You're making fun of me for getting a Martian beer on Mars?" I ask. "Why, what do you normally get?"

"Alexander Keith's," he says easily.

"They have Alexander Keith's on Mars?"

"You didn't even look at the menu? You came to a bar on Mars and you didn't even look to see what they have? For shame, Aspen. For shame."

"Why wouldn't someone want to get a Martian beer their first night on Mars?"

"Because it's so cliché," he says with a chuckle.

"And getting the same beer that you always get is boring. And probably expensive. How much is beer imported from Earth, anyway?"

"That isn't the point."

I laugh and tighten my grip on his hands. He pulls me back into him and kisses me slowly.

"I can't believe you're here," he says.

"Me neither. I've been here all day and I still can't believe it."

"So you wanna show me your apartment?" he asks.

"Oh. Yes. Yes, I do."

"You wanna try your Martian beer first, or you wanna go now?"

"Now," I say a little too quickly. "We can go now."

We stop about ten times during our walk to my apartment so that we can kiss, so it takes us much longer than fifteen minutes to get there. As soon as we do, we crash through the door and practically trip over each other as we find our zippers and buttons, all while not taking our mouths off each other.

"This is the living room," I mumble against his lips.

"It's a nice living room," he murmurs back.

"Yeah. And that's, that's the kitchen over there."

"Yeah," he says, kissing me and then pulling my top off. "It's a beautiful kitchen."

"And the bedroom…"

"Yes, show me the bedroom."

I walk backwards and pull him with me, into my room, and onto my bed.

"When do you start work?" Jack asks, the both of us sprawled across my bed, still naked, still sweaty, but the happiest I think we've ever been.

"Monday," I say. "But I have no idea what day it is today."

"It's Wednesday."

"Shoot. So you have to work tomorrow then?"

He nods. "I do."

"How's that going? Are you enjoying it?"

"Yeah, it's nice. A different flow from back home. I like it."

"That's good. I don't know what I'm going to do all day here for two more days without you."

"Miss me."

"Yes, I will definitely do that."

"Maybe you can come meet my students. I'll take you out for lunch."

"That sounds nice."

He sighs and nods, and we lie in comfortable silence together for a few minutes.

"I have an amazing view of the sunset out the back of my apartment. It's too bad we can't see the sunrise from it too."

"You can see the sunrise from my place," he says.

"You can?"

"Yeah. You want to go to sleep at my place? We can watch the sunrise before I go to work."

"That sounds amazing."

The compound is quiet as we walk along the path and between other apartment complexes to get to Jack's. I miss the idle sounds of crickets and get a sudden wave of homesickness. Jack puts his arm around me and pulls me into his side.

"Whatcha thinking about?" he asks.

"Crickets."

"Crickets?"

"Yeah. I'm kind of sad there are no crickets here. I always liked hearing them in the summer and stuff."

Jack sighs. "Yeah, I miss that too, sometimes. It is pretty quiet, isn't it? It's nice though. It's just a different kind of appreciation."

"Yeah."

"Anyway, this is me." He grabs onto my hand and pulls me up the stairs of an apartment complex that looks exactly like mine only the balcony is dark instead of light. I notice as he pulls out his keycard that he's got the Mars Bar keychain hanging off it. I smile as he unlocks the door and ushers me inside.

"I can watch the sunrise from my bedroom," he explains. "It overlooks the town and it's really nice the way the light glows on the buildings."

"I can't wait to see it."

He smiles and we head to his room, trying to get right to sleep, but of course we don't. Our goodnight kiss turns into making out, which leads to getting naked again.

"We've already done this in a bed tonight," Jack says with a bit of a laugh.

"Should we do it on your couch instead?"

He grins against my mouth and we move to the living room. I wish we could do this all night, but I'm exhausted. We move to the shower and I almost fall over once the hot water starts to fall over us.

"You alright there?" Jack asks, grabbing onto my elbow.

I nod and stand on my toes to kiss him. He kisses me back but then pulls away and grabs a shampoo bar from the side.

"Turn around," he says. "I'll wash your hair."

So I turn around and let him lather the shampoo into my short hair, massaging my scalp as he goes. I almost fall over again because it's so relaxing, but he catches me.

"You have to stop doing that," he says with a chuckle.

"Sorry," I say, smiling at him from over my shoulder.

I turn around to face him and he wraps his arms around my waist, pulling me into him.

"I wish we could stay here forever," I whisper.

"What, on Mars? Or in the shower?"

"In the shower."

"Hmm. That would be a little difficult, but I'll see what I can do."

I lean my head on his chest and let the water spill over us, too content to move.

"You're going to get shampoo in your eyes," Jack says.

"No, my eyes are closed."

"Still. Let me rinse it out for you."

And that's what he does.

We stand under the hot stream of water long after all our soap has washed off us and gone down the drain, but I think neither of us want to get out. I mean, I do want to get out because I'm so exhausted, but I also just want to stay here with him all night. When Jack finally turns the water off, I'm so content. We get out of the shower and Jack wraps a towel around me. He presses his forehead against mine and then rubs my arms up and down over the towel.

"I'm so tired," he says quietly.

"So am I."

"We should get to bed so we can wake up in four hours and watch the sunrise."

I laugh at that. "Good call."

So that's what we do. We curl up in his big bed with a fluffy comforter and I don't know about Jack, but I fall asleep against him immediately. I've never slept so well. He wakes me up in the morning with a kiss on the tip of my nose and hands me a tumbler cup with a straw.

"I made you an iced coffee," he says.

"Wow, thank you," I say, sitting up and taking it from him.

He opens his curtains and sits on the bed next to me. I lean my head on his shoulder, taking the occasional sip of my drink, and watch the sun come up, the blue light around it getting fainter as it rises.

"So what do you say?" he asks. "Your place for dinner? And we can watch the sunset from there?"

"Yeah. And then back here to sleep so we can do it all over again."

"Sounds like a plan."

So that's what we do.

ACKNOWLEDGEMENTS

Thank you to everyone who followed along with my Mars Story skit on Tiktok. It was my first time sharing a piece of fiction that way, and I really fell in love with it. I had always enjoyed doing reenactment and retail skits, and people seemed to enjoy watching them, so I was nervous to switch it up and post the first episode of one that had been completely and obviously made up. After writing and posting the first three or so episodes, I thought that this story would make a good book. One that I really wanted to write. So you can probably guess how excited I was when people started commenting on my videos asking if I would be turning the Mars Story into a novel.

I have never been so excited to get started on a first draft before, and writing it was so much fun. Using the skits as reference for dialogue and story progression was fun as well, and I hope you all enjoyed the extra story lines and pieces that I added. In the skits, a lot of the story is revealed through conversations, since it was just me in my living room, playing all the characters, so it was great to be able to write the actual scenes as they happened, instead of through people talking about them after the fact. I hope everyone liked how I did it.

Thank you to everyone for all your kind words and support on every episode of The Mars Story. Sometimes the love for it was overwhelming. Thank you for your patience as I turned it into a book, and thank you so much for waiting this long to be able to read it. Trust me, it was a hard wait for me too!

Thank you to everyone who read different versions of this story, to help make it the best that it can be. Sarah Jane Wetelainen, Elle Levesque, Lizzie, John Cuddington (my dad), and Stephanie Austin. Everyone's input was helpful and very much appreciated.

Also thank you to Stephanie Austin for coming up with the title! It was so hard for me to call it anything other than The Mars Story after so long, and it felt like any title I came up with just wasn't good enough. Also thanks to Lyndsay Beech and Rhonda Chartrand for brainstorming title ideas with me. Even though I didn't use any of your titles, the help is still appreciated.

Thank you to Laura Kulson, as always, for the gorgeous cover. I don't know what I would do without you and your genius artistic brain. And skills.

Listen to the Spotify playlist that I made to match the feels of the book! I made a short little link for you so it's easy to type

https://bit.ly/3KrMtxJ

Or you can scan the QR code here

Or you can just search for it on Spotify! It looks like this

Manufactured by Amazon.ca
Bolton, ON

39843239R00171